PRAISE FOR THE

"Gripping and powerful."
— Lifeofanavidmoviegoer.wordpress.com

"Freakin genius."
— Romance Bytes

"She's a brilliant storyteller."
— NetGalley Reviewer

"The plot is sheer poetry."
— Readers' Favorite

"A sassy, edgy page-turner."
— Wall to Wall Books

"A brilliant read."
— NaturalBri Reviews

"Best cloak and dagger thriller I've read in a while."
— NetGalley Reviewer

"A thrilling, suspenseful novel."
— Amazon Reviewer

"This is one wild ride. A very good psychological thriller that will keep you up until the wee hours of the morning."
— The Cubicle Escapee

ALSO BY GLEDE BROWNE KABONGO

Autumn of Fear
Game of Fear
Swan Deception
Conspiracy of Silence

Available in Audio
Conspiracy of Silence
Swan Deception

WINDS
A FEARLESS NOVEL
OF FEAR

GLEDÉ BROWNE KABONGO

BrowneStar
Media

BrowneStar
Media
www.brownestarmedia.com

WINDS OF FEAR

Copyright © 2019 Gledé Browne Kabongo

Notice: This book is a work of fiction. The names, characters, places, and incidents are products of the author's imagination or have been used fictitiously. Any resemblance to actual events, locales or persons, living or dead is purely coincidental.

Cover Design by Qamber Designs & Media

ISBN: 978-1-7333253-2-5 (paperback)
ISBN: 978-1-7333253-1-8 (eBook)

*"Revenge is the sweetest morsel to the mouth,
that was ever cooked in hell."*
— Sir Walter Scott

CHAPTER 1

THERE WAS NO spine-chilling fear or dark premonition in the air to warn Oliva Stewart that the stranger partially hidden behind the tree would one day destroy her life.

Yet, Olivia kept one eye focused on the average height woman sporting oversized sunglasses, a scarf, and newsboy cap, and the other on her three charges.

As the kids exited the car, waved goodbye, and headed for the playground, the stranger snapped photos of them and quickly dropped the small camera into the left pocket of her heavy winter coat. Her eyes darted left and then right to make sure no one had seen her.

Olivia had, from her vantage point.

With only seconds to decide on a course of action, Olivia's brain zeroed in on the most obvious question. Why would a random stranger lurk around school property during morning drop-off and take photos of the Rambally kids? Drop-off rules were straightforward: you dropped off at the curb and kept it moving.

Olivia was already agitated because she was cut off by another driver a couple of blocks away from the school—a gray Honda Accord with an out-of-state license plate—some state in the Midwest. She couldn't remember which because she sometimes got them confused. She only noticed the make and model because there was a huge decal of an animated rabbit and some cliché quote about believing in yourself on the rear window.

Clutching the driver-side door handle of the Volvo SUV, Olivia watched the stranger walk toward the playground, both hands in her pockets and her head down.

Olivia leapt out of the car, not caring about the rules, and hurried in the direction of the playground. As she got closer, she observed that the woman had positioned herself at an angle that allowed an unobstructed view of children running and playing. However, the stranger's attention was focused on Olivia's charges, Lucas, Blake, and Alexis. Her camera was out again, but she apparently spotted Olivia's approach, and lowered it.

Olivia slowed her pace, not wanting the woman to panic and disappear to avoid a confrontation. She stuck her hands into her jeans pockets and pasted a smile on her face.

"New to drop-off?" she asked, with forced casualness.

"Something like that."

The stranger's expression was unreadable, carefully hidden behind the sunglasses.

"You're a photographer?"

"Yeah."

A lot of vague, cryptic answers, Olivia thought. The woman had long, dark hair that cascaded past her shoulders. Her gray winter coat was buttoned all the way up, which Olivia found suspect. It was coming up on mid-March and unseasonably warm. A welcome sixty degrees Fahrenheit at eight-fifteen in the morning.

Olivia tried again to drag some scrap of information from the woman, who kept switching her weight from one leg to the other.

2

"Well, I'm Olivia," she said without extending a hand. "I watch the Rambally kids, the ones you were taking pictures of. If you're a parent or caregiver, you can understand why I came over. I'm sure you have a good reason for snapping photos of them."

Olivia detected a shift in the stranger's body language. One that said she didn't appreciate being interrogated.

"Excuse me, I have to go," she whispered.

Without thinking, Olivia grabbed her by the arm. "Why were you taking pictures of the Rambally kids? Don't deny it—I saw you. Answer me, or I'll make a big stink about it. You can't take pictures of little kids on a playground at school. It's creepy and inappropriate."

"I don't know what you're talking about. I don't know who these Rambally kids are."

Olivia placed her hands on her hips and glared at the woman. "Really?"

"I'm sorry. I didn't mean to cause any trouble. I was just snapping some pics of my niece. It's her tenth birthday."

Out of the corner of her eye, Olivia saw Alexis playing tag with her friend, Emme.

"Your niece?" Olivia asked. "Didn't look that way to me. Besides, why would you wait until your *niece*"—Olivia held up air quotes—"was at morning drop-off to take pictures of her?"

The woman dug for something in her coat pocket.

"This is my brother, Henry," she said, handing a photo to Olivia. "He's in hospice care. Cancer. Today is his daughter Kaley's tenth birthday. I promised him I would document her day. Just wanted to give him some happiness in his final days."

Olivia took the picture and studied the man staring back at her. He sported jeans and a T-shirt, dark hair and glasses. He smiled for the camera and made the peace sign with long, thin fingers, his back against a tree stump in a park environment.

A wave of guilt crashed into Olivia, and she wanted the ground to open up and swallow her whole. With shaky hands, she returned the photo to the stranger.

"I'm really sorry," she said, lowering her voice. "I guess I jumped to conclusions. You can't be too careful these days, you know what I mean?"

The stranger simply nodded.

"Well, I'll let you get on with your day…" Olivia hesitated. "Sorry, I don't even know your name."

"Jane. Jane Witherby."

"Have a good day, Jane."

Olivia did a visual scan of the area on her way out to see whether Jane had indeed vacated school premises. She saw no sign of her. Olivia shivered in spite of the brilliant sunshine baking the car's windshield.

CHAPTER 2

—◦—

ONE YEAR LATER

PERFECT DAY IN the Rambally household.

I should know however, from bitter experience, that perfect days can't be trusted. My ten-year old, Lucas, is working through one of two grilled cheese sandwiches at the kitchen table, while I tap away on the keys of my laptop, typing notes from the research articles splayed out on the table. The twins, Blake and Alexis, a year younger than Lucas, blast into the kitchen and join him. They both eye the remaining sandwich on Lucas' plate.

Blake smacks his lips. "Can I have that sandwich? I'll split it with Alexis."

"No way. Get your own."

Alexis looks in my direction. "Mom, Lucas is being selfish. He won't share, after everything I've done for him."

I shrug. I won't get in the middle of their quarrel. Then without warning, Blake grabs the sandwich off the plate and runs out of the kitchen with a squealing Alexis on his heels. Lucas takes chase, screaming at them.

5

"Give it back, Blake," Lucas bellows from the family room.

"I'll arm wrestle you for it," Blake says.

"Mom, Lucas and Blake are fighting," Alexis yells. "You said no hitting."

I let out an exasperated breath, annoyed that my concentration has been broken. The notes need to be completed before dinner, and there are several articles I have yet to peruse. I push back from the table, stand up, and traipse to the family room while counting to ten, a brief exercise to summon my patience, which is in short supply these days.

I fold my arms over my chest and give all three my sternest you're-all-in-trouble stare. Lucas and Blake are on the floor with matching guilty looks plastered on their faces. Alexis sits on the sofa twirling Mr. Snoopy, a stuffed bear that once belonged to Lucas, taking in the commotion. This scuffle has nothing to do with food. My kids never pass up an opportunity to get on each other's nerves. They could easily ask me to make them sandwiches of their own, but why do that when they can get a rise out of their older sibling instead?

Before I can scold them, footsteps approach. Ty appears and assesses the scene.

"What's with all the yelling?" he asks. "Didn't I tell you three I needed a little quiet to get some work done?"

Blake and Lucas get off the floor and straighten up. Neither one of them says a word. Alexis remains silent.

"Well, is someone going to tell me what's going on?" he demands.

Lucas, near tears, says, "Blake took my grilled cheese and ran off with it and he wouldn't give it back. I think that's really mean. I wouldn't do that to him. He could have asked Mom to make him one."

Ty turns his attention to the twins. "Did the two of you

gang up on your brother again? How many times have I told you it's not nice to do that?"

A remorseful Alexis replies, "We were just having a little fun, Daddy. We didn't mean anything by it. Lucas is too sensitive."

Lucas says, "I'm not sensitive, and you two aren't funny. I'm going to get you both. Then we'll see how funny you think it is."

I'm about to interject that we don't threaten each other in this family when the doorbell rings. I move to answer it, leaving Ty to deal with the kids. When I open the door, I jerk back briefly. A young couple stands before me with megawatt smiles that could light up Times Square on New Year's Eve. I recognize them from the neighborhood. We've waved on a few occasions, the way neighbors sometimes do, but I've never met them up close like this.

The woman looks to be in her late twenties or early thirties with copper-red hair styled in a French braid that runs down the left side of her head. Her enormous green eyes drown out her small, round face, giving her features a cartoonish manifestation, à la an animated Disney princess. The man has an impressive physique that could only be achieved by endless hours spent in the gym. He boasts a strong jawline, and his ash brown hair is parted on one side and brushed back to gleaming perfection, not a stray strand in sight. His glasses give him a nerdy yet confident look.

"May I help you?"

The woman says, "Sorry to show up out of the blue. We just moved in next door and wanted to stop by and introduce ourselves. I guess you could say we're on the get-to-know-our-neighbors tour. I'm Jenna Payne and this is my husband Charlie." She gestures to him.

"I'm Abbie Rambally." I extend a hand. After a long, awkward pause, I invite them in.

7

I usher the guests into the kitchen. This visit is an unexpected interruption to my work, but I don't want to make them feel unwelcome. I grab the files and laptop off the kitchen table, and place them on the kitchen island. Ty must have disappeared back into his home office because all three kids saunter in, appraising the visitors with curious stares. I introduce them to Jenna and Charlie.

"Very nice to meet you, Alexis," Jenna says. "Do you go by Lexie?"

My daughter responds with a dramatic eye roll. I'm pretty sure she gets it from me. I should quit that habit.

"Just Alexis. It's more sophisticated than Lexie." She makes a face.

"Thank you for correcting me. I'll remember that."

The boys introduce themselves to the couple with a firm handshake and eye contact, the way their father taught them. Blake first, then Lucas. When Jenna extends her hand to Lucas, her face brightens and her eyes lock in on him, as if some invisible force has taken her captive. She holds on to his hand as if she doesn't want to let go. I just met the woman, yet something about my son has her enthralled. Lucas slowly withdraws his hand from hers and says it's nice to meet her. The spell is broken.

"It's time to get started on homework," I announce to the kids and herd them out of the kitchen. Alexis, my procrastinator, lingers.

"Do you have kids?" she asks the couple.

Kids for her to play with—that's her litmus test to determine adult coolness. Apart from her cousins, Zoe and Gabrielle, who live almost an hour away, and her best friend from school, Alexis' circle of friends remains small. She's always on the hunt for new friends who will indulge her fondness for playing fashion runway. Her brothers refuse to participate and simply ignore her attempts at dispensing wardrobe advice.

A peculiar stillness floats in the air but Alexis stands her ground, waiting for an answer.

Jenna finally gives a forced smile. "No, I don't have kids, but I'm a children's book illustrator. That's almost as good as having kids, isn't it?"

"I guess so." A disappointed Alexis waves goodbye and takes off.

"I apologize for my daughter's rudeness," I say, grabbing two coffee mugs from the cabinet and placing them on the table. "Alexis thinks she's grown and doesn't have a filter. I'm trying my best to teach her boundaries, especially when it comes to adults."

Jenna waves a dismissive hand. "No need to apologize. I think it's great that she speaks her mind. You're lucky to have such bright, wonderful kids."

I thank her for the compliment, grab the recently brewed pot of coffee, and pour in each mug.

"Cream and sugar?"

"No, just black is fine," Jenna says.

"Charlie, what about you?"

He's been awfully quiet since they sat down. Jenna appears to be the dominant half of the couple, although I've learned over the years, sometimes painfully, that appearances can be deceiving. Or it could be that Charlie isn't much of a talker. Either way, it's time to chat him up, see what he has to say.

"I'll take mine black also," he says.

I sit across from my guests while they sip coffee and nibble on homemade scones. Before I can start my inquiries, Jenna says, "These are the most delicious scones I've ever had in my life. Did you make them yourself?"

"Thank you. Yes, I know my way around a kitchen."

I lob my first question at Charlie before Jenna has a chance to take over the conversation.

"So, Charlie, what brings you and Jenna to Lexington, Massachusetts? Where was home before?"

I keep my attention focused on Charlie. Engaging him might give me some insight into Jenna's odd reaction to Lucas.

"Colorado. I'm a software developer. I've built up my consulting business over the past few years and many of my clients are on the East Coast. We figured it made sense to move, and Massachusetts won out because it's a tech hub. A lot of innovation happens here."

"You've come to the right place," I concur. "There are a few tech companies right here in Lexington, as well as MIT Lincoln Labs. We're not far from the Route 128 high-tech corridor, and Cambridge is only a twenty-minute drive down Route 2, if you don't encounter heavy traffic. This is a sweet spot that puts you at the center of all the action."

"It strikes me as a good place to raise a family, too," Jenna says. "Great neighborhoods, prime location, great schools. Do your kids attend one of the local elementary schools or do they go private? I only ask because Charlie and I want to start a family soon and I would love to get advice from someone with actual experience. If you don't mind," she adds quickly.

"Lexington does have a great school system that ranks well both nationally and state-wide. We didn't see a need to send our kids to private school."

"Fantastic," she says.

I allow a lapse in conversation to envelope us. Jenna clears her throat and Charlie breaks off a piece of his scone. I sense there's more she wants to say and I'm curious.

"Is there a Mr. Rambally?" Jenna asks. Charlie gives her an

admonishing glare but says nothing.

"Sorry. I don't mean to pry. It's hard making new friends in a new place. I tend to go overboard," she says with a nervous giggle.

"Don't give it another thought. Yes, there is a Mr. Rambally. He—"

As if on cue, Ty enters the kitchen, fiddling with the cuffs of his dress shirt worn under a V-neck sweater.

"Cooper, I have to run out for a bit. Stevenson wants me on a consult for—"

He looks up and stops mid-sentence when he sees our visitors. "Oh, I didn't know we had company."

After introductions and handshakes, Ty says, "Welcome to the neighborhood. I think you'll like it here."

"Oh, I'm sure we will," Jenna responds, giving Ty a wide smile. I could swear she also batted her eyelashes at him, but I could be imagining things.

"Wish you could join us for coffee," she says.

"Sorry. Duty calls." Ty casts a sympathetic glance in my direction.

"Please don't get sucked into working another shift on your day off. You're hardly home as it is," I complain, not caring if the neighbors think I'm a nag.

He kisses me on the cheek and says, "I'll do my best."

"Another shift?" Jenna asks, curiously.

"Ty is a cardiothoracic surgeon at Massachusetts General Hospital," I explain.

"Barely," he responds. "One year of specialty training left."

Ty wrapped up a grueling, four-year general surgery residency a couple of years back and is now in year two of his cardiothoracic training. He maintains that only upon completion will he truly feel like he has arrived as a full-fledged surgeon, even though he's performed countless surgeries, and has emerged as quite the rock star.

"A doctor down the street. I feel healthier already," Jenna says. "Don't worry, Ty. I'm not one of those people who will be hitting you up for free medical advice all the time. Okay, maybe a little."

We all dissolve into laughter, even quiet Charlie. Ty bids goodbye to our guests and disappears from view.

A brief silence passes, during which Jenna and Charlie exchange glances. Then Jenna clears her throat and emits a nervous smile as she twirls the tip of her French braid.

"I hope you don't take this the wrong way or anything," she begins, leaning in closer. "You don't have to answer if it's uncomfortable, it's just that—"

I cut her off. "I promise I don't bite, and I probably won't feed you to the alligator in my back yard, but it depends on what you have to say."

Her eyes go wide, and I grin at her before taking a sip of my coffee. Charlie shifts nervously in his seat, as if the chair suddenly shrunk several sizes, and can't support his bulk.

Jenna blurts out, "Is Lucas adopted?"

"Why would you think that?" I ask, casually, keeping my voice even.

"Because he looks so different from Blake and Alexis, and all three of them seem to be the same age. And your husband is black, so I figure…"

"You figure something must be up because Lucas doesn't look like the rest of the family?"

"Well, yeah. I—I mean, he has blue eyes and fair skin. His hair is caramel blond. He's as pale as I am," she says, stretching out an arm.

"And here I am, thinking we lived in a post-racial society

where that didn't matter," I quip.

She adds quickly, "Please don't be offended, Abbie. I'm sorry if it came off that way."

"I'm just messing with you. We get asked this question often. When Lucas was a toddler, some crazy man came up to Ty and almost called the police because he thought Lucas was his son. He insisted Ty return his child, and Ty wasn't about to hand over Lucas. The two almost came to blows until they both asked the obvious questions, names, addresses, and such."

Charlie leans forward and Jenna's jaw hangs open. "Are you serious? That actually happened?"

I take another sip of my coffee. "Aha, true story."

"So he *is* adopted then," Jenna persists.

Why is it so important for her to know whether or not Lucas is adopted? I don't get it. We just met. What's her deal?

"No, Jenna. Lucas is not adopted. I'm his biological mother. I have the ultrasound pictures and everything. Do you want to call the doctor who delivered him?"

She shakes her head. "What about your husband?"

"What about him?"

"He can't be Lucas' biological dad."

"Ty is Lucas' father. Period."

Jenna looks down at her hands in her lap, her expression unreadable. Charlie breaks the stillness with a question of his own.

"Ty called you Cooper. Is that a nickname?"

Grateful for the question, I quickly respond. "Cooper is my maiden name. Ty has always called me that, since we met as teenagers, and he never stopped."

"Aww, that's so cute," Jenna exclaims, looking up. "You guys dated in high school?"

"No. We didn't date until college."

I can see the wheels turning as she tries to put together

a timeline that would make sense to her. How does Lucas fit into the picture?

Charlie pops the last piece of scone into his mouth and makes a production of chewing slowly. Jenna isn't about to give up that easily, though. I'll indulge her as long as it serves my purposes.

"Oh, I see. So you met Lucas' biological father in college then. Before you started dating Ty, I mean. Lucas must be what, ten years old?"

I experience a light bulb moment as the subject of her curiosity comes into sharp focus. Lucas' biological father.

"Why the keen interest in Lucas and his paternity? We just met and frankly, I find your questions intrusive, Jenna." I wrinkle my nose as if I had caught a whiff of a long-dead squirrel. "Did you and Charlie come here with an agenda?"

"Not at all, Abbie," Charlie says, his cheeks turning crimson red. "My wife says what's on her mind. She was lied to all of her life by her parents, and she has struggled with trust issues." He rushes through the explanation, wanting to get it all out in one go. "What you're witnessing is the result of years of therapy that encouraged her to be open and genuine about her feelings. You have an interesting family, and she was just curious. No harm intended."

"Is that true, Jenna?"

She doesn't answer, and nods.

"Okay then. You want to know about Lucas' biological father? I'll tell you. He's dead. And I say good riddance."

Charlie jerks back in his chair as if I've just slapped him, the chair making scraping sounds against the tiled floor. Jenna starts to breathe deeply and noisily.

She says, "My goodness, I forgot I have a conference call with a potential client in five minutes." She stands up and steps away from the table. "We should go, Charlie. I don't want to appear unprofessional in front of a new prospect. Abbie, thanks for your hospitality. We should do this again sometime."

What on earth brought on this visceral reaction? She's behaving like a petulant child whose parent refused an indulgence.

"What's wrong, Jenna?" I ask.

She doesn't answer and heads out of the kitchen. I look at Charlie and lift my palms in a gesture of confusion, as I follow them out.

"She'll be fine," he says.

Jenna doesn't bother saying goodbye. Charlie offers a weak *sorry* and takes off after her, closing the door behind him.

I return to the kitchen and pour myself my fourth cup of coffee of the day. Tendrils of steam from the dark liquid rise and disappear into the afternoon air, just as Jenna did moments ago. I take the mug in both hands and scent the rich brew, blowing atop its surface before taking a sip. The visit is on instant replay in my mind as I lean against the counter. Jenna's reaction to Lucas and pushing the issue of his biological father, pointing out that Lucas is as white as she is, wanting to know if he was adopted.

What a strange visit.

Charlie was quick to reassure me that they didn't come with a predetermined agenda, but given what I just witnessed, I'm not so sure.

I close my eyes and take in a deep breath. My comfort zone has now retreated behind a veil of paranoia and apprehension I can't afford. There's too much at stake in the coming weeks. As a Ph.D. candidate in clinical psychology at Boston University, my dissertation defense— the culmination of three-plus years of sacrifice, sweat, and tears— is one of the most important events of my life. My goal is to be become a neuropsychologist, which requires an additional year or two of postdoctoral training.

I've applied for several Postdoctoral Fellowships in Clinical Neuropsychology, including the program at Mass General Hospital where Ty works. I should know if I've been accepted soon. It would be disastrous if I were to snag a spot but fail my dissertation defense. I shudder at the thought. The pressure to graduate in May can be unbearable at times.

I drain the last of my coffee and pop the empty mug into the dishwasher. For the sake of my sanity and the need to remain laser focused in the coming weeks, what transpired this afternoon must be chalked up to nothing more than a curious encounter.

Yet, the sharp taste of foreboding clings to the back of my throat.

CHAPTER 3

C HARLIE PAYNE SLAMMED the refrigerator door shut after he grabbed a beer, twisted off the cap, and took a long gulp. When he banged the bottle down on the kitchen island, spilling a few drops, Jenna didn't flinch. She leaned against the island, arms folded and a granite hard expression on her face.

"What the hell was that about?" he exploded. "How could you lose it like that in front of Abbie?"

"Pop a chill pill, Charlie," she said. "You're making a big deal about nothing."

"No big deal, huh? Our first visit to the Ramballys, and you're already making waves. Do you not understand why we're here?"

Jenna unfolded her arms. "I understand perfectly well why we're here. This is my show, and we'll do it my way."

"So pressing Abbie about her son, and then throwing a temper tantrum when she said his father was better off dead, isn't a big deal? Do you even care that she will put up walls, that you just made it harder for her to trust us? You don't think before you act," he said, wagging a finger at her.

"I got her to reveal her true feelings while you just sat there like a useless oaf. Besides, if I came across too nice, she might have pegged me as a fake. I know what I'm doing, so stop judging me. It's annoying."

"We have to be careful," he said, taking his voice down a notch. "So tomorrow, you're going to march yourself over there and apologize to Abbie. Tell her you didn't mean to flip out on her, that her family is none of your business, and you want to make it up to her."

"I don't think so."

"Oh yes you will." He glared at her. "She seems like a nice lady, and I want her to think the same about us."

"Oh please." Jenna picked up an apple from the fruit basket on the counter and bit into it. "How nice can she be? Did you see that nosy little brat of hers? Alexis? How do you think she got that way? By watching, Mommy, of course."

"Don't get stupid," Charlie warned. "We agreed we were going to take this nice and easy. Stop stirring up trouble."

Jenna ignored him and took another bite of her apple. Then she said, "Lucas, on the other hand, was a perfect little gentleman. I think we're going to get along fabulously. I wanted to give him a big hug, right then and there. He just had that effect on me. Totally lovable."

"Tomorrow, Jenna," Charlie yelled. "You go to Abbie Rambally and tell her you're sorry for being a jerk."

Later that night, Charlie repeatedly punched his pillow as sleep eluded him. What a day. Abbie was nothing like he expected. He had been nervous about how he would react to meeting her for the first time, the woman he had heard and learned so much about over the past few years. He had expected a self-absorbed, self-righteous snob with a sense of entitlement. He didn't know how all of those qualities were supposed to manifest themselves in a twenty-minute visit in her kitchen, but he didn't pick up on any of that.

He prided himself on his ability to read people. His survival had depended on it in the past and still did. From their brief visit, Charlie gleaned several revealing pieces of information about Abbie Rambally. For one thing, she was a lonely housewife who was practically raising three kids by herself. While she was proud of her husband's accomplishments, she resented the amount of time he spent away from home. For another, she was a highly intelligent woman, not to be underestimated. Although Jenna didn't realize it, Abbie had played her. She used humor to find out why Jenna was asking questions about Lucas, questions Jenna had no business asking. Jenna fell right into her trap. And third, and perhaps most intriguing of all, Abbie was under a lot of stress. Charlie intended to find out why.

She was a willowy one, although he couldn't help but notice her soft curves and long, lean legs. She was almost as tall as Charlie, who was about five foot eleven. She wore no makeup and her hair was pulled back into a hurried ponytail, providing an unobstructed view of her face. Up close, she was even more stunning than in the photos he had seen of her.

Everything about Abigail Cooper Rambally fascinated him. After all, she was the reason he was here, on this street, in this town, at this juncture in time. He was worried about Jenna, though. That stunt she pulled this afternoon put him on notice that she had the potential to screw things up.

He wouldn't allow that to happen. No one was going to mess this up for him. As Charlie drifted off to sleep, the warning echoed in his head, a warning from the man who had given him the resources to reinvent himself. His instructions were clear:

If Jenna becomes a problem, eliminate her.

CHAPTER 4

FUNCTIONING ON JUST three hours of sleep, I hastily down my first cup of coffee of the day at six forty-five in the morning. I pray the caffeine kicks in quickly. The kids are up and going through the morning routine of getting ready for school. Liv will arrive soon to take over so I can head out to the Stanwick Rehabilitation Hospital in Boston, site of my field research for my dissertation. I observe and conduct experiments with patients who've suffered stroke or traumatic brain injury, focusing on how the injury affects memory, intellectual function, speech and language.

I hurriedly stuff some papers into my bag on the kitchen counter along with my laptop. Lucas strolls in, still in pajamas and rubbing sleep from his eyes.

"Can you make blueberry pancakes for breakfast, Mom?"

"I'm sorry, sweetie." My brain is already halfway down Route 93 South. "Mom has to go in a few minutes. Liv will get you breakfast."

"But I want *you* to make breakfast. Your blueberry pancakes are the best. Liv can't make them the way you do."

My children have the worst timing in the world, no exaggeration. I adore them, but sometimes, I'm glad to get away

20

from the house. In Lucas' defense, he doesn't usually make demands, which is why I feel guilt rising up from the pit of my stomach and getting lodged somewhere between my chest and my throat.

I kneel in front of him and palm his face. "I promise I will make this up to you. Besides, we're out of fresh blueberries. This week has been a little crazy, and Mom needs to go shopping soon. You understand, don't you?"

His eyes cloud over. His lips wobble and there's a sharp intake of breath. He must really be in the mood for blueberry pancakes. Lucas is much more controlled than his siblings, and quite mature for his age. Maybe it has something to do with him being the firstborn, and Blake and Alexis arriving while he was still technically an infant. He had to grow up fast.

"The sooner I get out of this house, the sooner I can get back and go to the supermarket to pick up the blueberries, okay? Pancakes for dinner. How about that?"

"It's okay, Mom. I understand. Bye." He turns to leave.

"Hey, why the long face?" Liv arrives and blocks his exit.

"Lucas wants blueberry pancakes for breakfast," I explain.

Liv knows this routine well enough to know I have to leave. I can't be late.

"Go," she mimes over Lucas' head.

I grab my bag and keys off the counter and head to the garage. I start the engine but don't back out right away. My little boy needed me, and I couldn't be there for him. No matter how much I tell myself that this is only temporary, that soon, I will complete my program, it hurts. Like someone took a sizzling hot knife and carved my heart in two.

CHAPTER 5

O LIVIA CAME TO work for the Ramballys five years ago when Lucas was in kindergarten and the twins still in preschool. She bonded with them instantly and felt connected in a way she hadn't with anyone outside her immediate family. She adored Lucas, Blake, and Alexis. She had worked for other families in the past but was always struck by how spoiled and entitled the kids were. But not these kids.

"It's okay, Lucas," Olivia soothed. "Wipe your tears. I'll pick up blueberries after I drop you off at school so it will be all ready for your mom when she gets home. I'll make sure she has all the ingredients ready to go. You're not missing out. It's just delayed, that's all."

"Dad's always gone and now Mom, too," he said. "It sucks."

His confession surprised her. She took his hand in hers and led him up the stairs. "Why do you say that, Lucas?"

"Because it's true."

"Well, it's only for a little while. Your mother is almost finished with her degree. These are the last two months before she graduates, so she's under a lot of pressure to make sure everything goes well. Just think, in a couple of months, she will graduate, and you, Blake, Alexis, and Dr. Rambally will be there to cheer her on at the ceremony."

"And then that will be it, she won't be gone so much anymore?" He looked up at Oliva, his eyes gleaming with expectation.

Olivia didn't want to lie to the boy. She wasn't sure if that would be *it*. She seemed to remember Abbie saying something about postdoctoral work, and obtaining a license to practice as a clinical neuropsychologist, and board certification. She had no idea how long all of that would take. A couple of years ago, when she was at a low point, Abbie had confided in Olivia that when she floated the idea of pursuing her Ph.D., Dr. Rambally had asked her to put it on hold because they couldn't afford to hire full-time care for the kids so she could tackle a rigorous academic program.

"I thought I deserved to have something of my own," Abbie had said with tears in her eyes. "I sacrificed so much, and once the kids were school age, it made sense for me to get an advanced degree if I wanted to ever have a career of my own. My dream of becoming a neurosurgeon was dead, but I figured I could still study the brain and help patients in a different way. I don't know why Ty wanted me to wait."

"Maybe he was worried that the kids were still so young and need you. Plus, you're only in your twenties. You have your whole life ahead of you."

"I wouldn't accept that, so I took matters into my own hands."

"What do you mean?"

"I asked my parents for help. For money to hire full-time care. I had applied for a fellowship to fund tuition and other expenses, and luckily was awarded enough to cover all expenses."

"What did Dr. Rambally say when he found out?"

"I didn't tell him right away. I had to apply and get in

first. It helped that I got my bachelor's degree from Boston University and had done well. He was livid that I went behind his back and asked my parents for help, but I stood my ground. We didn't speak to each other for a week. In the end, it was worth it."

OLIVIA WAS ABOUT to put away the groceries when the doorbell rang. She glanced at the microwave clock. It was ten in the morning. She left the shopping bags on the kitchen counter and headed for the front door.

When she opened the door, she came face-to-face with an unfamiliar woman. Olivia took an instant dislike to her, though she didn't know why. Something about the woman's demeanor rubbed her the proverbial wrong way. It could be the smirk on her face or the way she ran her fingers through her red-brown hair that fell past her shoulders, or the way she tossed her head back as if she and Olivia were engaged in some weird power struggle. She was pretty, but boy did she pile on the makeup: blush, eye shadow, and bright red lipstick. Who wears bright red lipstick and blush at ten in the morning? Her lashes were long and dramatic—at least fifteen coats of mascara, Olivia estimated.

"Can I help you?" Olivia asked.

The woman looked her up and down.

Olivia made no fuss when it came to her wardrobe. Simple jeans and a T-shirt, or a sweatshirt in this case. No makeup. Her dark brown skin didn't require it. Her hair was styled in a short bob and she wore no jewelry. She must appear bland and frumpy to this glamor puss, but Olivia cared little about her opinion.

"Is Abbie home? I need to talk to her. It's important."

"And you are?" Olivia didn't like how the woman intimated that she and Abbie were close.

She didn't answer but instead posed a question of her own. "Who are you?"

"Look, lady, we can stand here all day and play this silly game, or you can tell me who you are and I can pass along your message. Mrs. Rambally isn't home right now. I can tell her you stopped by, whoever you are."

"Tsk, tsk. You don't have to get all hostile. I didn't see you when we visited yesterday. You must be the help."

Several colorful responses formed at the edge of Olivia's tongue, but she dismissed them all. She liked her job and needed to keep it. The last thing she wanted was this woman causing problems for her.

"Well, I obviously didn't break into the house. I have things to do, so if you'll excuse me, I'll tell Abbie some random woman stopped by demanding to see her and I have no idea who she is. Goodbye."

Olivia started to close the door when an arm reached out and stopped it.

The pest of a woman forced a smile. "I didn't mean to snap at you. I was under the impression that Abbie was a stay-at-home mom, and I was expecting her to answer the door. When you did, it threw me off a bit. My apologies."

Olivia said nothing, content to let the pest do all the talking. She seemed to enjoy running her mouth, anyway. Olivia's dislike went beyond the snarky attitude, which needed a serious adjustment. Maybe Olivia had seen her somewhere before, but she would have remembered, wouldn't she? Goodness, her makeup screamed 'look at me, I'm desperate for attention'.

"Anyway," Ms. Snarky continued, "tell Abbie that Jenna stopped by to apologize, and I'd like to invite her and her family to dinner."

"I'll pass along the message," Olivia said in a bored tone.

"Now I must get back to work."

She didn't wait for a response. Olivia closed the door and returned to the kitchen to put away the groceries. She didn't know everything there was to know about her employer, but Olivia knew this was not the kind of person Abbie would be friends with. The two women were complete opposites. Where Jenna was obnoxious and overbearing, Abbie was thoughtful, generous and kind. And she didn't need makeup by the truckload to make herself attractive. She was naturally beautiful.

After the groceries were put away, Olivia took a short break before she started the laundry. She helped with light house-keeping, although she would do more if Abbie would let her. She texted Darya Petrov, a fellow nanny in the area, to see if she'd ever heard of this 'Jenna' person. Olivia figured Jenna was new to the neighborhood. And what had she done to Abbie that she needed to apologize for?

Olivia: Ever heard of a woman named Jenna who just moved into the neighborhood?

Darya: No. Why?

Olivia: No reason.

Darya: Then why do you ask?

Olivia hesitated, thinking of an appropriate response.

Olivia: She just stopped by looking for my boss. Majorly rude woman.

Darya: Oh. Ask Lucy. She might have heard something.

Olivia: Thanks. TTYL

Olivia texted Lucy and asked similar questions. Did any of the moms in their circle ever mention someone new named Jenna. She didn't know whether or not Jenna had kids, but Olivia was fairly certain she was new to the neighborhood.

Lucy replied that she never heard of her. A disappointed Olivia thanked Lucy and headed upstairs to the laundry room.

Was Jenna even this woman's real name, or did she give Abbie a fake name? She seemed like the kind of person who would do something shady like that.

Olivia shook her head as if getting rid of cobwebs. Her mother always warned her about her wild imagination. She needed to focus on her duties and erase Jenna from her brain.

CHAPTER 6

T HANKS FOR PICKING up the ingredients, Liv. Lucas will hate me forever if I don't make these pancakes."

"It was no trouble at all. Lucas will be a happy little guy tonight."

I'm exhausted as usual, and it's the time of day Liv and I change shifts, around four in the afternoon. The kids are upstairs wrapped up in homework and projects, and Liv and I are in the kitchen. She's about to head home to her apartment in Framingham. I plan on an early night so I can relax and attempt to get several hours of sleep. I'll be happy with six instead of my usual three or four. The coming weeks will be brutal as I get closer to defending my dissertation. So far, I'm on track with my research and my advisors haven't thrown any monkey wrenches in my work as of yet.

Liv grabs her coat off the back of a chair and says, "Someone stopped by earlier today looking for you."

"Oh, who was it?"

"Some lady named Jenna. All she would say is that she came by to apologize and something about a dinner invitation."

I groan. "Thanks for telling me."

Liv buttons her jacket as the doorbell rings. My heart

sinks. Plans for a peaceful, restful evening flee at warped speed. I have to get rid of whoever it is.

Liv follows behind as I trudge to the front door. When I pull it open, surprise and annoyance well up inside me in equal measure. Jenna and Charlie Payne stand before me with goofy grins on their faces. Or maybe it's a nervous grin. I'm too tired to care.

"Surprise," Jenna says, extending both arms.

Before I can speak, Charlie says, "Jenna has something to say to you and we figured the kids might be home and you would be, too. We really don't want to intrude. This will only take a minute and we'll get out of your hair."

Feeling deflated—or more accurately, displeased—I gesture for them to come inside. They do a double take when they see Liv behind me. And then a most peculiar interaction occurs in the foyer after I make the introductions. Liv, my friendly, outgoing, nice-to-everyone nanny barely mumbles a greeting to Charlie, scowls at Jenna, and gives her a handshake so lackluster, I'm not sure it happened at all.

"Liv, is everything okay?" I ask.

Her face transforms back to the one I'm used to, and she says, "Sure, everything is fine. I'll leave you to your guests, Abbie. See you tomorrow."

And with that, she walks out the front door and into the balmy March afternoon.

BY THE TIME Olivia merged onto Interstate 95, also known as Route 128, heading south, her brain was in overdrive. She was so distracted when she left the Ramballys that she forgot about taking the backroads to her place in Framingham and ended up on one of the most congested routes in the state. On a weekday afternoon, during rush hour traffic. It would be a slow, painful slog to get home. She had no choice. She would suffer through the gridlock traffic and take exit 20B to Framingham. Olivia put her Bluetooth headset on and asked the virtual assistant to call Lucy.

"Hey, it's Olivia again. Remember that woman I asked you about earlier today, Jenna? Now I have a last name. Payne. Her name is Jenna Payne, and her husband is Charlie Payne. Heard any of the parents talk about them?"

"I'm not paranoid, Lucy. I think I've seen her before."

"No, I'm not a hundred percent sure. You think I'm making this up? I could tell Abbie was annoyed when they showed up this afternoon. It's like they're stalking her or something."

"Fine, Lucy. You could have just said you haven't heard anything."

Olivia whispered under her breath.

"No, I wasn't using a Jamaican curse word under my breath. You're hearing things. No. Look, this argument is stupid. I have to go. Traffic is moving again."

Olivia hung up from Lucy and drove a couple hundred yards. Traffic came to a crawl again. She took a deep breath. Something about Jenna and Charlie Payne bugged her, and the fact that she couldn't figure out why amplified her frustration. But what if Lucy was right and Olivia was being paranoid for no reason? The situation unnerved her, and now she was sniping at her friends. Anytime she used Jamaican slang or curse words, she had moved past simple annoyance.

Olivia was a first-generation American born of Jamaican immigrant parents, and the culture was deeply ingrained in her: hard work, no excuses, respect for parents and authority figures, and all that. That's why she was so grateful for this job with the Ramballys. She had her own goals and dreams. She wanted to be a pharmacist and already had a two-year college degree. Her plan was to attend Massachusetts College of Pharmacy to earn her bachelor's.

The Ramballys paid well, and Olivia figured she had another two years with the family before they would seek other arrangements. The kids were getting older and Abbie would be working as a professional in her field by then. With what she earned as their nanny, Olivia would have saved up enough to avoid going into student loan debt to pursue her pharmacy degree. Plus, Dr. Rambally's specialty training was also coming to an end. Changes were inevitable, and she wanted to be prepared.

Dr. Tyler Whistler Rambally. Olivia sighed. *He was so dreamy.* The first time she met him, she was immediately struck by how young he was. And then how hot he was. He had that undeniable magnetism about him—full, sensuous lips that looked like they were only made for kissing. When he smiled, he made you feel like the two of you shared some intimate secret. Olivia had taken in every detail about him, including the cologne that made her want to inhale the scent of him all day, and the way the sleeves of his dress shirt were rolled up to his elbows, revealing smooth, brown, muscled forearms.

And his hands. He had the most beautiful hands she had ever seen on a man, young or old. He had caught her staring and mistakenly believed she was admiring his watch. He said his wife had bought it for him when match day results came in and confirmed he had been accepted as a surgical resident at Mass General Hospital.

But the most attractive thing about Dr. Rambally, Olivia discovered that day, was the way his hazel eyes came alive like fireworks when he talked about his wife and kids. He confessed to her that he wouldn't have made it through medical school if Abbie hadn't held things together at home and encouraged him to fight for his dream when he felt like giving up.

He said he owed her a debt he could never repay, so if Olivia was hired to help her take care of the kids, she had better be good. Olivia had lived through a couple of bad relationships and seen enough marriages tank, but the Ramballys made her believe in love; that it could be powerful and long-lasting and filled with mutual respect and admiration.

A truck horn blared from behind and startled her. She was so caught up in her reverie that she hadn't noticed traffic was moving and the nearest car was now hundreds of yards in front of her. She needed to stop obsessing, especially about the Paynes. Just because she didn't like them didn't mean they were a threat. She refused to be the girl who cried wolf and embarrass herself out of a job she loved and needed.

CHAPTER 7

"Y OU SURPRISED ME," I say, resignation clouding my voice. "I was about to start dinner and call it a night, an early one. When you showed up without calling first, it threw me off."

Charlie and Jenna are back in my kitchen. I'm not about to slow down my plans to give them my undivided attention, and I don't care how it makes me look. I busy myself mixing the ingredients together for the pancake batter: flour, eggs, baking powder, a splash of almond extract, salt, and sugar. I place the butter to be melted on low heat on the stove. Whipping the ingredients together in a large bowl, I turn around to face my unwanted guests.

"We understand," Charlie says. "We didn't want another day to go by without setting things right. Isn't that so, Jenna?"

"Yeah." Jenna clears her throat. "I made a mess of things. I'm really sorry about the way I acted yesterday, asking intrusive, personal questions about your family. It was none of my business, and I shouldn't have said anything. You were so gracious to Charlie and me, and you didn't deserve to be interrogated."

I stop stirring and shut off the heat under the butter, which is now melted.

"So why did you ask those questions?"

Jenna shrugs. "Honestly, Abbie, I don't have any answer or excuse that would make what I did okay. I'm ashamed, if you want to know the truth."

I'm not exactly sure what's going on here. Jenna says all the right things and looks appropriately remorseful, down to the staring at the floor as if she were too chagrined to look me in the eye. I don't buy it for one second. Too contrived, too practiced, like they decided exactly what she was going to say before they came over. My guess is, Charlie let her have it after they returned home and was the catalyst for this staged apology. That's why he accompanied her over here—to make sure she laid out the apology just the way they had planned.

"Everyone makes mistakes," I say. "I appreciate you coming over to make things right."

"Thank you, Abbie," Jenna says. "It would mean a lot to Charlie and me if you and your family came over for dinner soon. My cooking doesn't come close to yours, but I hope you'll give me a chance to prepare you a decent meal as an olive branch. One less dinner to make, right?"

"That's not necessary," I say and return to my pancake batter. I pour in the melted butter and fresh blueberries.

"It's absolutely necessary," Jenna insists. "We're neighbors and I couldn't live with myself knowing that I hurt you and didn't try to make amends. I want us to put this incident behind us and start over."

Before I can respond, Lucas barges into the kitchen with Blake and Alexis on his heels. Lucas gives me a big hug and thanks for making the pancakes. The twins high-five him. Lucas is the reason they are having breakfast for dinner.

"You're welcome, honey," I say to Lucas. The kids then turn their attention to Jenna and Charlie, whom I pray will leave so

34

I can focus on dinner and that warm bed calling my name.

"Are you staying for dinner?" Alexis asks. "My mom makes the best pancakes in the world, and tonight is a special treat. We only usually have it for breakfast."

My heart drops to my stomach. Alexis is like a dog with a bone when she gets an idea in her head, and right now, she has decided the neighbors should stay for dinner.

"Mr. and Mrs. Payne have to get home," I say to Alexis. "They just stopped by for a minute, but maybe we'll get to have dinner with them soon."

I hope my response will placate her. No such luck.

"Come on, Mom. It will be fun. We'll be good and Mr. and Mrs. Payne can keep you company."

I make a show of searching for the pancake griddle as if I've misplaced it. My favorite movie star could plop down in front of me right now, and I wouldn't know what to say and forget they were even here the minute they left. That's how bone-tired I am. The thought of coming up with a viable excuse for the Paynes' benefit makes my head hurt and my ears ache.

"Alexis, sweetie, another time," I say wearily. "Mrs. Payne—"

"Mom, you promised to help me with my compare and contrast essay on the Inca and Aztec civilizations tonight," Lucas interrupts. "My teacher says she won't give us extensions, and I haven't even started yet. It's due in two days." He holds up two fingers for emphasis.

Thank you, Lucas. Charlie and Jenna are taking it all in, not saying a word, as if they're enjoying my discomfort and can't wait to see how I squirm my way out of this awkwardness they caused. Lucas is an honor student who does his best to get ahead of his schoolwork. He hates leaving things for the last minute, unlike his brother who will come to me about a project the day before it's due. That essay was completed three days

35

ago. It's in tip top shape.

Charlie stands up and so does Jenna. Charlie says, "Well, then Lucas, we'll leave you to it. Schoolwork is very important, and if you need your mom's help, we don't want to get in the way."

I escort them out and before I close the door, I provide my mobile phone number, which Charlie repeats for confirmation. "I'll let you know about that dinner at your house. Just text me some dates that work for you."

When I return to the kitchen, I wink at Lucas and he gives me a big, wide, co-conspirator grin. By the time I finish with the pancakes and we sit down to dinner, it's five-thirty. The kids devour the pancakes as if it were their last meal. I suddenly have a burst of energy, and it has nothing to do with the coffee I drank earlier. An idea is forming in my head. After dinner, I go through the evening routine but it's still early. I leave the kids to occupy themselves for a while and head upstairs.

I hop in the shower off the master bedroom and quickly towel off, then get dressed in an oversized T-shirt and leggings. I pick my phone off the dresser and dial Layla's number. Layla St. John is my brother Miles' on-again, off-again girlfriend, but we get along great. She's a successful real estate broker.

The phone rings three times, and I'm about to be disappointed that it will go to voicemail when she picks up.

"Hey Abbie," she says. "Long time no speak."

After some brief chit chat about how the real estate market is treating her, an inquiry about whether she and Miles are on or off this time around (they're taking a break), I explain the reason for my call.

"Looking for information about the property four houses down the street from me, three fifty-one Cherry Blossom Lane. I want to know who bought it most recently and when, as in the month and year."

"Sure, I can look that up for you. Is everything okay? Why do you need info on that specific property?"

I can't afford to set off alarm bells with Layla. I must be careful what I say and how I say it. Despite her pronouncement that she and Miles are taking a break, they speak often. The last thing I need is for her to go blabbing to my brother about this. He will tell our parents and everything will be blown out of proportion.

"No, everything is fine," I say, my voice taking on a reassuring tone. "The new owners came by yesterday. Nice people. Just making sure they're on the up and up since they took a shine to the kids. Can't be too careful these days. You know what I mean?"

"I hear you loud and clear. Especially with your history. I would do the same thing if I were in your situation." She pauses then says, "Look, I'm in the middle of something, but give me a couple of hours. I'll see what I can find out."

I stare at the phone in my hand after Layla hangs up.

Especially with my history? What does that mean?

It means your brother is a blabbermouth who tells her everything.

As promised, Layla gets back to me two hours later. What she tells me has me flopping down on my bed in confusion. She couldn't find any information on the purchase or owners of three fifty-one Cherry Blossom.

"I don't understand. Shouldn't that information be public record? I only called you to check because I figured you could get the information faster than me, from some special real estate database only brokers have access to or something."

I'm whining and probably sound unhinged to Layla. It's because my brain is still churning and hasn't yet fully processed what I heard.

"It could be that the new owners bought the property under an LLC. People do it all the time, especially celebrities. They don't want nut jobs and stalkers looking up their addresses."

"So you're saying we need the name of the LLC to get any information on the property."

"You got it."

After the conversation ends, I sit up and tuck my legs underneath me. It doesn't mean anything, I reason. There has to be a perfectly good explanation as to why the Paynes just moved into a home where the transactional history is cloaked in secrecy.

CHAPTER 8

"T HE NANNY COULD be a problem," Charlie said to Jenna. He was watching a sports program on TV and Jenna sat on the couch at the far end, scrolling through her phone.

"Did you hear what I said?" he asked, incensed by her lack of interest.

"I heard you." But she didn't look up.

"This is important," he said, louder this time.

She let out a dramatic sigh as if he were keeping her from solving world hunger. She finally looked up at him.

"She doesn't like me because I got under her skin the first time we met, when I went over to apologize to Abbie like you wanted me to. We got into it a little. I told you that. She's just the help. No threat at all."

Charlie rose from the couch and began pacing. His eyes landed on the wedding photograph above the fireplace. Jenna knew how to push his buttons better than anyone in his entire life and sometimes he had to work overtime to keep himself in check.

"I disagree with your assessment. I didn't like her attitude, the way she looked at you. Are you sure she didn't recognize you?"

Jenna threw her phone at him. He ducked in the nick of

time. It landed near the fireplace with a thud. The thick rubber protective case prevented any damage.

"What do you take me for?" she scolded. "Some dumb idiot? If she had recognized me, she would have blabbed all to Abbie by now. She's Abbie's little poodle who does her bidding and is anxious for her approval."

Charlie didn't trust it. His gut told him something was off with that nanny. Success heavily depended on his ability to identify and eliminate threats before they become a problem. Olivia Stewart was a problem. Abbie didn't trust them yet. That was also a problem.

He moved toward the sofa and stood over her. "If as you say she's Abbie's poodle, then it stands to reason that she would tell Abbie she doesn't like you, wouldn't it, Jenna? If that's the case, it makes our job that more difficult, wouldn't you say?"

She glared at him. Her eyes emitted pure defiance like an electrical charge. "You need to calm down and stay focused on what matters. If things go sideways, our boss will be angry. You know what he's capable of when he's angry. Don't make me call the boss, Charlie."

He flinched, then backed away from Jenna. The mere mention of the boss was the equivalent to being kicked in the groin by a two-thousand-pound stallion. Jenna had known the boss much longer than Charlie. The threat was a not-so-subtle reminder that if things got too hot, the boss would side with Jenna and Charlie would be expendable. But he was a survivor. What Jenna didn't know was that she was expendable, too.

Charlie left the room without saying another word and headed for his home office. He shut the door behind him, booted up one of his high-end laptops, and opened up an encrypted folder that contained photos. He scrolled through, studying each one intently. Maybe the pictures would give up some nugget of information, something he may have missed the first hundred times he looked at them.

He had some decent photos of all three kids. The boss was only interested in one of them, though. The remaining two were to be used as insurance if things went south.

CHAPTER 9

◆

I SHOULD FEEL awful about the deception, but I don't. The not so subtle hostility between Liv and the Paynes in my foyer days ago is stuck in my brain. Liv is as polite as they come, yet she was downright rude to a couple she had never met before. What's that about? I'm hoping tonight will provide answers.

I loop my arm around Ty's as we make the brief trek down the street to Jenna and Charlie's. We reside on a quiet, leafy suburban street with large colonial-style houses and green, manicured lawns. Lexington's claim to fame stems from the fact that it was the site of the first shots fired in the American Revolutionary War during the Battle of Lexington in April, 1775. The town is consistently named one of the most affluent communities in the country, while preserving its rich history. We like it here because the town offers city amenities—numerous restaurants, coffee shops, parks, and access to public transportation—while sustaining its high quality of life and family-friendly values, including its top-rated school system.

At six o'clock on a Friday evening, several residents are pulling into their garages after the long work week. We wave to Graham McNair, a patent attorney whose wife ran off with one of the former partners at his law firm and left him to raise two little boys on his own.

We walk up the long, winding driveway and the kids quicken their pace. A race to see who gets to ring the doorbell first. I don't have the energy to tell them stop running. Liv takes off after them but then stops cold. Ty catches up with her while Blake rings the doorbell.

"You okay, Liv?" Ty asks.

"Yeah. I panicked for a second. Thought I forgot my phone at the house but it's right here," she says, patting the front of her purse.

When I get closer, the expression on her face suggests everything is not okay, so I press her.

"Are you sure you're okay? Is there something bothering you?"

She nods vigorously and says, "Yeah, sure. Everything is fine."

Just then, Jenna flings the door open and gestures for us to come inside. She lets out a small gasp when she sees Liv. I offer a swift apology as we all head inside.

"Sorry, Jenna. Something came up and I asked Liv to stay overnight. It would have been rude of me to leave her in the house all alone while we had dinner with you and Charlie. You don't mind, do you?"

The white lie slides off my tongue like a gentle summer breeze while my heart hammers in my chest like a raging storm, the kind that downs power lines and topples large tree trunks.

Our hostess forces a smile. "The more the merrier. I made plenty of food."

The layout of the house is similar to ours. The entryway leads to a grand staircase to the right, closets to the left, and kitchen and family room further down the hall.

She wasn't kidding about the food. I scan the spread before us in the dining room: roasted chicken and red potatoes, macaroni and cheese for the kids, garden salad, wine for the adults, and juice for the kids, and that's not even counting the bread rolls and fresh fruit platter.

"Jenna, this is way too much," I say as we're all seated. "I hate that you went through all this trouble just for us."

"Don't be silly. It was no trouble at all."

"I could eat," Blake says.

"Me, too," Lucas chimes in.

"Glad you could make it, Ty," Charlie says, as everyone digs in. "I told Jenna not to get her hopes up. With your busy schedule, we thought you would still be at the hospital."

"I had to come. Cooper threatened to leave me and take the kids if I didn't."

"I was only kidding," I say, grinning.

We all chuckle. Except for Liv. She's been moving around the same piece of chicken on her plate, head down, not saying a word. Something has clearly upset her. I don't want to push the issue, especially in front of everyone. It could be personal. So I let it go for now.

"Your wife's a tough cookie," Charlie says, addressing Ty. "Raising three kids is no joke."

"You're a lucky man, Ty," Jenna adds. "The kids are lucky too, having their mom home with them I mean."

"Cooper has her own dreams and goals. She won't be able to stay home with the kids much longer," Ty says. "She's almost done with her Ph.D. She defends her dissertation in a few weeks."

Ty looks at me in that way of his that makes my heart do more back flips than an Olympic gymnast.

"Abbie, you've been holding out on me," Jenna squeals. "I had no idea you were so ambitious. Raising three kids while enrolled in a Ph.D. program and making it look easy. That's pretty badass if you ask me. What are you studying?"

44

"Clinical Psychology. I'm not out of the woods just yet. I have to pass my dissertation and worry about postdoctoral training if I want to make it as a licensed neuropsychologist."

"Congratulations," Charlie says. "What you're doing is nothing short of amazing."

"I have help. I wouldn't be able to do any of this without Ty's support and Liv helping me with the kids."

I peek at Liv. She finally lifts her head. I smile at her, letting her know that it will be okay, whatever has her down.

"You're doing the heavy lifting, Abbie. The kids are a joy. It doesn't feel like a job at all."

"That's sweet of you to say, Liv," Ty exclaims. "But the truth is, we'd be in dire straits if it weren't for you."

Liv beams at Ty, the first time she's smiled since we arrived here and even before that. Charlie glances at her and a peculiar look comes over his face. He catches my eyes on him and quickly shifts his gaze to the kids, landing on Blake's almost empty dish.

"Would you like more mac and cheese, Blake?" Charlie asks. "There's plenty left."

"That's okay," I interrupt. "The kids could do with a little more salad and fresh fruit."

Then Blake asks, "Mrs. Payne, can we see some of your books?"

Jenna looks like a deer caught in the headlights. Her voice is shaky when she asks, "I'm sorry sweetie, what books?"

"The ones you work on," Alexis explains. "You said you were a children's book illustrator."

All eyes turn to focus on Jenna. She fidgets with her scarf then says, "Of course. I would love to show you my work some time. But we just moved here, and all of my books are in storage still. But when I get them out, I will come right over to show you."

45

My mind jolts at the statement, reminding me what Layla said about the property: there's no public information available.

"I hope you and Charlie got a good price for the house." My eyes scan the space. "The real estate prices in this town are out of control."

I wait for one of them to take the bait dangling before them, and offer up a logical explanation as to why information about their home is unavailable.

Charlie sits stiffly in his chair. His Adam's apple bobs up and down. Jenna chews on her bottom lip. Neither one of them says anything for a beat.

"What, did that get too personal?" I ask, feigning innocence. "I didn't mean to pry. Ty and I know what it's like to be a young couple just starting out. If it weren't for our parents, I don't think we could live in this town."

"How do you mean?" Jenna asks, leaning forward, her eyes eager with anticipation of some juicy tidbit about to drop in her lap.

"Our house was a wedding present from our parents," Ty says. "It turned out to be a blessing. The kids came quicker than we had planned, so it worked out that we were already in a town with great schools and neighborhoods. We lucked out."

"That was a generous wedding present," Jenna says, side-stepping my original question all together.

"Yes, it was," I agree. "The house has increased in value as real estate prices continue to rise in this town. Great for us. Not so much for new people moving in who get saddled with the higher priced listings."

My comments have zero effect on the Paynes. Their expressions remain carved neutral. I have no doubt they understand that I'm trying to bait them into a discussion about the purchase of their home, even if they don't know why. They're experts at playing the caution game. Well, three can play that game.

After dessert, we move into a sparsely decorated living room: a white sofa and couch with a few throw pillows, two lamps on either side of the fire place, and no curtains in the bay windows. The kids entertain themselves with a game of cards while Ty and I continue conversing. Liv excuses herself and heads to the bathroom. I make a mental note to find out what's going on with her.

"Charlie, I don't want to be too presumptuous, but if you're looking to grow your client list here in Massachusetts, I may be able to help," I offer.

His face lights up. "You would?"

"Sure. I come from a family of entrepreneurs, and I don't mind helping out whenever I can."

"Thank you, Abbie," he says with genuine feeling. "Tell me about your family."

"Well, my mother owns several restaurants, has written multiple bestselling cookbooks, and once hosted her own top-rated show on the Cooking Network, *Shelby's Kitchen.*"

"Wow," Jenna says. "That's pretty awesome. No wonder you're so driven to accomplish your goals. It runs in the family."

I ignore her comment. "Then there's my dad. He has a lot of contacts in the corporate world. He used to be CFO for Orphion Technologies. I'm sure you've heard of them."

Charlie's eyes widen, and his mouth falls partially open. "Are you serious? Your father is Jason Cooper? *The* Orphion Technologies?"

"That's right."

"I had no idea. They're one of the most innovative companies in the world. I even applied for a job with them and didn't get it. Working for Orphion was my dream job as a developer. It just didn't work out."

"My dad worked for the company a long time ago, but he's on the board of directors now. He also has a lot of tech clients, long-established juggernauts and start-ups that are changing the landscape. He's a good person to know for a young tech entrepreneur like yourself."

"She's right," Ty says. "Jason Cooper is a good person to know. If he likes you, he could be a golden ticket to bigger and better opportunities."

"Do you have a website?" I ask. "He will check you out before he agrees to an introduction."

"I do." He asks for my email address. After I provide it, he says I can check it at my leisure.

"My father is ridiculously busy and still travels a lot, so don't be surprised if it takes a couple of weeks or longer to set up a face-to-face introduction," I explain.

"No problem, Abbie. I'm just happy you're willing to do this for me."

"That's really nice of you, Abbie," Jenna adds. "It could take the business to another level if this works out."

"We're happy to do it," I say, squeezing Ty's arm.

I do a mental summersault. Charlie just gave up an important piece of information without realizing it.

CHAPTER 10

"W HAT IS IT?" Ty probes.
"Nothing."

"Come on, Cooper. Something's been on your mind all night, and it has to do with Charlie and Jenna. Tell me."

It's a few minutes after eleven at night. Ty is sitting up in bed reading a medical journal. The moment I appear, he places the journal down on the nightstand and concentrates his gaze on me. He gestures for me to join him in bed. I climb in and rest my head on his chest. The rhythm of his heartbeat is so calming. I wish I could stay like this and drift off into blissful rest. I could use a few days of uninterrupted sleep. However, sleep is the last thing on my husband's mind.

I sit up and position myself on the bed, yoga style. I recap the events that transpired after he first met the Paynes and had to take off for Mass General: Jenna's reaction to Lucas and her questions about his paternity, how upset she was when I said Lucas' biological father was dead and I was happy about it, and what Layla told me about the house they live in. Then the apology the very next day.

He listens quietly, not interrupting, then gestures with his arm. "Come here."

49

I return to his arms and he kisses my forehead. Then he says, "Sounds like you've had an interesting past few days. But I wouldn't worry too much about it. People have been reacting to Lucas like that for years. The Paynes didn't do anything we haven't seen a dozen times."

"Wait a minute," I say, as I squirm out of his embrace. "How can you be so dismissive? You don't find any of it strange?"

"Not really." He shrugs. "I wouldn't use up too much energy worrying about it if I were you. As for the house being purchased by an LLC, it makes sense if Charlie is looking to expand his business. Owning the property will help add value to the business."

How can he be so casual and logical about all of this? Am I seeing things that aren't there, losing touch with reality? Maybe the stress of my upcoming dissertation defense is getting to me.

"Something is off about Jenna and Charlie," I insist. "You weren't there. You didn't witness the rest of the visit that day they showed up here for the first time. And how Jenna ran out of the kitchen like the house was on fire. Even Liv gave them the cold shoulder, and she likes everybody."

"Maybe Liv's attitude had nothing to do with them at all. They could have caught her at a bad time."

I contemplate his words, yet refuse to give in. "I think you're wrong to downplay this."

A bewildered look crosses his face. He slips the watch off his wrist and places it on the nightstand.

"Cooper," he says firmly, "you're stretched thin as it is. Right now, our family and your dissertation defense are your top priorities. You've being doing a great job so far, and I know the road has been difficult. Please don't get sidetracked by the Paynes. I think they're just trying to make friends in a new town."

He climbs out of bed and begins pacing, a habit ever since

I've known him. The ritual helps him gather his thoughts.

"Then answer me this: Why was Jenna so upset when I said Lucas' biological father was better off dead? She kept pushing, Ty, wanting to know about him. So, I told her. Then she bolted out of the house like she was trying to outrun a cyclone. The very next day, she shows up with Charlie, apologetic and conciliatory, like she was coached."

"You don't think the apology was genuine?"

"Not for a second."

"Do you think Jenna knows the truth about Lucas?"

"No way."

I reach for a pillow and squeeze hard, drawing in a frustrated breath. "I hate this. The constant suspicion and worry."

He rejoins me in bed and squeezes my shoulder. "I don't want you getting upset over something that could turn out to be nothing more than nosy neighbors. You've overcome too many obstacles to get to this point. Don't stumble now."

"I guess you're right. My focus should be on my goals, not some random side show."

"I know how hard it was for you to say that, so I'll prove to you that you're getting anxious over nothing."

"How?"

"Remember my friend Eric from college?"

"Of course. He and your other friend Hak ate as if it were their last meal whenever I cooked at your apartment."

"Yeah. Those guys could eat. They always asked when you were coming over so they could 'accidentally' drop by."

I almost smile. I've spent years erasing the memory of my days as a student at one of the nation's most elite universities. It was there, during my sophomore year, that my world was turned upside down, never to be the same again. Prior to that, I was unstoppable, full of life and endless promise. Maybe even a little cocky. I was nineteen years old and had the world at my feet.

My carefree, perfect life didn't come to an abrupt halt. It was more of a slow, excruciating unraveling. There were times when I sat alone in bed at night and allowed my feelings to run amok. I grieved. I grieved for the girl I was. The promise of that girl, and what could have been. Ty and I are only two years apart. If things had turned out the way I planned, I would be a surgical resident heading into neurosurgery specialty training soon.

I worked through my grief over late-night feedings, sick children, the cooking and cleaning and laundry, and all the things needed to run a household.

Eventually, acceptance seeped in. My family had to come first. Yet I couldn't see myself as a housewife forever. What would I have once the kids got older and started doing their own thing? I wasn't willing to part with all of me, so I had to find another path. The field of neuropsychology seemed a good fit. It just about killed me to take on that program while raising three kids. But I was determined. And now, my sacrifice is about to pay off. So Jenna and Charlie Payne can just go back to Colorado and stay off my radar.

"What does Eric have to do with anything?" I ask, stepping out of the past.

"He's a federal agent. DEA."

"What's the connection to the Paynes?"

"I thought he could use his contacts within the government to see what he could find out, to put your mind at ease. To tell you the truth, I think this whole thing will blow over soon and we can resume our normal lives."

CHAPTER 11

SUMMER, THREE YEARS EARLIER

"ARE YOU IN?" Iceman growled.

"Yeah. I think so."

"Not good enough. I need to know if I'm wasting my time with you. In or out, yes or no?"

Archie took a drag on his cigarette to calm his nerves. This was it. If he refused, he would be dead by midnight. If he said yes, there was a fifty-fifty chance he would make it on the outside. Iceman only pretended to give him a choice as they sat on the sidelines and observed a pickup basketball game in progress.

"What do I have to do?" he asked.

Iceman's lips parted slightly. Most people would think he was going to smile. They would be wrong. It was more of a predatory look, a cat that caught a canary and decided to toy with it before it became dinner. He was a tall, skinny dude, and Archie wouldn't have believed what he was capable of until someone made the mistake of calling him pretty boy. Iceman lifted the guy over his head and threw him across the mess hall, full force. The guy suffered a concussion and so many broken bones, he was in a body cast for months. Archie tried not to shiver at the memory but failed.

"Are you getting cold feet?" Iceman asked.

"Nah, man," Archie said. "But you still haven't told me what I have to do."

Iceman didn't answer right away. A helicopter passed overhead. An argument amongst the players in the basketball game heated up. Shouting, threats, swearing, and punches followed. Both men ignored the commotion as gun-toting guards broke up the melee.

"It's really simple," Iceman said. "I want you to get something for me. Still interested?"

Archie nodded as if he understood. He still had no idea what Iceman wanted. Iceman had saved him on a couple of occasions. He had clout in this place. The guys on the cell block were afraid of him. Even the guards didn't want to mess with him. The guy was fearless. Nothing fazed him. Not even being sent to the hole for months at a time. He was a terrifying machine. No feelings. No emotions. His face was a solid mask of ice.

He never swore, not like most of the guys. When he spoke, he was all proper, like some pompous college professor with an axe to grind. So no, Archie wasn't about to tango with this guy and unleash his inner crazy.

Besides, Iceman had some chick on the outside who could get him stuff. She was loaded, from what Archie could tell. He wouldn't mind getting a piece of that pie, although he had no idea where this chick got her money from. It didn't matter, though. Whatever Iceman was proposing, it would be high risk and could possibly land him back in prison. But Archie figured he should hear the man out, listen to the whole plan.

Darkness crossed Iceman's face. "I also want the perpetrator to pay. Dearly."

Archie looked at him. "So in plain English, you want revenge on some dude who played you foul?"

Iceman nodded.

"I can do that."

"Good."

"So how long before I have to nail this guy?"

"Patience, my friend. It will take a lot of training and finesse for what I have in mind."

"You don't have a plan?" Archie asked, kicking the dirt in front of him.

"I have a plan."

"How am I going to help you if I'm stuck in here?"

"I've already taken that into account. You won't be in here much longer, will you?"

"No, but—" Archie didn't finish his sentence.

Iceman cut him off with a detached "We're done. For now." Then he stood up and walked away.

Archie stumped out the cigarette even though he'd only had one drag. He didn't want to think much about what Iceman was proposing. Archie only focused on the end result— enough money to disappear and start over.

By the look in his eyes, Iceman wanted payback. *Bad.* He felt sorry for whoever this dude was. He was about to get iced.

CHAPTER 12

WEDNESDAY MORNING FINDS me pacing the kitchen floor like a madwoman. Liv is ten minutes late. Liv is never late. Not even a Nor'easter of epic proportions could keep her away. Apparently, her subdued demeanor during dinner at the Paynes' last Friday evening lasted throughout the weekend because when she returned to work on Monday, she wasn't in a talkative mood and I couldn't drag anything out of her. Now, she's taken the strange behavior up a notch by not calling to let me know she'd be late.

I've called three times already and each call went straight to voicemail. The kids are already up and going through the morning schedule. Soon, they'll be down, expecting breakfast.

I glance at the microwave clock for the hundredth time. Now she's twelve minutes late. She knows how important today is. I meet with my advisors, most of whom will make up the committee that judges my dissertation defense. Men and women who will determine if I've wasted the past three years of my life. I'm already riddled with fear and doubt about whether I can be successful as a neuropsychologist. I don't need to compound the problem.

Decision time. If I don't leave home in the next ten

56

minutes, I will be late. They won't wait around for me. Traffic from Lexington to Boston on a weekday morning is challenging. Panic rises inside of me like a torpedo speeding toward its target. Swallowing several times, I beat back the dread by sheer force of will. Distracted, I reach for my phone on the kitchen island to call Liv again and instead knock over a cup of coffee. The mug shatters on the tiled floor. Lucas and Blake walk into the kitchen and assess the mess, their eyes wide.

"Don't come in any farther." I hold up a hand to halt their movement. "Mom needs to clean up the spill. I don't want either of you accidentally stepping on broken pieces."

"Mom, what's wrong?" Blake asks.

I ignore the question. I don't remember where I placed the rubber gloves needed to protect my hands while I pick up the broken ceramic fragments and wipe up the liquid.

"Have you guys seen the pair of lavender rubber gloves?" My eyes dart from one child to the other.

They're dumfounded by the question. "Well don't just stand there, answer me," I yell.

"We don't know, Mom," Lucas responds, looking like he's being falsely accused of a horrible crime.

"Mom, you're freaking us out," Blake says.

Get a grip, will you? Work through this calmly and rationally.

I take a deep breath, shake the panic from my face, then school my features into a façade of calm and control. At least, I hope that's what's outwardly projected. I pull my boys into my arms for reassurance.

"I'm sorry. Mom is a little anxious this morning. I didn't mean to yell. Everything will be fine."

I release them from the hug and gauge whether my reassurances have had any effect, because my anxiety level is pushing DEFCON 1 levels.

They both nod and move toward the kitchen table.

"Liv is running late, so our morning routine is a little off today," I inform them with forced cheerfulness. "No biggie. I'll clean up the spilled coffee and broken mug and get breakfast started."

By the time I find the gloves and clean up the spill, Alexis has also arrived in the kitchen, and all three kids have solemn looks on their faces. Liv still hasn't made an appearance. I can't call Mom to help me out. She's away and even if she were home, it would take her an hour to get here.

The kids take charge of breakfast. I hear a waffle pop from the toaster. Alexis and Lucas pull out the plates and a jug of milk from the refrigerator and set the table. I can't call Ty. He's doing rounds and besides, it's not like he can abandon his patients to take the kids to school.

The ringing of the doorbell slices through the controlled chaos of my morning. I ignore it. Liv has keys to the house and never rings the bell. Alexis leaves to get the door while I stand at the kitchen sink, biting my nails and trying not to have a nuclear meltdown in front of my children. I can feel the tears pooling as I envision my advisors walking out the room in disgust at my failure to appear for the second-most important meeting of my graduate academic career. I see my future plans circling the drain, ready to disappear for good.

When Alexis lumbers into the kitchen, Jenna at her heels, my panic turns to anger, a large plume of black smoke bellowing from a blazing inferno.

"Whatever it is Jenna, I can't deal with you right now. I'm sorry, but you have to leave. Now."

Her face is crestfallen as she takes a step back. "Did I offend you, Abbie?"

"Liv isn't here yet and Mom has to go," Alexis says. "Mom's

upset. Today is really important and she can't miss school. Isn't that right, Mom?"

I simply nod at my daughter because at this point, my energy reserves are taking a nosedive.

Alexis joins her siblings at the table, and they eat breakfast in stone-faced silence. Jenna takes a couple of steps closer to me.

"Abbie, I know we're just getting to know each other, but if you're in a bind, I can take the kids to school for you."

Silence scatters around the room. My eyes laser in on the refrigerator door, a holiday photo of the family.

"Abbie," Jenna says gently. "I'm sure Olivia has a good reason for not being here, but I hate to see you so upset. Tell me where the kids go to school and I can drop them off. If you want me to pick them up after school in case Olivia is sick or something, I can do that too, no problem. I work from home and my workload is light today."

"Why are you here?" I ask, rudely. "You could have called first."

"Sorry, Abbie," she says, her tone flat. "It was a split-second decision. I was on my way to the supermarket. I thought I would drop in to see if you needed anything."

"We'll be okay, Mom," Blake says. "Mrs. Payne can drop us. School's not far."

"And we have our phones," Lucas says. "You can track us."

"I'll call you after we get dropped off, before we head to class," Alexis adds.

I look at my babies. I'm about to start bawling right there in front of them. Instead, I walk over to the drawer near the refrigerator and open it. A yellow sticky notepad is right on top a pile of writing utensils and other office supplies. I lift the pad and hand it to Jenna.

"Write down your license plate number. And I also need to see your license so I can take a photo."

"Why?" she asks, offended.

"A lot of bad things have happened to me, Jenna, from people who pretended to be nice to me, pretended to care. Now I'm the mother of three, and I have to protect my kids. This is not about you. I do appreciate you helping me out. You want to be a mother one day. Maybe then, you will understand my overprotectiveness."

"I understand." She writes down the requested information on the sticky note. I take it from her and wait expectantly for the license to come out. She digs through her purse and then hands it over. I take a photo with my phone.

"The kids know how to get to school. They'll show you the way," I inform her.

I kiss each of my children on the cheek and tell Alexis to make sure she calls me.

"I'll be back right after my meeting, so you won't need to get them this afternoon," I say to Jenna. "Hopefully, I will hear from Liv before then."

CHAPTER 13

A FEW MINUTES PAST one-thirty in the afternoon, I'm back home in the kitchen, leaving what seems like my hundredth message for Liv. Jenna didn't kidnap my children as I feared during my early morning meltdown, though self-recrimination plagued me most of the day. *Did I place my ambition ahead of my kids by having Jenna drive them to school?* All three arrived safely, and that was the only highlight of my day. I picked them up before dismissal, and I'm glad the school didn't make a fuss about it. They're upstairs getting homework done.

Now I'm officially afraid that something truly awful has happened to Liv. There were no major car accidents in Framingham or on any of the major routes or back roads she takes to work. Ty hasn't heard from her either, and neither did Lucy or Darya, her friends in the area. I tried the local hospitals, and nothing. I want to find out from her parents if they've heard from her, but I have no contact information for them. All I know is that they split their time between Brooklyn and a suburb of Kingston, Jamaica.

I contemplate filing a missing person's report, while running through multiple scenarios in my head that could explain Liv's absence and lack of communication. Maybe she had a personal emergency and hasn't had time to call me. No. Liv wouldn't leave us stranded without an explanation. A death in the family? What if one of her parents died? She's an only child, and that would be enough to send her over the edge. If that's the case, she would call once the initial shock started to wear off.

She's fine. No need to panic and take away police resources by jumping the gun to file a missing person's report.

I pour myself more coffee and sit at the kitchen table. I don't feel like cooking dinner tonight, so it will be pizza delivery. I'm sure the kids will be all broken up about it. I limit their junk food intake, but after the day we've all had, they deserve a treat.

The doorbell rings. I slowly rise to my feet and drag my exhausted bones to answer it. A young guy in his twenties asks if I'm Abbie Rambally. When I confirm that I am, he asks me to sign the digital, hand-held device. Once I do, he hands me a large, manila envelope and tells me to have a nice day.

I rip the envelope open as I head back to the kitchen table and my coffee. I extract a single sheet of white paper with a typewritten message on it. My knees almost buckle when I see who it's from. I sit down and read its contents in their entirety.

Dear Abbie,

I can't begin to tell you how sorry I am. You and Dr. Rambally have been kind and generous to me but I can't pretend anymore. I've tried my best to hide it but my feelings for him have grown from a simple crush to fantasizing about him day and night. I can't continue to disrespect you like that. It's not right. For this reason, please consider this my official resignation letter. I've given this a lot of thought. You deserve a nanny you can fully trust. Please don't call or try to find me. I've decided to join my parents in Jamaica. My mother is sick and my father can't take care of her by himself. Tell the children I'm sorry and I love them. I'm truly sorry, Abbie. I hope one day you'll forgive me.

Sincerely,

Olivia

CHAPTER 14

I SIT AT the kitchen table dumfounded. The letter has hit me like the proverbial ton of bricks, and said bricks have flattened me out.

I force myself to slow down my breathing and reread the letter again to make sure I understand what my loyal, dependable caregiver—a woman I considered a dear friend—is saying to me. I want to be certain there's no room for misinterpretation. The words remain unchanged. I've long suspected that Liv had a little crush on Ty, but nothing to warrant a decision of this magnitude.

Ty blossomed after college as though some Fairy Godmother responsible for sex appeal waved her magic wand at him. He was always a good-looking guy, but something happened after he started medical school. He morphed into this gorgeous, sexy man with magnetism to spare. Shocked the heck out of me. At the time though, I was too stressed and miserable to pay much attention to the fact that women flirted with him wherever he went. Even teenage girls and old ladies.

However, I've never witnessed any odd interaction between him and Liv. Did she dote on him? Sure. Did she respect and admire him? Absolutely. But Liv always conducted herself with professionalism. Now I'm wondering if I missed something.

What she describes in the letter hit me like a thunderbolt. There were no indications that her feelings for Ty had so intensified that she would quit her job. It doesn't ring true. There has to be something else at play, some explanation that would shed light on this mystery.

I hear a car pull into the driveway. The door slams shut, and then keys jangle in the front door. Ty is home. I texted him after I allowed Jenna to take the kids to school, but I didn't go into details about the situation. Only that Liv had some kind of emergency. He arrives in the kitchen and takes off his jacket, which he drapes over the back of a chair. He kisses me on the cheek. I gesture for him to take a seat. He does as he loosens his tie and rolls up the sleeves of his dress shirt.

"What's going on, Cooper? Is everything okay with Liv?"

"I'm not sure."

He frowns. "What do you mean?"

"Liv quit on us, Ty.

"What?"

"It's true."

"But why? I thought everything was going well."

"So did I."

"Did she say why when you spoke to her?"

I open the envelope, take out the letter, and push it across the table toward him. He reads the contents then places the sheet back on the table.

"What do you think?" I ask. "Does this sound plausible?"

Ty shakes his head in bafflement. He removes his tie completely and unbuttons the top two buttons of his shirt. He gets up from the table and starts pacing.

"That doesn't make any sense, Cooper."

"Tell me about it. You never suspected she had a crush on you?"

"A crush, sure. I'm not stupid. But what she describes in this letter is another story. Not that I'm home much, but I never noticed any change in her behavior toward me when we interacted. Nothing to indicate she was distressed, or that her feelings had escalated."

"That's what I thought. She certainly did a good job of hiding it if what she says is true."

Ty pulls out the chair and sits once more. "You're saying you don't believe what's written in the letter?"

I shrug. "I don't know, Ty."

I flash back to what I observed last Friday evening at the Paynes'. Then days later, she ups and quits. Coincidence? *If I share my concern with Ty, he'll just tell me I'm being paranoid.*

"Isn't it interesting that Jenna happened to show up right when you needed help, right when Liv was supposed to arrive but hadn't?" he says.

A rush of adrenaline surges through me. In my panic, it never occurred to me to question Jenna's reason for popping over in the middle of my meltdown. I bought her story about heading to the supermarket and wanting to see if I needed anything. Her timing was flawless. I let my guard down. Now I'm pondering if I was a fool for believing her. If I can't tell when my own neighbor is lying to my face, how am I supposed to help my future patients who might use deception to build walls around painful truths? I haven't even graduated yet, and I'm already a failure.

"Cooper, what's wrong?" Ty asks, his brows knitted together.

"I never questioned it."

"Questioned what?"

"Her sincerity. I was so focused on getting the kids to school and making my meeting that I took her explanation at face value, and took her license plate info."

"Don't beat yourself up. You had the presence of mind to get that information from her. That means we can do some more digging if we need to."

"She didn't anticipate me asking for her driver's license."

"How do you know that?"

"She hesitated when I asked, clearly uncomfortable. In fact, she asked me why." *Yet, like a fool, I allowed her to take the kids to school, despite my reservations.*

Ty rubs his chin and leans back in the chair.

"I'll give Eric a buzz. See what he can find out about the Paynes."

"What are you going to tell him? We don't have much to go on."

"I'm telling him the truth. I want to find out if Jenna or Charlie has any type of record, anything that would cause them to pop up on law enforcement radar."

"He's going to ask a lot of questions."

"Don't worry about it. I'll take care of it. Now comes the hard part. We have to tell the kids."

"I'm dreading it."

"Do you want me to do it?"

"We'll do it together." I reach over and caress his arm.

Ten minutes later, three solemn faces stare back at us from across the kitchen table. Lucas keeps his head down. Blake stares off into space, and Alexis is trying to stop her lips from trembling, unsuccessfully.

"Don't be afraid to ask questions, and it's okay to be mad," I say. "We all loved Liv, and her leaving is a big blow to our family."

"Your mother is right," Ty says, backing me up. "Liv left us for a good reason, to take care of her sick mom, but that doesn't make it hurt any less. It's okay to be upset. You don't have to hide how you feel."

More silence. Alexis starts to hiccup, as the tears escape.

"Come here, Pumpkin," Ty says, opening his arms wide.

Alexis buries her head in his chest and starts sobbing. The boys won't look at either one of us.

Blake asks, "Can we go now?"

Ty and I exchange glances. "Um…"

They don't wait for a fully formed response. My boys flee the kitchen as if they were being chased by a cheetah in the jungle.

CHAPTER 15

"THIS REALLY STINKS," Lucas says.

"I know."

"Who's going to take care of us when Mom has school?"

"I don't know, dude."

Lucas threw the rubber ball against the wall repeatedly, knowing full well that it aggravated Blake. They each had their own room but hung out in each other's space often. They could share secrets without Alexis running off to tattletale. When their parents announced that Liv left and wouldn't be coming back, Lucas couldn't believe it. Liv was cool and funny, and he thought she liked them. He guessed he was wrong, because look what happened.

He knew he wasn't supposed to be selfish. His parents were always telling him and his siblings they had to be considerate of others and it wasn't always about them. Right now, though, Lucas didn't care. What about them, now that Liv wasn't around anymore? What about his mom, who was always so stressed out that sometimes she cried in the bathroom when she thought no one was around and could hear her? He hated when his mom cried. She used to do it a lot when he was younger but lately, not so much. Liv bailing on them was going

69

to make her sad.

He didn't want to think about a new helper for Mom. Lucas didn't like strangers, and the idea that a stranger would soon be taking care of them made him uncomfortable.

With Liv, it was different. They liked her right away. They didn't think of her as a stranger. She was more like a family member who went away for a while but then she came back and everything was fine.

Blake, who was sitting on the large toy chest, suddenly gasped.

"What?" Lucas asked, popping into a sitting position so he could face his brother.

"Do you think Liv leaving has anything to do with last weekend?"

"What do you mean?"

"When she was asking us about Kaley Witherby."

Lucas frowned at his brother. "Who's Kaley Witherby?"

"Dude, you really need to pay attention."

"I do pay attention. You're the one who's not making any sense."

"Liv asked us on the way to the movies last Saturday if there was a Kaley Witherby in our class."

"Oh yeah, Lucas said, remembering how Liv kept asking them if they were sure. He hadn't paid much attention because he was excited to see the latest superhero movie.

"Her mom is sick. That's why she left."

"I guess," Blake said. "It was just weird, that's all. Do you think we should tell Mom?"

"Tell her what?"

"About Liv asking about Kaley."

"Why would we do that?"

"I don't know. Maybe she knows something about Liv

70

leaving that she didn't tell us."

Lucas stiffened at the thought of holding on to secrets. He had one of his own that he couldn't tell anybody. Well maybe he could tell Blake. But he wasn't sure yet. When Mr. and Mrs. Payne came to the house for the first time, Lucas overheard something he wasn't supposed to. He knew he wasn't supposed to hear that because his mom thought he was upstairs doing homework. Lucas *was* doing homework, but then he got thirsty and headed downstairs to get a drink. As he got closer to the kitchen, he could hear his mom yelling at Mrs. Payne.

You want to know about Lucas' father? I'll tell you. He's dead. And I say good riddance.

He just stood there, frozen. If his mother had left her seat at the kitchen table, she would have caught him eavesdropping, that's how shocked he was. He couldn't move. He couldn't even feel his legs under him. Everything went numb.

Lucas knew he looked different from his brother and sister, but his parents never made a big deal about it and neither did he. He never asked why Blake and Alexis had brown skin and big brown eyes like their mother and he had blue eyes and pale skin. He just thought his family was different and that was okay.

His dad was always his dad. So when his mother said his dad had died, Lucas was confused. He had the same dad as Blake and Alexis, so who was this other dad? Was he mean to his mom? Is that why she's glad he's dead? Was he a bad man and his mom got him a new dad?

"Lucas, what's wrong?"

Lucas was so caught up in his mind, he forgot Blake was sitting right there in the room with him.

"Nothing."

"Why are you crying, then?"

Lucas swiped his hand under his eyes.

"I'm not crying, stupid."

"It looked like you were. Are you upset about Liv?"

Lucas didn't answer. Most of his friends who had brothers hated them, especially Liam McSweeney. Liam and his little brother, Jack, didn't get along because Liam said Jack got away with everything and he got blamed for everything, even stuff that wasn't his fault. But Lucas liked his brother. Blake was easygoing and helpful. Lucas could tell him when he was scared or mad about something and Blake would understand, even though Lucas was older. Blake was a good little brother, and Lucas was lucky.

"Maybe. I don't know. It's confusing."

"About Liv?"

"Yeah, that and other stuff."

"What other stuff?"

Lucas shrugged. He wasn't sure if he wanted to tell Blake what he overheard in the kitchen. Then he just blurted it out.

"Mom told Mrs. Payne that my father died and she was happy about it."

Blake tugged at his ear. He stayed really quiet. It seemed like a long time. Then he said, "I don't understand what you mean, Lucas. How can your dad be dead? Our dad is downstairs with Mom and Alexis."

"I don't understand it either."

Blake shook his head slowly then said, "Do you want me to ask Mom about it?"

"No."

"Why not?"

"She'll know I was eavesdropping, and I don't want to get in trouble."

"Then what should we do?"

Lucas shrugged. "How should I know? I'm ten, dude."

72

Blake folded his arms and his eyes squinted. Lucas knew that look. Blake did that when he was thinking hard about something.

"If you had a different dad, why wouldn't Mom tell us?"

Lucas had thought about that question a lot, ever since he heard the conversation between Mom and Mrs. Payne. He wondered if he was adopted. His classmate Caleb Anderssen looked different from his parents and sister, Dylan. Caleb was Chinese, and he told Lucas during recess one day that he was adopted. But Lucas didn't want to think about that. Plus, he was too afraid to ask his parents, anyway.

"Adults have a lot of secrets," he said to Blake.

"Says who?"

"Says adults. And the movies, and TV and books. Come on Blake, you know it's true."

"Yeah, I guess you're right."

"I don't want to talk about this anymore," Lucas said.

"Me neither."

"You want to play video games?"

"Sure."

CHAPTER 16

C HARLIE PAYNE STROLLED into the Hawthorne Bar, tucked underneath the Commonwealth Hotel in Boston. It was strange being in a bar that looked like someone's living room, complete with sofas, throw pillows, armchairs, and multiple photos and artwork lining the walls. Chairs, not stools, were perfectly lined up at the bar. The counter boasted vases of flowers. He had heard that the ambience and drink menu here were fantastic, so he decided to check the place out. Told her to meet him here.

The place was hopping, busy enough but not overly crowded. Several bartenders were mixing drinks for the patrons seated at the long counter. However, it didn't take him long to spot her, seated near a cluster of armchairs with a glass coffee table in the center. He trudged over and sat next to her. She ignored him and focused her attention on the group of young professionals knocking them back and having a good time. He didn't care. They both knew what this meeting was about.

She was in her late twenties with light brown hair piled high on her head in a loose chignon. She wore a powder-pink, long-sleeved, open-collared blouse and black pencil skirt. On her feet, were black, sling-back pumps. She would do quite nicely, Charlie thought.

He asked, "Are we just going to sit here all night, not saying anything?"

She turned to look at him. Even in the dim light, he could detect her hostility.

"Works for me," she said, then returned to people watching.

"We had a deal. It's time to collect. And it's not as if it doesn't come with perks."

"Perks that depend on my cooperation."

"That's what we agreed to. Don't make it complicated, Katie."

She pinged her gaze back to him. Angry sparks shot from her eyes, her body tense like a large jungle cat about to pounce. Charlie was surprised she didn't hiss at him.

"What exactly do I have to do?" she asked.

"Whatever you're told."

"What does that mean?"

"What do you think it means?"

"Don't be a douche."

Charlie let out a deep sigh. She was deliberately trying his patience.

"It's very simple. You help out a mom with her kids. It's only a temporary assignment. You will be paid very well for a job that's easy and rewarding."

"What kids, which mom, and where?"

"Three school-age kids. They're no trouble at all. You like kids, don't you?"

If Katie were a guy, she would have punched him in the face and a brawl would have broken out right then and there. That's the vibe he got from her, the way she kept balling her fists that she tried to hide in her lap.

"Where exactly is this assignment, and how long will it last?"

"Lexington. A few weeks, a month or two. No more."

"I don't have a choice, do I?" Her tone was softer, defeated.

"How about I get us a drink?" Charlie offered. "It may help this go down a little smoother."

"You really think a drink is going to help me deal with your blackmail?" she snarled.

"Be right back," Charlie said. "I'll pick out something special for you."

A few minutes later, Charlie returned with two drinks that he deposited on the table, a champagne cocktail comprised of white rum, honey, lime, and bitters.

"You do have a choice," he said, picking up the conversation where they left off. "Nobody is holding a gun to your head."

She picked up the drink and took two big gulps, then swiped the stray drops from her mouth with the back of her hand. Charlie took his drink and had a few sips.

"How long do you intend to hold my mistake over my head?" she asked.

Charlie scoffed. "I'm asking for a simple favor. I did you a solid, and now it's your turn. Working in a beautiful home in the suburbs with a nice family is not exactly doing hard time. You will be well compensated," he reiterated. "I fail to see the downside here."

She leaned forward, disapproval gleaming in her eyes. "You make it sound so simple, but it isn't. What's really going on, Charlie?"

"I will contact you with further instructions. Be ready to move when I do."

He didn't wait for a response. He stood, finished off his drink, placed the empty glass on the table, and left the bar.

CHAPTER 17

M Y MOTHER, THE indomitable Shelby Cooper, sits next to me on the sofa in the family room, her tiny frame draped in a pretty, embroidered top and black slacks. At fifty-four, people often mistake her for my older sister. I inherited Mom's big sable-brown eyes, which are now trained on me with a combination of warmth and concern.

"What is going on around here, Abbie? I turn my back for a minute, and Liv quits?"

"I don't know, Mom. One minute everything was fine and the next, she was gone."

I recap the letter and Liv's explanation for quitting us, how Jenna came to the rescue, but that I'm still in a bind because I have to find a replacement for Liv, at least until the school year is over. The summer will give us time to think about a more permanent solution.

"That doesn't sound like Liv at all, does it?" she says.

"What do you mean?"

"She quit a job she loved because she had a crush on your husband? What about her plans for pharmacy school? Didn't you say she wanted to save enough money to enroll at Mass College of Pharmacy?"

"Well yes, but maybe it's as she says. Her feelings for Ty grew and she couldn't handle working for us anymore."

"It just doesn't add up, Abbie."

"What are you saying?"

"Are you holding something back?"

"Like what? I told you everything I know."

"Abbie?" Her tone implies I'm holding out on her and she won't let me get away with it.

"I swear, I'm not holding back. I tried calling Liv's phone again yesterday, even if she said in her note not to contact her. The line was disconnected."

"Really?"

"Yes. Why is that strange?"

"I guess she really is making a clean break. But Liv loved this family. Disconnecting her line seems extreme."

"Maybe she didn't want me to talk her into coming back, especially since her mother is ill."

"What does Ty have to say about all this?"

"He's as shocked as I am."

"And my grand babies?"

I rake my hair back and take a deep breath. "They're struggling. The boys say they don't want to talk about it, and Alexis just sulks. I dread having to bring someone else on board. The kids don't get out for summer break until June. That's almost three months away, so I have no choice but to replace Liv."

"I see your dilemma. There's also your dissertation defense to consider. The time is approaching fast and you need these last few weeks to get everything in tip-top shape. Have you heard from Mass General about the post doc fellowship?"

"Not yet, but I expect to hear soon. Gosh Mom, what if I get the fellowship and something goes wrong with my dissertation? I can't walk into Mass General come September without a Ph.D."

She reaches out and strokes my hand. "You will do fine. You've sacrificed so much to get this far. The next few weeks are just to cross the t's and dot the i's. You got this."

Her encouragement floods me with warmth and gratitude, the feeling that her belief in me will carry me through to the finish line.

"Thanks, Mom. But I'm still in a pickle. I just started researching potential candidates to replace Liv. I found two reputable agencies, but it might take a while to find the right person. In the meantime..."

I trail off and let the statement hang in the air. I don't want to outright ask her for help. If she wants to, it has to be her decision. Maybe I'm being a coward, but my parents have done so much for me already. I can't take their generosity for granted.

"I can't help much," Mom says. "You know we're expanding the business. I'm working deals with a few gourmet food chains and high-end supermarkets to carry our products."

Many moons ago, Mom gave up her career as a scientist to focus on her true passion, and has parlayed it into an empire. She's a five-star chef who started out by opening a high-end restaurant in the highly competitive Boston market. It really took off, and soon she opened another. Next thing, she got her own nationally televised cooking show.

Those years were special. Mom and I worked together on *Shelby's Kitchen*. Bestselling cookbooks followed. After the show wrapped, she continued experimenting with different food products and expanding her restaurants into major cities around the country. She's up to six. Now, she's taking her gourmet frozen foods to supermarkets and food chains all over the country.

"I know you're busy. I appreciate you even considering

helping us out. Ty has to interview all potential candidates the agency sends our way. You know he has a tough schedule. That could delay hiring a replacement."

Mom shoots me a sympathetic glance then says, "How is my son-in-law?"

"I can't wait for specialty training to be over. They overwork the residents."

"You two knew what you were in for," she points out.

"It's extreme, Mom. Sometimes he goes thirty days straight, working day and night, no break. The reality of it is different from the idea of it."

"I know it's been a tough road, sweetie. I so admire your strength and determination. You're one of my heroes. Did you know that?"

I smile. "I learned by watching you. You didn't have it easy either."

"Look where we are now, though. Just hang in there a little longer. You're almost at the finish line. Next year around this time, Ty will have put specialty training behind him, and you will be completing your postdoctoral work. The kids will be a year older. Soon, they will be able to stay by themselves until you get home."

I cover my mouth to suppress a yawn. "You paint a great picture. I just hope it works out that way."

"Of course, it will," she says with confidence. "Look at me. I am living the life I've always dreamed of. Complete freedom to do what I love, with the love of my life at my side. We have a lot to be thankful for. All of this is just for a season. Soon, you'll enter a new, wonderful phase in your life."

I open my mouth to speak but my words are drowned out by the kids bounding into the family room and shrieking, "Grandma!"

They all tackle her at once, except Lucas who stands hesitant, wringing his hands. That's odd. Lucas adores his grandmother.

Blake and Alexis pepper my mother with a slew of questions about her trip but mostly want to know what presents she brought them. They're so spoiled. I signal for Lucas to come closer.

"What's wrong?" I ask him softly.

"Nothing."

"Are you sure? You haven't seen Grandma Shelby in a while, and you're usually excited to see her."

"Come here, Lucas," Mom says.

He obeys and Mom gives him a great big hug and big, wet kiss on the cheek the way she usually does. Only then does a tiny smile appear on his lips.

"Who wants presents?" Mom asks.

"I do," the kids shriek, and then follow their grandmother out to the car where the gifts are stashed.

CHAPTER 18

"I SPOKE TO Eric briefly," Ty says.

"And?"

"Charlie and Jenna came back clean."

"Really?"

"You sound disappointed."

I look away, fixing my gaze on the atmosphere of Newbury Street in Boston—the last of the day's sunshine reflecting off cars and buildings, the heavy traffic, both of the motorized and pedestrian variety, the upscale boutiques and retailers blended in with pricey condominiums housed in multi-story brownstones.

Mom was kind enough to watch the kids so Ty and I could have a date night, a rare treat these days. I guess she felt sorry for me when she visited yesterday and I unloaded my sob story about finding care for the kids. We're heading to her flagship restaurant, Shelby's Place, a couple of blocks down. Ty is on call tonight, so I'm hoping we get through dessert before his pager goes off.

"Does this mean we can trust them?"

"I don't know," Ty says, slowing down to avoid hitting a couple crossing the street. "We wanted to find out if they were ever in trouble with the law, and according to Eric, everything checks out. It lines up with what they told us. They came from Colorado, which is on both their licenses and on the license plate of their car. Neither one has so much as a parking ticket."

"But Eric didn't have time to do any serious digging," I say, turning to him. "All this is just surface stuff. It doesn't mean they're not dangerous."

"Well, he stuck his neck out to get the information he was able to provide as a favor to me. Federal agents can't go around doing random background checks on civilians. It's illegal. Besides, what exactly have the Paynes done?"

"Absolutely nothing."

TY PULLS UP in front of Shelby's Place, puts the car in park, and hands over the keys to the valet attendant once we exit. The restaurant has won every major accolade imaginable: *Boston Magazine's* Boston's Top 50 Restaurants (numerous times), AAA, Five Diamond Award, and Gayot Top 40 Restaurants in the U.S. to name a few. Mom found a way to infuse her sophisticated New American Cuisine with a southern flair, homage to her Louisiana roots.

Rich Escada, the general manager, gives us a warm welcome and seats us immediately. The place is busy as it is every Friday night with waitstaff tending to the eclectic clientele who frequent the establishment—power brokers, (the mayor and Governor who have been known to show up with their entourages from time to time), corporate executives and young professionals, or couples like us, out for date night.

With its floor to ceiling windows, high-end fabrics, and lit candles on every table, the warm, modern ambience never gets old. We're seated in a cozy nook that gives us a view of the dining crowd and busy Newbury Street.

"Glad to have you with us tonight," Rich says. "Shelby said it's your first date night in a long while, so we're going to take good care of you."

"Thanks, Rich," Ty says. "It's nice to have some alone time. We might even run away together if this evening goes as well as we hope."

He chuckles and asks how the kids are doing, and how my graduate studies at BU are coming along. Mom can't stop bragging about her kids and grandkids and must have told the entire restaurant staff, which is quite large, what's going on.

Rich takes off, and he's immediately replaced by not one, but two of the restaurant's best waiters, Claude and Ivy. Claude is focused on our drink order and Ivy on appetizers. Neither one has a pen and notepad, but their service will be flawless.

A short while later, I reach into the bread basket and break off a piece of a flaky, buttery roll. I pop it into my mouth, close my eyes, and savor the warm deliciousness melting on my tongue.

"Sooo good," I exclaim with a sigh, and reach for more.

Ty looks at me, amusement flickering in his hazel eyes.

"What?"

"Nothing. I like seeing you like this."

"You like seeing me turn into a little piggy? If you don't stop me, I'll eat the whole basket."

"Go right ahead," he says, gesturing. "But I meant I like seeing you relaxed like this, enjoying yourself. And that outfit is killer on you. Don't think I didn't notice heads turning as we walked to our table."

I allow my gaze to linger on him and moisten my lips suggestively. "Why thank you, Dr. Rambally. You're making me blush."

He blows me a kiss, and I giggle. I was glad to ditch my day-to-day uniform of jeans or leggings, plus a tank top or T-shirt underneath a zip-up sweatshirt. For this occasion,

I paired a black, short-sleeved lace sheath dress with strappy sandals. I went glam with the makeup too—smoky eyes, dark red lipstick, flawless matte foundation, and dramatic lashes.

Against the backdrop of clanking silverware, conversations at various volumes and the waitstaff navigating the crowded space, Ty and I catch up. His job is getting more stressful as he appears on the schedule for more and more complicated surgeries. He's happy Dr. Stevenson, his mentor and supervising physician, has total confidence in him, but he's worried about burnout and losing his passion for medicine. I assure him that won't happen and once he's a full-fledged cardiothoracic surgeon, he will have more flexibility to navigate his career.

When it's my turn, I decide to address the giant, pink elephant that has lived in our house since the kids were born.

"We have to talk about Lucas."

Ty frowns. "What about him?"

"You know, that issue we've been avoiding for years."

Ty looks out the window for a beat then returns his gaze to me.

"What happened?"

"Nothing. I just don't think we can hold off any longer."

"Come on, Cooper. I know you better than that. Out with it."

I recap yesterday's incident, how Lucas hesitated to embrace my mother like he usually did, content to stand off to the side until Mom called him out. That raised a flag with me. It was odd behavior. All three of my kids adore their grandmother and love interacting with her.

"Are you sure you're not overthinking the situation?" he asks, his forehead wrinkling. "It's kind of your thing."

"Is it a stretch to imagine he's more keenly aware of the differences between himself and his siblings, and other family members?"

"Maybe he was in a mood. You know he gets that way sometimes."

"With Jenna asking questions about his paternity and the fact that he's getting older, it's time. I don't want to be blindsided one day. It's better he hears the truth from us."

"You're talking about altering his life and possibly causing long-term issues."

"We can't put on blinders and pretend it's not an issue, Ty. Lucas isn't stupid."

"Well, we can't tell him the truth. It would devastate him."

"I'm not saying that. Maybe we give him shadings of the truth."

Ivy arrives with our appetizer order and places them on the table, quelling our conversation. Smoked salmon salad for me and lobster guacamole for Ty. My stomach growls. I haven't eaten much today, and I'm sure Ty is starving too. He hardly ever has time to eat.

"What version of the truth do we give him?" he asks, after Ivy disappears.

I dig into the salad, combining greens with a piece of salmon. *Delicious.* Ty digs in too.

After I've chewed and swallowed, I say, "We reinforce that *we're* his parents. Nothing else matters."

Ty tips his head to one side. "And then what?"

"We edit the past."

"Meaning what exactly?"

"We get creative. We tell him that a long time ago, his mother was in a relationship with another man, but he died in a horrible car accident before I had a chance to tell him Lucas was on the way. Then, you and I got married. We've always been close friends who loved each other and decided that we would become a family."

There. I think that's a pretty good explanation. Then Ty blows up my neat little story with a heavy and unwelcome dose of reality.

"What are you going to say when he starts asking questions about this man? What happens when the nightmares come back, Cooper? It took years for you to feel safe again, to be convinced that monster wasn't going to reach from beyond the grave and violently assault you again."

I was about to reach for my fork again, but stop short. I wouldn't get a firm grip on it, anyway. My brain feels waterlogged and the sudden urge to use the bathroom is overwhelming. I stand up and immediately sit down. My knees won't support me. I wipe my clammy hands on my dress.

Ty comes around the table and kneels beside me. He turns my face toward him so we're at eye level.

"I'm sorry, Cooper. I didn't mean to bring up painful memories, but if we go down this road, there's no turning back. We can't predict how Lucas will handle things. If he's beginning to feel as if he doesn't belong, or that we're withholding important information from him on purpose, giving him 'shadings of the truth', as you say, will either ease his mind or make things worse. Do we really want to do this now?"

I open my mouth, but nothing comes out. When I try again, it's but a squeak.

"We have to, Ty. Otherwise it could blow up in our faces in terrible, unforeseen ways. We have to tell him to control the narrative, look him in the eye and let him know how much we love him. Do you honestly think he hasn't wondered why he looks white and his siblings are black? You think people don't talk, kids at school haven't said things?"

"I know, I know," he says, rubbing his chin. "We also have to think about Blake and Alexis, how this will affect them."

"Exactly. Although, I think they will be okay."

"Yeah. Kids are resilient. The truth is, they won't care who Lucas' biological father is, or that he looks different from them. He's their brother, and that's not going to change anything for them."

"Will it for Lucas, though?" I ask.

"In the long run, he will be fine. He's known my face since he popped out of your womb. Remember, you thought he winked at us? I'm the only father he's ever known, the only one he needs."

"There's another piece to this you haven't considered."

"What?"

"Christian is Lucas' uncle."

"Oh man," Ty says, massaging the back of his neck. He gets off his knees and heads back to his seat. He leans back in his chair, careful not to crash into diners at the next table.

"It's complicated," I say.

"Very."

CHAPTER 19

O N SATURDAY MORNING, I receive a text message from Jenna. She wants to know how I'm doing and if it's okay to come over. She volunteers to pick up some freshly baked goodies from one of the bakeries in town. My fingers hover over the screen. Doubt gnaws at me. Is it a good idea to invite her back in? She hasn't done anything to me, or our family. According to a federal agent, she's not a criminal. She did take my kids to school and handed over her driver's license, and her car's license plate number. *Liv didn't like her. Liv is gone.* I brush aside the cloud of uncertainty and respond to the text.

A half hour later, Jenna arrives with enough food to feed a small army. We set out the food like a Thanksgiving spread on the kitchen island: pastries, croissants, cannolis, muffins, Danish, and bagels.

"You went overboard, Jenna. We can't eat all this food."

"You can freeze the leftovers and pop them in the oven to eat at a later time."

I had already made oatmeal from scratch, so at least there's fiber and protein to balance out all the carbs.

The kids barge in, spy the goodies, and immediately start stuffing their faces as if they haven't eaten in weeks, and I haven't taught them proper table manners.

"Get dishes, please," I admonish. "You're not bears in the wild foraging for food."

Jenna and I lean up against the edge of the island while the kids grab plates and glasses and sit at the table. I gesture for Jenna to follow me and leave the kids on their own. We head into the hallway.

"What's going on?" I ask.

"Have you found anyone to watch the kids yet?"

"No. I'm working with a couple of reputable agencies but haven't interviewed anyone yet. I'm running out of time. My mother is busy, although she volunteered to watch them as much as she can until I find someone."

"Maybe I can help with that."

"How so?"

"I know a girl at church who might be a fit. I'm not sure because I only met her recently. The pastor's wife introduced us. Said Katie just moved here and is looking for a family."

"Really?" I try to keep the excitement out of my voice. She's handing me a lifeline. "What do you know about Katie?"

"Not much. She's our age. The last family she worked for moved back home. They were French Canadian. Pastor's wife told me to ask around the neighborhood and see if any of the families needed someone. I thought of you right away."

"You didn't say anything to Katie, did you?"

"No. I wanted to talk to you first."

"Good. I'm not looking forward to this process. For five years the kids had stability, and now all that has changed."

"I don't know how you do it, Abbie. I can't imagine the stress you're under, trying to earn your Ph.D. and having to worry about care for your kids. Being a mom is really hard."

"It is. Are you sure you want to be one?"

I meant it as a half joke, but Jenna's face crumples.

"What is it, did I say something wrong?"

She waves me off, but tears pool in her eyes.

"Jenna are you okay? Let's move to the family room."

"It's stupid, nothing to worry about," she says, plopping down on the sofa. She sniffles and wipes her nose with her forearm, and then gives me a weak smile. "I've wanted to be a mom since I was a little girl. It's been hard. I suffered two miscarriages in two years. I'm scared to try again."

"I'm so sorry, Jenna. I had no idea. If I did, I wouldn't have made that insensitive remark."

"Don't worry about it. You couldn't have known. To tell you the truth, I think that's why I like being around your family. It gives me hope. As if hanging around you guys it will rub off on me and Charlie, and we will finally have a family of our own."

Fertile Abbie. That's my secret nickname in the family. Lucas was barely three months old when I got pregnant with the twins. Ty and I were beside ourselves. He had just started medical school that fall. I was still nursing Lucas. We'd been careful, or so we thought. I don't know if we would have made it if Grandma Naomi Cooper, my paternal Grandmother, hadn't been there to help me stay sane. Now, I sit here next to this woman who's obviously desperate for a child and can't have one. Life is so strange sometimes.

"You can't give up, Jenna. You and Charlie are both still young. Not everything comes easy in life."

"It did for you."

"Children came easy for me. But in all other aspects of my life, I've had to fight. Sometimes the battles were fierce, but I didn't give up. Neither should you."

"Thanks for saying that, Abbie. It means a lot coming from you."

"So how do I get a hold of this Katie? No point in wasting time. Between her and the agency, something is bound to work out, right?"

"For sure. I can make a call and let Muriel, that's our pastor's wife, know I have a family who's possibly interested in talking to Katie. We can take it from there, see if she's game."

"Sounds like a good plan. Thanks, Jenna, for coming to my rescue again."

"Like I said, you give me hope. And it's not as if I have a ton going on. Charlie is starting to travel again, so I'm left to my own devices."

"Welcome to HAG," I say. "Husbands Always Gone. I'm the founder and CEO."

Jenna giggles, and so do I.

Perhaps it's time I put my paranoia to rest.

CHAPTER 20

TWO WEEKS AFTER Liv resigned, Katie Nicholson came to work for us on a beautiful April morning.

Tragedy followed in her wake.

The kids file into the kitchen where Katie and I are waiting for them. She hovers nervously, as if she's afraid to talk to them. The kids spent time with her before we made the decision to hire her on a trial basis. But they're still getting over Liv quitting us. I told Katie not to worry, that they would come around.

"Can I get you guys anything for breakfast?" she asks, with a too bright smile and nervous energy.

"We got it," Lucas says, opening the refrigerator door. Looks like Blake is about to make toast, and Alexis settles for cereal.

"I'm heading out," I announce to the kids. "Please listen to Katie. She's here to help us. I know it's hard, Liv leaving, but we have to make the best of the situation. Katie is nervous too, so maybe we can be kind and patient with each other to make the transition smoother, hmm?"

"Okay, Mom," they say in unison.

I turn to Katie. "You have everything you need?"

"Yes. I have your cell number and Dr. Rambally's, as well as your parents' and Jenna's in case anything happens and I can't reach you."

"Good. I'll be back in a few hours…"

My voice trails off when my attention is drawn to Lucas who has his head down instead of eating his breakfast.

"Lucas, how many times have I told you, no electronics in the morning, especially at the breakfast table. That includes your phone."

He raises his head slowly, guilt clouding his face.

"Hand over the phone, please."

I take the device from his outstretched palm and venture a look at the screen to see what content has him so fascinated that he was willing to get into trouble. He was doing an internet search on Liv. Looks like the search just popped up and he didn't get a chance to follow any of the links. I tap the first one.

What the browser opens up paralyzes me.

CHAPTER 21

I HEAR MUFFLED sounds but I don't quite register them. I stare at the phone, but the image and letters in the words seem to be scrambled, appearing as a glob of blurred spots. There's a persistent ringing in my ears. Someone takes me by the hand and leads me to a chair where I sit. I slowly blink so the words will come into focus. When they do, I feel my throat closing up and my heart pounding in an erratic rhythm.

WOMAN'S BODY FOUND
AT COCHITUATE STATE PARK

The headline is accompanied by a photo of Liv, taken from her driver's license. My mouth goes dry. A cold, numbing sensation clamps around my chest and squeezes. I gasp for air. I barely record the concerned looks of everyone in the kitchen, the kids and Katie.

She's supposed to be in Jamaica, taking care of her sick mother. That's what she said in her note. The headline is wrong. It has to be a case of mistaken identity. Perhaps Liv's license got stolen and the thief is the one who was murdered.

"Mom, what's going on?" Lucas asks.

"N-nothing, baby," I say, my voice cracking. "Stay off the

web, okay. That goes double for the both of you." I give Blake and Alexis a stern look and slip the phone into the pocket of my dress coat.

They described Liv as a murder victim. *Murder.*

The whole world seems to be moving in slow motion, a nightmarish fog so thick, it may swallow me whole. I say something to Katie, not sure what. The kids leave the breakfast table. Feet shuffle. Doors slam. The roar of an engine coming to life sounds strange and distant. I go limp in one of the chairs surrounding the table.

Liv is gone. Just like that. My heart is clogged up with grief, yet my mind makes a straight line to the obvious questions. *Who killed Liv and why?*

I place my head on the table, silent streams of tears pooling on the floral, water resistant tablecloth. Did Liv know her killer? Was her death a random act of violence? I think about her parents who have lost their only child. I don't know the last time she saw them. She often took off to New York on weekends or holidays to see them or visit her cousin Alvin who lives in Hartford. She was twenty-eight years old, never got the chance to do all the things she wanted to do—become a pharmacist, get married, raise a family, retire to Jamaica, and open an upscale bed & breakfast near the beach.

She promised she would always have a stash of Jamaican Blue Mountain coffee ready for me. She said Ty and I could retire there, too, part of the year. Ty could spend his days fishing out on the open ocean and I would cook his catch. I didn't have the heart to tell her Ty is terrified of open water. He fell off a boat and almost drowned in the ocean when he was twelve on a family trip to the Bahamas. He hasn't gotten over the phobia yet.

How am I going to break the news to the kids? Their father and I told them Liv went to Jamaica to care for a sick parent. This will be the most devastating blow they've ever had to deal with in their young lives. When Grandam Betty, my mother's mother died, the kids were little. They never had a relationship with her. They were too young to understand what death truly meant. Now, that has changed. Liv was such an integral part of their world, it will be difficult for them to adjust to life without her.

Lucas will take it the hardest. He doesn't handle change or disruptions very well. He was doing a web search on Liv, for crying out loud. He threw a fit when his first kindergarten teacher left because her husband got a job out of state. It took him a month to get over it. Liv was with us for five years, half his life. Blake is the one who adapts to situations more easily.

I walk over to the sink, open the faucet, and splash water on my face. After I pat my face dry with paper towel, I fish the phone out of my pocket. I didn't finish reading the story. I force myself to continue. I owe it to Liv to find out what happened to her.

The backstory reads like an episode of a TV crime drama. A local man was walking his dog in the park. The dog started barking wildly. He followed the dog and came upon the body. Police were able to immediately make an identification, because the victim had her purse and her wallet, which contained her driver's license. The victim had a single bullet wound to the head and one to the chest. Framingham Police is investigating the murder.

I wonder if there was something I could have done. The only sign that Liv was in any distress was the dinner that night at the Paynes'. I should have pushed, forced her to unburden herself. I let her down, and that's a stinging failure I will carry with me for the rest of my life.

CHAPTER 22

TWO DAYS LATER, after reading tons of articles on how children handle death, we're as ready as we'll ever be to deliver the inevitable blow. We're gathered in the family room, all three kids seated on the sofa, their faces bursting with inquisitiveness. Ty takes the lead. He works at a hospital. That makes him better equipped to discuss death than I am. That's what I told myself when I flat out refused to be the one to tell the kids that their beloved caregiver is gone.

"What is it, Daddy?" Alexis asks. "Why do you and Mom look so sad?"

Ty squats so he can meet them at eye level. I stand beside him. "You're right, Alexis. Your mother and I are sad."

"Did something bad happen?" Blake asks.

"Yes, Blake. Something bad happened."

Lucas remains quiet. An air of gloom emanates from his whole being.

Ty continues, "It's about Liv. Liv is gone to heaven. She died two days ago in an accident."

All three of my kids have frozen looks on their faces. They hold that position for a solid couple of minutes. Their father and I are trying our best to model for them. They will take their cues from us, and if we don't handle this well, they won't, either.

Alexis is the first to react. She shakes her head with such force, I'm afraid brain cells might come tumbling out.

"No. It's not true, Daddy. It can't be true. You and Mom said Liv went to take care of her mother in Jamaica. That's where she is. She can't be dead. It's not true." She continues to shake her head, the tears already rolling down her cheeks.

Lucas and Blake look at each other. They're both hunched in their sitting positions, seconds away from blubbering. Their breathing is erratic, their clenched facial expressions a sure sign they're trying to hold it in.

"I wish it weren't true, Pumpkin," Ty says to Alexis. "Mom and I don't want it to be true either, but it is. You know something, though? Liv will always be in our hearts. We will never forget her. Right, Mom?" he asks, looking up at me briefly.

"Your father is right," I say, looking all three of them in the face. "Things are going to be hard for a while. We will miss Liv because we all loved her, but she won't really be gone because the love we have for her will live inside us always."

Ty stands up and joins the kids on one end of the sofa and I sit on the other. The look of incredulity and devastation hasn't left their faces. The coming weeks and months will be difficult for us as a family. But we'll get through it together.

CHAPTER 23

THE NEXT DAY, two detectives from the Framingham Police Department sit in our living room. My parents have taken the kids out for the day to help keep their minds occupied—no easy task. After the initial shock of learning Liv was no longer with us, my kids oscillated between normalcy one minute and a flood of angry, bitter tears the next, their emotions a never-ending seesaw. We expect this behavior will continue as we work through our grief.

The questions were many and difficult to answer at times. Ty and I decided on a little white lie. We couldn't tell our children that their nanny was violently gunned down by an unknown assailant. It was more merciful to explain she had been in an accident. Are we bad parents for lying? Only time will tell.

Detectives Robert Hunt and Rebecca Stiles occupy chairs across from me in the living room. Ty stands off in a corner near the window where he can survey the action. Hunt is white, early fifties, and sports a neatly trimmed moustache and a red patch of skin on his face that's most likely psoriasis or some other skin condition, further highlighting his already ruddy cheeks. He has a nervous habit of clicking and unclicking his pen. Stiles is a petite African-American woman, with an afro-sized head of curls and smooth, sandy-brown skin. Her posture is strong, shoulders back, chin high. The scent of her perfume floats in the air.

"What happened to Liv?" Ty asks, before either detective can begin the interview.

"That's what we're trying to find out, Dr. Rambally," Hunt says. "We're hoping you and your wife can help shed some light on the investigation."

Ty sticks his hands in his pockets and looks out the window. Liv's death hit him hard. He told me it was such a waste and he couldn't wait for the authorities to catch the bastard who did it. I told him it could have been a woman. He was doubtful. He didn't know anything about ballistics, but because Liv was shot in the head and chest, Ty is convinced a man pulled the trigger. He has no explanation as to why.

"Ms. Stewart was your nanny?" Hunt asks.

"Yes. I'm a full-time graduate student, so she would come in the mornings to see the kids off to school, pick them up from school, take them to activities, stuff like that."

"How long had she worked for your family?"

"Five years. Our oldest, Lucas, was in kindergarten at the time. The twins were still in preschool."

"Do you know of anyone who would want to harm her?" Hunt probes.

"No. Liv was nice. Didn't have a mean bone in her body."

"When was the last time you saw her?" Stiles asked.

"A little over two weeks ago, Tuesday. That Wednesday morning, she didn't show up for work."

"How did she seem to you? Did you notice any changes in her behavior? Did she say anything out of the ordinary?"

I shake my head slowly. Ty and I exchange glances from across the room. I know we're both thinking the same thing.

How Liv was acting strangely during dinner at the Paynes.

The two detectives pick up on our non-verbal exchange.

"Is there something you want to tell us?" Hunt asks. "We need you to be forthcoming so we can help catch her killer."

Ty leaves his spot in the corner and joins me on the sofa. "We noticed Liv was acting strangely during dinner at the neighbors' two weeks ago."

Stiles leans forward. "Strange how?"

"Liv had a bright, confident, and outgoing personality," I explain. "The night of the dinner, she had this downcast, world-on-her-shoulders kind of attitude. She barely spoke at all. The same thing happened when she showed up for work the following Monday."

"Did you ask her what was going on?" Hunt asks.

"I did, but she kept reassuring me that everything was fine. I should have pressed her. I regret not doing so."

"Why do you say that?" Stiles inquires.

The agony of losing Liv hurts like a dozen sharp knives stabbing me all at once. There's no escaping the pain and guilt, the endless loop of what-if questions. What if I hadn't backed down and forced her to tell me what was wrong? What if Liv would still be with us if I weren't so caught up in my own issues? What if she'd been in trouble for a long time and I completely failed to notice, and it all came to a head that night of the dinner? She panicked when she thought she had forgotten her phone. Was she expecting an important call that had to do with her change in mood? She did excuse herself from the dinner table to go to the bathroom. Did she call someone and if so, who?

Stiles waits expectantly for my answer. I inhale sharply and say, "I failed to act on a gut feeling that something big was bothering Liv. Had I followed my instincts, I wouldn't have taken her note at face value."

"What note?" Stiles asks, exchanging a curious glance with her partner, before focusing her attention on us once more.

"Liv was supposed to show up for work as usual. When she didn't, I got concerned," I explain. I walk the detectives through what transpired that morning in late March.

I stop to catch my breath and halt the tears about to pour out of me. Ty picks up the story.

"Then my wife received a note by messenger. Liv said the letter was her official resignation and we shouldn't try to find her. Said she was moving to Jamaica to help take care of her sick mother."

"Do you have the note?" Hunt asks.

I reach for my purse next to me, extract the note, and hand it over to Detective Hunt.

He scans the contents then hands it over to his partner, who does the same.

"Says here she quit because she had a crush on Dr. Rambally," Stiles says. "You never mentioned that a few moments ago."

Before I can answer, Ty takes control of the question. "When we first read the note, we thought that reason was odd. We never saw any signs of what she describes in the note. Knowing what we do now, we're convinced she didn't quit for that reason."

"Are you saying you don't believe the note, that she never had a crush on you?" Stiles presses.

"I didn't say that," Ty says. "We suspected Liv had a little crush, but nothing serious, nothing that would cause her to quit."

"How can you be so sure?" Hunt asks.

"Because I'm hardly home," Ty snaps. "I work long hours at the hospital. When I do make it home, Liv is usually gone for the day. And now that I think about it, I'm not sure Liv wrote that note."

"What are you saying, Dr. Rambally?" Stiles asks, an assessing frown creasing her forehead.

"I'm saying, do your job and find out whether Liv really wrote that letter or not. The answer could lead you to her killer."

As soon as the words leave his lips, I grip his arm. I don't know why I didn't see it before. Something about the letter always bothered me. Now that Ty expressed his doubt, it hits me with the force of a ten-pound bowling ball.

"What is it, Cooper?" he asks, turning to me.

I don't answer right away, weighing the pros and cons of revealing the red flag that just popped into my head before I have a chance to discuss it with Ty first. On the other hand, we're desperate for answers. Withholding information could be detrimental to that goal.

"Liv didn't write that letter," I assert.

"How do you know?" Stiles asks.

"It's signed, *Olivia*."

"But that was her name," Stiles says. "What's so strange about that?"

"We never called her by her full name," I explain. "We called her Liv. Ty, I, and all three of our children. She would never sign a note to us using her full name."

Hunt writes something in his tiny notebook. Stiles leans back in her seat, her brow creased. She reads the note again then asks, "Does the rest of the note sound like her?"

"I don't know," I respond.

"What about text messages and such?" Hunt asks. "Do you have any kind of communication from her that we could use for comparison?"

I promise the detective that I would go through my text

messages and get back to him.

"If Olivia didn't write the note as you suspect," Hunt says, scratching his head with the pen, "then the killer knew she worked for your family. They took the time to type up a note so you wouldn't go looking for her. Do you know anyone who would do that?"

I break eye contact with the detective and begin to twist my wedding band. A slow ache builds in the back of my throat. I glance at Ty. He swallows several times. What the detective is asking, well, I don't want to think about it. Did the killer spy on Liv, learn her routine, her comings and goings? Did they gather information on our family, too?

"No, I don't know anyone who would do something like that."

"Are there any leads in the case?" Ty asks. "Have you looked at her cell phone records, did you get a hold of her parents?"

"Easy, Dr. Rambally," Hunt says. "We have our best on this case. It's not every day we have a murder in our city. We're taking this seriously. It's a top priority."

"Has the coroner established a time of death? How long had she been in the park before they found her?"

"Did Olivia confide in anyone that she had romantic feelings for you?" Stiles cuts in.

"Why would I know that?" Ty snaps. "As I told you earlier, I'm hardly ever home."

I can see where this is going, and it's not a good place. I squeeze Ty's arm to calm him down. He's frustrated.

"Why so defensive, Dr. Rambally?" Stiles asks, her eyes brightening as if she just stumbled upon a major clue. "Do you have something to hide? It's not unusual for a nanny to have feelings for her employer, especially if that employer is a young, handsome doctor. Have you ever interacted with Olivia outside of work?"

They think he might be a suspect. Why didn't I keep my mouth shut about the note? If he gets in trouble…

Ty shoots a venomous glare at Stiles. "You can fish all you want, detective, but everyone in this room knows I had nothing to do with Liv's death."

"We don't know anything," Hunt counters. "The investigation is in its early stages. It's our job to leave no stone unturned."

Stiles adds, "You still haven't answered my question. Have you ever interacted with Olivia Stewart outside of work? Maybe you met up for coffee or she came to see you at the hospital."

Boiling with fury, I grit my teeth so hard that my jaw aches. I can hear the blood rushing through my head. How dare they think he had anything to do with Liv's horrific murder? Ty faces life and death decisions every day and has been trained to withstand unimaginable pressure without losing his cool. But right now, my husband isn't a rock-star surgeon. He's a human being, grieving the tragic and unexpected loss of someone important to our family, and having a cloud of suspicion cast over him by the police is more than I can stand.

"Was that necessary?" I ask Stiles, pinning her with a defiant stare. "So far, neither one of you asked us for alibis. You can't, because you don't know when she died, how long she'd been in the park, exposed to the elements like some piece of trash someone threw out." The tears burst forth like a raging storm, dual streams rolling down my cheeks in torrents. I feel the hiccups coming on. Ty wraps his arm around me and pulls me close.

As Ty works on soothing my anger, Hunt clears his throat and says, "We didn't mean to upset you. We understand you're grieving. We're not heartless. But this is a murder investigation, and we're not in the business of making people feel good. It's our job to solve crimes. Sometimes that means asking uncomfortable and even distressing questions."

"We told you we don't think Liv wrote that letter," I insist, wiping my tears and sitting up straight. I'm not backing down from this fight. It's too important. We will cooperate because catching Liv's killer is more important than our anger. But we're not about to get bullied by the police, either. "Darya Petrov and Lucy Hale were friends of Liv's. They worked for two families in the area. Maybe Liv said something to them about what was going on with her."

Can you provide us with their details?" Stiles asks quietly, toning down the earlier brashness.

"Not really," I say. "All I know is that Darya works for the Coleman family on Oak Drive, and Lucy works for the Levys on Rosewood."

Ty stands up, slips his hands into his pockets, and returns to staring out the window in the corner he occupied at the beginning of the interview.

"Everything okay, Dr. Rambally?" Hunt asks. "You seem a little nervous."

Ty turns around and looks straight into Hunt's face. He says, "I am nervous that the woman who took care of my children was found murdered in a park with two bullet holes in her body. I'm nervous that somebody knew she worked for our family and took it upon him or herself to write a note and messenger the note to my wife. I'm nervous that my family could be in the sights of a killer. I don't care how much you dismiss the idea, Liv did not write that note. So yes, detective, I'm nervous."

Ty is as laid back as they come, but when he's upset, he can be intense.

"We understand you're upset," Hunt responds, as if trying to calm a toddler. "It's a stressful situation and your family is grieving. We just want to cover all angles."

Stiles looks at the letter again. "The letter is deeply personal. It talks about her parents and returning to Jamaica. Who would know those details about her family if, as you suggest, Olivia didn't write the note?"

Ty glares at Stiles, ignores her question, and then returns to staring out the window. I jump in to fill the silent, hostile void.

"We didn't know every detail of Liv's personal life. She could have been dating someone who got violent and killed her. It's sad to say, but it happens all the time."

Hunt says, "We have looked into it. As far as we can tell, Ms. Stewart was not in a romantic relationship at the time of her death. We have spoken to an ex-boyfriend she dated over three years ago. He wasn't able to tell us much. The relationship ended amicably, and he's had no contact with Ms. Stewart since. And he lives in Florida. Hasn't traveled by any means in the past year. He checks out."

"What about her parents?" I ask.

"They can't think of anyone who would want to harm Olivia. They're devastated, obviously."

"You said Olivia was—" Hunt flips through his notebook. "Subdued the night of the dinner at your neighbors?"

"She was."

"Who are these neighbors?"

I provide the names and address for the Paynes.

"This is a baffling case," Stiles says. "We have no motive, a young victim shot twice and left in a park, and everything about her background has come up clean so far."

"That's why you're the detective and we're not," I say. "We can't explain this senseless murder any more than you can."

"Are there any problems in your marriage?" Stiles asks out of the blue.

If I could reach across the room, choke Detective Stiles, and get away with it, I would. This woman is relentless. She won't let go of the idea that Ty had something to do with Liv's death. Asking about the state of our marriage is another way to try and make Ty a suspect. Ty heard the question but doesn't react. He's smart enough to know they're baiting him, and if his anger explodes, it will only serve as confirmation in their minds that he has something to hide.

I say, "No, there aren't any problems in our marriage. As my husband pointed out more than once, he's hardly home, so there is no time to develop 'problems in the marriage,'" I say, using air quotes. I glower at both detectives then say, "We'll cooperate fully with the investigation. Liv was like family, and for our sake and that of our children, we want her killer found and locked up for life."

My gaze continues to focus on them. "However, if you ever hurl an accusation at my husband again, subtle or otherwise, without proof, all bets are off. We'll lawyer up and have your department drowning in so much litigation that even your dogs will need lawyers."

I almost hate myself for playing that card, but no way they're getting away with trying to railroad us. I've read too many horror stories and seen too many reports about cops locking in on one suspect, refusing to consider alternate paths to solving the crime, often ignoring evidence that points elsewhere.

The not-so-subtle threat hangs in the air for a moment. Neither detective says anything. Hunt has a constipated look on his face and continues his habit of clicking and unclicking his pen. Stiles straightens her back in the chair, her face sour, as though an infant just vomited all over her starched blouse.

Hunt recovers first. "No need for threats. We're not accusing you or Dr. Rambally of anything. We're simply trying to under-stand the dynamics of your relationship with Ms. Stewart." He says it with a hint of derision, as if my calling them out has ruined the flow of the interview.

Stiles pipes up. "It's still very early in the investigation and it takes time to get answers and turn up evidence."

"Thanks for clarifying," I say. "It's good to know we're not being accused of killing an innocent woman."

Neither detective responds to my sarcastic outburst. After a few more questions about when and how we heard the news of Liv's murder, our whereabouts at the time, and nailing down the timeline when each of us last saw her, the interview wraps up. The detectives promise to be in touch, provide their business cards, and ask us to call if we remember any additional details or information that could help catch Liv's killer.

CHAPTER 24

SUMMER, THREE YEARS EARLIER

ARCHIE'S GAZE LANDED on Iceman as he sauntered into the prison library, tablet in hand. Archie should have known Iceman would be one of the inmates allowed the privilege of having a tablet. It was part of a pilot program to help inmates stay connected to the outside world. Though heavy restrictions applied, the program was gaining in popularity amongst state prison systems across the country.

Iceman hauled out a chair, plopped down in it, and gestured for Archie to join him at the table. A few inmates were scattered around the small space, searching bookshelves for their next read, knowing that at any time, their reading list could be flagged by corrections officers.

"What's cooking?" Archie asked.

Iceman pushed the device across the table toward Archie. "The woman in the picture, she's your target."

Archie stared at the photo. A stunning black woman, who was so hot she could melt steel, stared back from the screen. He traced the contours of her face with his finger. She wore a glamorous, expensive-looking evening gown with a long train in sparkling gold. She stood on carpeted steps of some building he couldn't see. There were people behind her and off to the side.

Her skin glowed like there was some magical lighting that came from inside of her and spilled outward, complementing the gold coloring of the dress. Her bright red lipstick and million-dollar smile made his heart stop for a moment. Who was she, and what did she do to Iceman?

Iceman snatched the tablet from Archie and gave him the stink eye. He said between clenched teeth, "You can stop drooling now."

Archie didn't know why Iceman had an attitude about it. As far as he knew, Iceman didn't have a wife or girlfriend or anything like that, but then again, Iceman wasn't exactly the confiding type. But this woman was important to him. Otherwise, why would he cop an attitude? For the first time since Archie had known him, Iceman exhibited emotion. *Jealousy.* That was the shocker of the day. Maybe the ice was melting. If it was, that would be a significant benefit to Archie.

"Sorry, man. She's beautiful. Don't get to see women like that locked up in here. How do you know her? Is she an ex-girlfriend?"

"The only thing you need to know about her is what I tell you. Got it?"

Archie splayed his palms and held them up. "Got it. I just think the more I know, the easier it will be to pull the job. You are going to tell me her name, right? I kinda need to know that."

Iceman crossed his arms over his chest. He didn't say anything, which made Archie uncomfortable. The dude was unpredictable. But Archie couldn't show weakness. He had his own goals to think about. And Iceman was the ticket.

"I haven't spoken her name in eleven years, to be precise.

The picture you just saw was taken at the Met Gala four years ago. It's the most recent photo I have of her."

"The Met Gala?" Archie asked, feeling like an idiot. "What's that?"

Iceman rolled his eyes, stretched, and leaned back in his seat.

"It's an annual fundraising gala that benefits the Metropolitan Museum of Art Costume Institute in New York City. It marks the beginning of the Costume Institute's annual fashion exhibit."

"Oh, so the girl in the picture is a model?"

"No. She had a show on the Cooking Network some years ago. But she was probably attending the gala with Callie and Nicholas Furi."

Archie drummed his fingers on the table. Furi. That name rang a bell for some reason, but he didn't know why. He thought hard about it. Then he snapped his fingers.

"Nicholas Furi, the movie director?"

"And his daughter Callie, the fashion designer."

Archie pondered that statement for a moment. Iceman made it clear he would only share information he wanted Archie to know. That wasn't good enough for Archie. He would find a way to do some research. He just needed a name.

"So what did this chick, whatever her name is, do to you?"

"She ruined my life. And now, since I'm stuck in here, it's your job to make sure she pays."

Archie scratched his temple. "I thought you said she stole something from you."

"My life! And she has something else I want. Something I want taken away from her so she feels what it's like to have something valuable snatched away."

Archie was still confused. Iceman was speaking in riddles or circles or something. His skin tingled as sweat began to form on his body. He flexed his index finger repeatedly. Iceman swiped the screen of the tablet. When he found what he was looking for, he handed the tablet once again to Archie.

He saw a kid, maybe four or five years old with wavy, blondish hair and blue eyes. He held an ice cream cone the size of a basketball in one hand.

"Cute kid," Archie said, handing Iceman the tablet. "What does the kid have to do with the woman in the picture?"

"He's her son. I want him taken from her. I want her world utterly destroyed."

Archie swallowed hard. Maybe he didn't hear correctly. Neither scenario made sense to him. The woman in the picture being the mother of the kid or even more disturbing, the fact that Iceman wanted the boy taken from her. That was some ice-cold shit.

Archie was in prison for killing a man, but it was an accident. Got into a stupid fight and pushed too hard. The guy cracked his skull and died. Archie got four years for manslaughter. But this guy, Iceman, he was a complete psycho. Who takes a kid from their mother for revenge? That's the kind of stuff you see in movies, not in real life. But Archie knew better than to voice his concerns. If he did, Iceman would have him killed. Best to keep his attack of conscience to himself.

"Are you sure that's her son? No offense, but she's black and the kid is white as rice and you didn't say he was adopted."

"Half-white," Iceman corrected. "And I assure you, she *is* his biological mother."

"How do you know that?"

Iceman leveled a gaze at Archie that could slice through concrete. He threaded his fingers together and placed them on the table. He said nothing. The silence made Archie want to leave, but that would be a terrible mistake. He would wait

Iceman out.

"Your only concern should be following my instructions precisely. These are not simple instructions. This job will require finesse, polish, and sophistication, the ability to be a chameleon. The guts to be detached and ruthless when necessary, and to think on your feet. If you succeed, you will be well compensated and we never need to see each other again."

He paused for dramatic effect. Then he said, "If you fail to accomplish this mission, well...have you ever seen the movie *Casino*?"

Archie blinked hard. Then his head bobbed nervously. He had never seen the movie, but he had a feeling that the fact that Iceman mentioned it was a bad omen.

"Well," Iceman continued, "it's a gangster movie about a casino manager and a mafia enforcer duking it out over a gambling empire in Vegas. Came out decades ago. A classic in my book. But the enforcer, Nicky Santoro, pissed off the mafia bosses."

Archie was afraid to ask the next logical question, but he shoved his fear deep down and would deal with it later.

"What does the movie have to do with my assignment?"

"When you get out of here, watch it. Nicky Santoro meets with a rather unfortunate end. It was my favorite scene in that movie. He was taken out to the Vegas desert and beaten to a bloody pulp with a metal baseball bat by several men. I believe he was still breathing when they dumped him into a shallow grave and started shoveling dirt on top of him."

A thunderous, black as midnight expression marred Iceman's face. He leaned in, and Archie tried not to tremble.

"If you cross me in any way, what I'll do to you will make Nicky Santoro's death at the end of *Casino* look merciful."

Archie forced his trembling limbs to remain still. Iceman's

words had grown legs and kicked him hard in the belly. He could push through the panic he told himself. There was one important question left to ask. Iceman's response would confirm once and for all whether Archie had the guts to pull this off.

"What do you want me to do with the kid once I take him from his mother?"

"Kill him."

CHAPTER 25

L UCAS KICKED THE ball into the net and scored.
"In your face," he bragged to Blake as he held up his
arms in a victory pose, the way he saw the pros do on TV.

"Lucky shot. Big deal," Blake countered.

"Skills, dude. Not luck."

"We'll see. I'm going to beat you next time around," Blake
promised.

The siblings were in the backyard getting fresh air and
exercise because their mother made them. Well, Lucas and Blake
were getting exercise, kicking around the soccer ball. Alexis was
only getting the fresh air. She sat up against a tree stump with
a tablet. Her fingers were working overtime on the screen.

Lucas assumed she was creating her own wardrobe with
that app she was obsessed with. Ever since their mom took her
to one of Aunt Callie's fashion shows in New York when she
was six, his sister became convinced that one day she would
become a famous fashion designer like Aunt Callie.

Lucas sat on the still-cold ground next to the soccer goal
net. He placed his head between his legs and tried not to think
about Liv being gone. That's all he thought about these days.
That, and the whole his-father-being-dead conversation he

overheard. Lucas didn't like to say the word dead. It was scary and meant forever. It meant Liv would be gone forever, and he would never see her again.

"Are you okay?" Blake asked. He took the spot next to Lucas.

"Just thinking about Liv. It's weird that she's gone. I hope they catch the bad guy soon."

He and Blake had been naughty. They'd disobeyed their mother when she warned them to stay off the web. Once their parents delivered the news about Liv, Lucas had snuck into Blake's room when they were both supposed to be asleep and secretly did a search for Liv's name. They wished they hadn't. It was like being told the horrible news all over again. They'd read the story and found out that Liv was shot, and hadn't died in an accident like their mother had said.

"Me too," Blake said, pulling him back to the present. "It's not fair. Why would someone want to kill Liv? She was so nice. Whoever did that to her is evil."

"I know." Lucas raised his head and looked at Blake. "That's why I don't want to get too friendly with Katie."

"What do you mean?"

"What if something happens to Katie, too?"

Blake frowned and looked at Lucas like he was nuts.

"What? No way."

"How can you be sure? Look how Liv ended up."

"But that wouldn't happen two times in a row," Blake said.

"But we don't know for sure, do we?" Lucas said, his voice a raspy whisper.

They remained quiet for a minute. Then Lucas said, "What if it's like one of those horror movies where they start killing people in the same family?"

"You're crazy," Blake said.

"What if I'm not? What if the bad guy who killed Liv

comes after all of us?"

"Lucas, you're scaring me," Blake said. "Stop saying stuff like that."

"Saying stuff like what?" Alexis asked.

Neither Blake nor Lucas had heard her approach. Their conversation was so intense, they weren't paying attention.

"Nothing," the brothers said in unison.

"Are you guys keeping secrets again?" Alexis asked, and sat next to Lucas.

"No, we're not," Blake said guiltily. "We were just talking about Katie."

Lucas nudged his brother, a signal to keep quiet about what they were discussing.

"What about her?" Alexis asked. "She's nice."

"Yeah," Lucas said. "That's what we were saying."

"But she's not Liv," Alexis said.

"Lucas is scared that whoever killed Liv will come after all of us," Blake blurted out.

"Blake! You weren't supposed to tell."

Alexis placed her tablet beside her. "That's ridiculous, Lucas. Why would you say something like that? Liv's death was an accident. That's what Mom said."

"No, it wasn't," Lucas said. "I read the story on my phone. Somebody shot her twice. That's not an accident."

Alexis' eyes went wide and her mouth hung open. Then her bottom lip started trembling.

"Maybe she was shot by accident," she said, her voice squeaky.

Lucas knew what was coming next. The tears.

"I'm sorry, Alexis. Maybe I'm wrong, and Mom is right."

Lucas pulled his sister close to him and hugged her. "Please don't cry, Alexis. Maybe I didn't read the story the right way. Look, this is really hard."

He looked over at Blake, whose eyes were glazed over with unshed tears, but Lucas knew his brother. He would pretend that he wasn't about to burst into tears like their sister.

"It's going to be okay, Lexi. No one is going to hurt us. Right, Blake?"

Alexis only allowed her siblings to call her Lexi and no one else, not even their parents. And when they did, it usually meant something serious was going on.

Blake told her to wipe her tears, and Lucas tried to convince her to head inside. Lucas and Blake were close, but he was Alexis' twin and they had a special bond. Lucas knew that later on, Blake would go to her room to make sure she was okay.

After Alexis went inside, Blake and Lucas remained in the back yard for a while longer. It was getting chilly and they would soon leave, as well, before their mother came yelling for them.

"So," Blake said. "What do you really think about Katie? You can tell me."

Lucas shrugged. He didn't quite know what to make of Katie. Sure, she was nice, but he just didn't know. He didn't have the same connection with her that he did with Liv, although Katie had only been with them for a little while.

"She's okay, I guess."

"Wanna know something funny?" Blake asked.

Lucas inched closer to his brother. He recognized the look in Blake's eyes. He was about to tell Lucas a secret.

"What?"

"Katie. Well, sometimes she's on the phone a lot, whispering."

"Whispering to who?"

"I don't know, dude."

"What did she say when you busted her?"

"Nothing. She didn't see me."

"Does she do it a lot?"

"I don't know. I only caught her two times."

"Why would she be whispering?" Lucas asked.

"Because she didn't want anybody to hear what she was saying."

"But why?"

"Adults have a lot of secrets. You said that."

"I don't like this, Blake. Katie is a stranger. I don't like strangers."

"I know, dude. But Mom and Dad think she's okay. Otherwise, they wouldn't have found her to help take care of us."

Lucas thought about that for a moment. What Blake said was true. He started disliking strangers when he was five. At the park once, a stranger came up to Mom and said something. Mom got really upset and started crying. Lucas saw the whole thing. When he got closer to his mom, she wiped her tears on the sleeves of her blouse. He asked her why she was crying, and she said it was nothing.

"Just a mean person, sweetie," she had said. "Nothing to worry about. How about a snack?"

What if Katie made his Mom cry? he thought.

"We should spy on Katie," he said.

"What? Why would we do that?" Blake asked.

"Because I don't want her to make Mom cry. Mom's not herself when she's sad. Plus, we need to find out what she's hiding."

"How are we supposed to spy on Katie? She's not around on weekends, and we're at school during the week."

"I have an idea," Lucas said.

CHAPTER 26

WHEN JENNA TEXTED to say we should have breakfast at the cute little bakery and café that just opened in Bedford, the next town over from Lexington, I jumped at the chance to do something normal. The past week was chaotic and difficult. The police still have no leads on who killed Liv and why. Her funeral was especially heartbreaking. I couldn't look the Stewarts in the eye or any of her other relatives, including a handful of aunts and uncles who had flown in from Jamaica. Ty and I didn't stay for the repass. Maybe we were cowards, running from our guilt.

Part of me feels that her death could have been prevented, although I have no rational basis for that thought. I keep going back to the night at the Paynes. I've played that scene in my head a million times, round and round, and I still can't figure out what she saw that night. It's obvious now that the story about forgetting her phone wasn't true.

My real motive for accepting Jenna's invitation isn't exactly pure. I want to know what the detectives asked when they interviewed her and Charlie. Not sure how forthcoming she will be, since I didn't warn her that the police may want to talk to her and Charlie.

I walk into the Princess Bakery and Café, where the mouthwatering aroma of fresh coffee brewing assails my senses. The place is bustling as patrons place their orders at the counter and others look for a seat. I stand off to the side, close my eyes, and tune out everything but the strong whiff of freshly baked bread competing with the brewing coffee, to transport me to a different place and time: Mom and I working side by side in the kitchen at home, kneading the dough for homemade bread, laughing and bonding. My brother Miles popping his head in to ask if the bread is ready yet as the delicious-smelling aroma wafts throughout the house.

Those were happy, simpler times. I never realized how much I missed those days until just now. The stressors in my life may be finally taking a toll: Liv's death and murder investigation, preparing to defend my dissertation, my temporary childcare situation, and such.

I slide into the seat across from Jenna, who arrived before me. She's dressed in a blue pastel top, floral scarf, and jeans.

"Thanks for suggesting we meet here," I say. "I love this place already." I cast a sweeping glance across the space. The walls are peppered with life-sized photos of delectable desserts, pastries, and various caffeinated drinks.

"You have a lot going on," she says. "I thought you could use a break from preparing your dissertation defense and all the other stuff."

"You can say it, Jenna. Liv was murdered and my family is grieving, struggling to come to terms with it."

"I'm so sorry, Abbie. I know I've said it a thousand times, but I just don't know what else to say or do."

"There's nothing to say. I only hope the police catch her killer, and soon. I don't understand the motive behind it, though."

"There are a lot of psychos out there. Maybe Liv was unlucky and crossed paths with one. Sometimes people kill because they can, no logical explanation."

I shake my head. "Not in this case. At least, I don't believe that's what happened."

"What do you mean?"

I don't answer her and instead pose a question of my own.

"What did the police ask you and Charlie when they interviewed you? Did you sense that they had anything to go on, or were they just fishing?"

Jenna digs into her purse and comes up with gloss, which she generously slathers all over her lips. She places the gloss back into her purse.

"The police didn't really ask us that much. The fact is, Charlie and I didn't know Olivia. We met her twice, once at your house and then the night of the dinner at ours. She barely spoke. That's pretty much what we told them."

"Did they ask any unusual questions?"

"Unusual how?"

"I don't know. Anything that seemed odd to you."

"Nothing comes to mind."

"I want to know if they have an angle to pursue, you know what I mean? I had the feeling they weren't going to tell us much until they had something solid, but it would be nice to know where they're headed."

"Abbie, I don't think you should take this on," Jenna says, leaning in.

"What do you mean?"

"You have enough pressure in your life. Your stress levels must be off the charts. I'm sure Ty wouldn't want you adding to that. Let the police do what they do. That's why I asked you here this morning, to get away from it all, even if it's just for an hour or so."

"You're right. But Liv was like family. When something tragic happens to a family member, you want to know why. Don't get me wrong, Katie is great and I'm so grateful to you for sending her our way, but Liv worked for us for five years. You don't just let go of that and move on."

"I can't imagine what you're going through. And I'm not going to pretend I do, but I worry about you, Abbie."

"Why is that?"

"Your stress levels. And I know it's none of my business, but you don't seem to eat much and you're on the thin side. *Really thin.* I don't mean it in a negative way. I just want you to be okay."

"So you thought bringing me here would fatten me up with all the delectable treats in this café?"

She's right. It's none of her business, but I can't yet determine if her comments came from genuine concern or something else. I have no idea what that something else could be. Not yet, anyway.

"I just thought you could use some down time, that's all."

"Well, we came here to eat right? So let's get some food."

We return to the table with our orders. Scalding hot, freshly brewed coffee and a large caramel sticky bun for me.

I cradle my coffee and take a sip. *Heaven.* Tastes like brown sugar and cherry had a baby. Jenna pours cream into her coffee and stirs. I observe her. She hesitated before giving me an answer regarding their police interview about Liv and used the simple act of putting on lip gloss as a stalling tactic. What do I really know about the woman who sits before me, a woman who had the guts to comment on my appearance and inform me she's afraid I'm falling apart?

"So how did you and Charlie meet?" I ask, breaking off a

piece of my bun.

She stops stirring and looks up at me.

"Pardon?"

"How did you and Charlie meet?" I repeat, louder this time. Perhaps the chatter and noise of the café drowned out the question.

"Oh. We met in college."

"Cool. Where?"

"Where what?"

"Come on, Jenna. Is it a state secret? I'm just asking where you and your husband met, where you fell in love. You act as though I've asked you to divulge your bank account and social security numbers."

Jenna coughs violently. Several drops of her coffee hit the table. A few patrons glance in our direction and then continue on with their conversations.

"Are you okay?" I ask, once the coughing subsides. "Do you want me to get you some water?"

"I'm fine," she says, dabbing her nose with a napkin. "I think I'm coming down with a cold or allergies or something. I hear the pollen here can be pretty intense this time of year. I guess my system isn't used to it yet."

I lose the chance to probe further. A woman our age, with a toddler in tow, approaches our table.

"Maren, is that you?" The woman shrieks with excitement, grinning at Jenna. "Maren Dinsdale, oh my goodness, how are you?" The woman opens her arms wide for a hug, but her arms remain empty. She drops them to her sides.

Jenna sits ramrod straight, stiff as a block of ice. "I'm sorry, I think you mistook me for someone else," she says. She starts chewing her lips and refuses to look the woman in the eye.

The woman's face goes somber. I can see the hurt in her

eyes. "Maren, it's me, Corrinne Beal. We met last year in Lexington, when I went to pick up my son—"

Jenna cuts her off. "Ma'am, you're mistaken. My name is Jenna Payne. Sorry, maybe this Maren is my doppelganger. It happens. But please leave us alone. I'm having breakfast with my friend."

The woman backs away slowly, seemingly devastated. "Okay. I'll leave you alone. Sorry for interrupting. My mistake."

She grabs hold of her daughter's hand and leaves.

Jenna shakes her head. "Some people."

"That was strange," I say. "She was adamant that you were this Maren person."

"I know, right? I've never seen that woman before in my life. I guess the mind can be tricky sometimes. People see what they want to see."

Right. People see what they want to see.

I shiver from the wake of a sudden chill snaking its way up and down my spine.

CHAPTER 27

A FTER THE PECULIAR experience at the café with Jenna, I did some research on "Maren Dinsdale" and nothing useful came back. Ms. Dinsdale is a ghost, an alias most likely. I'm convinced the woman at the café, Corrine, knew Jenna. She was telling the truth.

But what disturbed me even more than Jenna having an alias and denying she knew Corinne was what Corrine said. They met in Lexington last year. Corinne would have revealed more details, but Jenna threw a wet blanket all over that exposé.

Last year. As in the same timeframe when Charlie's company, Affirm Technologies LLC purchased the home at three fifty-one Cherry Blossom Lane, down the street from us. Ty's contact at DEA said the Paynes came back clean. Yet something Jenna said sends chills up my spine every time I replay it in my head.

People see what they want to see.

I take one last look in the bedroom mirror. I visited the salon yesterday and got a deep conditioning and a blowout. My hair runs past my shoulders and has a fullness and shine I haven't seen in a long while. My makeup is somewhat under-stated with a touch of playful glamor: mascara, a dash of eye shadow, colored lip gloss, and eyeliner, which gives me a dramatic, doe-eyed look.

My wardrobe is of the bespoke variety, thanks to my best friend, Callie Furi, fashion designer to celebrities and the uber rich who can afford the sinfully exorbitant price tags on her clothing and accessories. I've known Callie since high school, the days she walked around with her sketch book and used me as her human mannequin. She designed my wedding gown, and everyone wanted to know who the designer was. That match lit the fire to her blazing hot career.

I picked a royal blue, short-sleeved, fitted bodycon dress and three-inch black pumps. For accessories, glamorous hoop earring, and a crocodile leather Furi bag complete my ensemble.

I arrive downstairs in the middle of morning routine. The kids are having breakfast, and Katie is warning them that they don't want to be late so they had better hurry up. Looks like everyone got a late start this morning.

When I walk into full view, jaws drop and eyes pop.

"What, you kids have never seen your mother before?"

"Mom you look beautiful," Blake says.

"Wow, Mom, you look amazing," Lucas agrees.

I curtsy. "Thank you, my little gentlemen."

I can't afford to show up to my meeting looking like the overstressed housewife and student that I am. The women who work in those offices have the fab look on lockdown and resemble cover models, everyone from the assistants to the senior executives who occupy the C-suite.

"Oh, my goodness, is that a Callie Furi hand bag?" Katie squawks with delight. "I saw one of those while I was window shopping in New York a few months ago. I almost fainted when I saw the price tag. I promised myself never to look at one again."

"Mom and Aunt Callie are best friends," Alexis informs her. "I'm going to be a designer just like her when I grow up."

Katie looks at Alexis like she's just a kid with an overactive imagination. Then she turns to me. I confirm my daughter's statement.

"Wow. Do you know her dad, too, Nicholas Furi? I love his movies."

"Yes, Nicholas and I go way back. I met him when Callie and I were in high school together."

I glance at the microwave clock. If I'm going to make my flight, I have to leave soon.

I turn to the kids. "I'll be back early this evening. Uncle Miles will be over to watch you when Katie leaves for the day."

"Where are you going, Mommy?" Alexis asks. "You never dress up like this when you leave for school."

"Mommy has a very important meeting today. As I said, I'll be back this evening. And don't think you can goof off because your uncle lets you get away with everything," I say, eyeing each of them.

I won't elaborate about where I'm going. It's mostly for Katie's benefit. Now that my suspicion radar is on high alert, I can't trust that the Paynes, especially Jenna, won't use Katie to gain information about my movements. After all, Katie may feel indebted to Jenna for getting her this job, albeit temporary.

No one but Ty and the person I'm visiting know that my destination is New York City.

CHAPTER 28

THE LEVITRON-BLAIR TOWER, or LB Tower as it's affectionately known, looms before me at its busy midtown Manhattan location, a stone's throw away from Times Square. The noise and busyness of New York City always reminds me that I should take life by the horns, live a little. That I'm still young and have my whole life ahead of me. I turned thirty a few weeks back and would have barely remembered it was my birthday if not for Ty, the kids and my parents.

Liv will never get to see thirty.

The fifty-three-story glass behemoth that is Levitron-Blair holds its own against the ever-expanding cluster of skyscrapers that make up the New York City skyline. As the second largest media company in the world, LB owns over forty networks in the U.S., fifty-two internationally, in addition to nineteen field entertainments assets, including film and video game companies and amusement parks.

I tip the driver, exit the car, and head for the lobby bustling with employees, deliverymen, and visitors. I check in with security and receive a visitor's name tag, then take the elevator up to the fiftieth floor.

Expensive art lines the walls of the sleek hallway, some

of them shots of popular characters from film and TV shows produced by media entities owned by Levitron-Blair. The kids have toured this place before and didn't want to leave. Once they discovered an entire floor was dedicated to characters from their favorite shows, they were hooked.

The suite that houses his office and that of his administrative assistant is massive— expensive carpeting, dark brown leather sofas and tall plants. And most impressive, is the spectacular view of New York City.

Courtney Chen, Christian's posh-looking, thirty-something assistant, is impeccably groomed in a sapphire-blue pencil skirt, white silk blouse, and a navy-blue and white Chanel scarf. She hurries from behind her neatly organized desk with panic in her eyes.

"Abbie, I wasn't expecting you. Oh, my goodness, Christian is going to fire me. I don't have you on his calendar for today. What a screw up, I can't believe I did that. I'm so embarrassed."

I make the time out gesture with my palms. The poor woman is about to have a coronary over something she didn't do.

"Breathe, Courtney," I say, with a reassuring smile. "You didn't do anything wrong. This meeting with Christian was last minute, and it's obvious he forgot to tell you about it or just didn't want it recorded on his calendar. Either way, don't worry. You're not going anywhere. Christian can't do his job without you and he knows it."

"Ain't that the truth."

Christian Wheeler appears at the door to his office with a big grin on his face. Just shy of six-foot two, he possesses what one would call the All-American, boy-next-door good looks: thick, wheat-blond hair, luminous, Spanish-blue eyes and warrior physique—lean, toned and wiry. He sports a tailored, designer suit that could take care of a semester's worth of tuition at some universities, a white open-collar dress shirt, a pocket square, and no tie.

"I'll move around some things on your calendar," Courtney says, as she heads back to her desk.

Christian adds, "Make sure we're not disturbed."

His massive office boasts a spectacular view of New York City from all angles. Blades of morning sunlight slice through the windows. The space is a cross between a mini conference room and a penthouse suite at the Plaza. Potted plants occupy all four corners of the space. The décor is masculine yet sleek and modern.

I remove my coat, which he takes from me and drapes over the chair at his desk. He gestures for me to have a seat on the two-seat sofa and joins me. I look out the window and spot a blimp for a life insurance company floating through the sky.

"Is it everything you thought it would be?" I ask, gesturing to the expansive space and views. "You've been chief operating officer for what, a couple of years now?"

"To tell you the truth, I'm still learning, and I don't think I'll ever stop. Dad is angling to retire soon."

"You don't feel ready, do you?"

He chuckles. "You know me so well, Abbie. You're the only person I can admit my insecurities to."

"It's not going to get any easier. Surround yourself with people you trust implicitly. Sometimes that means having people on your team who are smarter than you. See it as an asset, an opportunity. Not a threat. Great leadership is about service. You know what I mean?"

A look of distress flickers across his face, just for a moment. He looks out the window, then shifts his gaze back to me.

In an almost inaudible voice he says, "I wish things had turned out differently."

"Maybe they turned out the way they were supposed to. We're exactly where we're supposed to be."

"How can you say that, Abbie?"

"It's life, Christian."

"Can you honestly tell me that if things hadn't gone down the way they did when you were at Yale, that you would have married Ty?"

His question is perplexing. I just didn't see it coming, even with our history.

"Why are you bringing up the past?"

This is not the conversation I thought we would be having, considering the reason for my visit. I've known Christian since high school. In fact, we dated senior year and chose to remain friends once we headed off to college that fall.

"You know what I mean, Abbie." He stands up and walks toward the window closest to us. He sticks his hands in his pockets and stares out the window again.

"I'm not sure I do. Why don't you tell me?"

Without looking at me he says, "I've always regretted that I missed my chance. For too many years, I kept my feelings bottled up and hidden. I was too scared to tell you. I was afraid of how you would react, afraid it would jeopardize our friendship."

I open and close my mouth. I clear my throat and attempt to speak again.

"Why now? What is it about this time in our lives that makes you want to confess?"

He walks away from the window and comes to stand in front of me.

"Because you're the only person who can help me become the best leader I can be."

I leave my spot on the sofa, and head for the window

to collect my thoughts. The view doesn't seem so impressive anymore.

"That's what your father is for, Christian. Alan can teach you what you need to know. You've been at his side for years, studying how the business operates. You went to Wharton and earned an MBA to help prepare you. Besides, you can hire an army of executive coaches if you feel you need polishing."

"Are you deliberately playing dumb or you truly have no idea?" he asks.

I spin around to face him. He stands only a few inches away from me.

"Have you ever known me to play games? You caught me off guard with this confession. I'm married to Ty. You know I've always loved him. The circumstance that brought about our marriage matters not. It's okay to be afraid of the unknown, Christian," I say, moving toward him. "The responsibility before you is staggering. You're only thirty-one, and it must seem like a colossal endeavor. But you can't pretend that, somehow, it would be less daunting if we were together."

"You're wrong," he says, clutching both my arms and looking me dead in the face. "I've told you things I've never told another living soul. You don't judge me for my mistakes. You've given me invaluable advice. You know who I am."

His arms drop to his sides and he apologizes for his intensity. Then he says, "I've always respected your marriage and would never compromise you. Ty is a lucky man. But I had to be honest with you. I had to put it out there in the hopes it would stop messing with my head every time I see you. I know it's selfish, and that's not why you're here, but I had to take the opportunity. Twelve years is a long time to wait to tell someone how you feel."

I allow his words to wash over me, wondering if bringing

it out in the open will free him, asking myself whether this revelation will make things awkward between us. I don't want it to. I never suspected he felt that way about me all this time. We kept in touch after high school. Life happened. We each followed our own path. I became a wife and mother when I was barely out of my teens. He went off to graduate school after college and lived the life of a pampered prince who would one day inherit the kingdom.

"You're right. That is a long time to carry around something like that. We were just kids back then, Christian. How could we have known what life would throw at us?"

"I thought we had time, Abbie. Then everything changed. The world got flipped on its axis for both of us. You married Ty and that was it. The door slammed shut. I've never spoken of it until now."

"That was brave of you. I had no idea. And for what it's worth, I thought after high school that was it. I never allowed myself to entertain the idea that we could have had a future together. We were on different paths. I was going to medical school after college, and then I'd study to become a neurosurgeon. That dream didn't come true for me, but your destiny, your legacy is to run Levitron-Blair one day."

"I think we're destined to be in each other's lives. Lucas coming into the world ensured that. It's going to have to be enough for me."

I take a seat and gesture for him to join me. "Speaking of Lucas, I didn't give you a lot of information over the phone, but we have ourselves a situation."

"What kind of situation?"

CHAPTER 29

"I S LUCAS IN danger?" he asks, his face anxious.

"I'm not sure. But there have been several coincidences, if you can even call them that. For instance, Liv was found murdered a couple of weeks after she got spooked in the Paynes' driveway. She saw something disturbing, but I don't know what."

I stand, and roam around the room, gathering my thoughts so I sound coherent and not like a raving lunatic. I land near Christian's desk and lean against it.

"How can you be sure Liv freaking out had anything to do with the Paynes?" he asks. "You told me on the phone they came back clean."

"There has been a new development. I came to see you because I'm petrified something bad is about to happen and I need your help."

He approaches the desk and sidles up next to me. "Talk to me, Abbie. What's going on?"

"All of these little incidents by themselves don't amount to much. But when you throw in what happened at the café a few days ago, huge red flags went up."

"What happened?"

I fill him in on the incident in the café with Jenna and Corinne Beal, the so-called case of mistaken identity.

Christian frowns. "Could the woman have been mistaken?"

"That's what Jenna said, but Christian, that woman was sure of what she was talking about. I believe her. She knows Jenna as this Maren person. She started to say they met at her son's school and Jenna rudely cut her off. The woman was disappointed. She knew she was right, but she apologized anyway for her mistake. It *wasn't* a mistake."

He strokes his chin. "You said you found out nothing unusual, yet, Jenna has an alias, and this woman, Corinne Beal said they met at her son's school a year ago?"

"Right. But Jenna and her husband just moved in next door a few weeks back, or at least, that's when they came by to introduce themselves. Up until that point, I had only seen them a couple of times before, a week or so before they dropped by the house. But," I say, holding up my index finger, "their home was purchased a year ago under Affirm Technologies, LLC, the husband's software consulting firm."

He tilts his head thoughtfully. Then he says, "How did you find out his company was listed as the owner of the house?"

I explain how I contacted Layla to find out when the Paynes purchased their home, and the incident that led me to do so: Jenna's curiosity about Lucas. I also fill him in on how Jenna came to the rescue the day Liv didn't show up for work, and ultimately helped me find a temporary replacement for her.

"Unless you're working for the CIA or undercover in law enforcement, an alias is usually not a good sign. I don't know too many suburban housewives who have aliases."

"I don't believe in coincidences," I say. "I've had enough of them to last me a lifetime."

But Christian isn't listening. He's in some far-off place, his eyes distant and worried.

"What is it?" I ask

"What were you going to ask me? The reason for your visit?"

"Well, I was getting to that."

"I need to know, now."

His gaze is so intense, I think his eyes may have changed colors on me.

"It's kind of a huge favor, and if you can't do it, I'll figure out something else."

"Just tell me," he implores.

"Do you think I could borrow the Wheeler jet, and your pilot?"

"I'm listening," he says.

"April vacation is in a few days. I would feel better if the kids weren't around while I figure out what's going on. I hate to even say it out loud, but it's been eating away at me."

"What has?"

"I'm willing to bet that Corinne Beal's son goes to the same school my kids do. Jenna doesn't have kids, and I can see no logical reason for her to be at the same elementary school as my children. She was there to do recon, Christian. She just happened to run into Corinne."

I force my brain to slow down, and take deep, calming breaths.

I continue, "Then she and Charlie show up a year later, pretending they just moved in next door, but Jenna zeroed in on Lucas. Something about him had her out of sorts. She became emotional when she was introduced to him."

Christian rakes his fingers through his hair. His jaw clenches. Then he says, "You paint a compelling portrait of suspicion."

"It's more than that. Something is up with that couple, and

it's not anything good. I don't want my kids, especially Lucas, around this school vacation if I can help it."

"You're sending them to the Bahamas, to Ty's parents?"

"Yes. Jenny and Bobby won't be back in the States until next month. The timing works. The kids have a ball when they're down there, and I'm sure their grandparents would be thrilled to have them. It's too risky flying on a commercial airline. I want this trip to be top secret so they don't have time to make new plans or alter existing ones. That's why I'm asking for use of the jet."

"Consider it done. But a thought just occurred to me. It's probably going to add to your anxiety."

"What is it?"

"If Charlie and Jenna have bad intentions, we have to consider that they timed whatever they're planning to coincide with spring vacation."

CHAPTER 30

"W E'RE RUNNING OUT of time. We need to move soon."
Katie looked at Charlie, wide-eyed and confused.

"What do you mean by soon? You told me this job was for a couple of months."

"Something came up. The plan changed."

"What came up?"

"You're on a need-to-know basis. That's the deal. You don't need to know why the plan changed. Just be ready to move within seventy-two hours. Did Abbie discuss spring break plans with you, what she intends to do with the kids?"

"No, she hasn't. I figured she would let me know when she was ready."

"No time to wait. Make her tell you."

Charlie rolled the swivel chair away from the desk of his home office. Having Katie here was risky, but he had an excuse at the ready in case anyone saw Katie leave, and by *anyone*, he meant Abbie's brother Miles, Abbie returning from her all-day meeting, or one of the kids. He would have preferred to meet Katie as far away from here as possible but he needed to stay put. He had work to do in his office.

Katie leaned up against the closed door, arms folded with a

thoughtful expression on her face.

"Seventy-two hours is not a lot of time for me to do whatever it is you're planning."

"How do you know that? I haven't told you what your assignment is yet."

"I'm not stupid, Charlie. This is about Lucas, isn't it? What are you going to do to him?"

"Stop with the paranoia. I'm not going to do anything to Lucas." He removed his glasses and placed them on the desk. He didn't need them, anyway.

Technically, he was telling the truth. Just not all of it. A wild idea had occurred to him last night, when Jenna confessed yet another screw up. The walls were closing in with this latest debacle of hers. Charlie was forced to improvise, so he came up with a new plan. One that would get him what he wanted and spare Lucas. That would enrage the boss, but the truth was, Charlie reasoned, the boss would have him killed, anyway.

This new plan would make Charlie a millionaire many times over and set him up for life. He would start over in a place where the boss couldn't touch him. Where no one could.

"Why won't you tell me what I'm supposed to do, exactly? Lucas doesn't trust me. I caught him snooping around my things the other day."

Charlie's head popped up. "What? When did this happen?"

"Last week. Caught him digging through my bag. I think he was looking for my phone."

Charlie stood up as alarm bells pummeled his brain. He was right to change course and wrap this up in three days. With this latest revelation, it would make it even more difficult for Katie to accomplish what he had in mind. He needed Lucas for the plan to work. Charlie had thought it was going to be as easy as taking candy from a baby, as the saying goes, but he underestimated the kid.

"Why is Lucas suspicious of you?" Charlie asked, accusation thick in his voice. "He's a ten-year-old boy who had never met you until recently."

Katie gave a non-committal shrug. "Not sure. They're still grieving the loss of their nanny. It's normal that they would be suspicious of any new person coming into their lives. Those kids are going through a lot. The mother is high-strung. Sweet woman but gosh, she acts like she's carrying the world on her shoulders. I'm worried about her, to be frank."

"Why would you care? You've known her for all of five minutes."

Charlie didn't want any attachments. It made things complicated. The last thing he needed was Katie growing a conscience. He would simply remind her of the consequences.

"Stay focused, Katie. If you screw this up for me, I'll make sure the police know who killed Ramon Diaz."

Katie's arms dropped to her sides. She closed her eyes and shook her head slowly.

"I told you that was an accident. A terrible, tragic accident I will regret for the rest of my life."

She opened her eyes. Tears pooled in them, but Charlie wasn't moved. Too much was at stake.

"But not regretful enough to turn yourself in. You left him on the road like a dog to die and then went on with your life as if nothing happened. Isn't that how it went down, Katie?"

The tears flowed freely now. It was cruel, putting the screws to her like that, but he was on a limited timeline.

Two years ago, Charlie strolled into a Denver bar and ran into Katie. The pretty girl who sat in the corner all by her lonesome, throwing them back like alcohol was about to be outlawed had caught his attention. He'd grabbed the stool next to her and introduced himself, turning on the charm in spades. He didn't have to do much. Soon, the whole sad story had come pouring out of Katie as smoothly as the alcohol had poured into her.

She was driving late at night, drunk and stoned. Her boyfriend had dumped her at a party, so she'd left. It was dark. The road wasn't well lit. She didn't see him. Only heard the impact. She'd gotten out of the car and when she saw what she had done, she'd panicked. Gotten back into her car and drove off.

Charlie was appropriately sympathetic. Said all the right things, soothing words of comfort and advice. He managed to get her phone number, but not before he distracted her long enough to poke through her purse and read her driver's license. He had memorized every detail.

When the time came to track her down, coincidentally, she had moved to Boston. Charlie believed in signs. What were the chances they would eventually end up in the same city?

Katie sniffled loudly, ending his stroll down memory lane. She swiped her nose with the back of her hand. "I guess I don't have a choice, yet again."

"This will all be over in three days, and you'll never hear from me again. Accident or not, you killed a man and kept going. What I'm asking is a small price to pay to avoid going to prison."

Katie stared at him miserably, but he knew he had her.

Charlie was experienced at reinventing himself. In a few days, he would do it again and disappear forever.

CHAPTER 31

M Y INTERNET RESEARCH on Corinne Beal yielded enough information that I was able to contact her through social media. We agreed to meet at a local bookshop in Concord later today. I explained that I was the person with Maren Dinsdale at the Bedford café three days ago and that I believed she didn't make a mistake. I told her I would bring her up to speed on what's been going on with Maren, and I had a few questions for her. I was surprised when she agreed to meet right away. I thought she would put up more of a resistance.

I sling my backpack over my shoulders, amble down the stairs and head for the kitchen. Blake and Alexis are present, but not Lucas. Katie is helping Blake stuff a fat slice of bagel down the toaster.

"Morning," I say breezily. "Blake, is Lucas getting ready for school or am I going to have to hurry him along?"

"He'll be down soon," Blake says.

"Did you two stay up past your bedtime again?" I ask, my gaze locked on him.

Blake has the deer-in-headlights look. His eyes pop wide. My kids are terrible liars. Something is causing Lucas to have a late start this morning.

"It's school vacation soon, Mom," Alexis pipes up, biting into a slice of toast. "Only today and tomorrow and that's it."

"Oh, Abbie," Katie cut in. "We never talked about it, but do you need me around next week? I don't know if you're taking the kids anywhere, so I wanted to ask in case you needed me."

"To be honest Katie, spring break kinda crept up on me and I don't have anything planned. I'll figure something out over the next two days. Maybe I'll take the kids to my brother Lee's house so they can spend time with their cousins. Or maybe I'll leave them with my parents. My dad loves to take them golfing when the weather gets nice."

I take an exaggerated breath, as if it's one more thing to add to my overflowing to-do list.

"No problem. I'll be available if you need me. Just let me know."

"Thanks Katie, I will."

Lucas barges in, barely awake with his shirt not buttoned all the way up and pants that look crooked.

I pull him close and adjust his pants. He missed a loop with the belt.

Once I straighten out his outfit, I say, "That's what happens to little boys who stay up late. They're tired and feel awful in the morning." I ruffle his hair, and he doesn't say a word as he heads to the kitchen table where a glass of orange juice is waiting for him.

"You guys are so busted," Katie says, with a playful grin aimed at the boys. Blake joins his siblings at the kitchen table and I pour coffee into a mug.

Katie adds, "Were you two up late trading scary ghost stories? I used to do that a lot with my sister. Boy did we get in trouble."

"I didn't know you had a sister," Lucas says sharply. "What's her name?"

A heavy silence blankets the kitchen. All movement and activity have ceased, waiting on Katie, whose voice is now on mute. She lowers her gaze slightly, her cheeks crimson.

Then she looks up and says, "She died when I was younger. Her name was Molly."

"Oh," Lucas says. I can see the guilt etched on his face, his regret at asking the question. I regret that he asked, too, for different reasons. They're already dealing with death. I don't want them having to confront it again, even if it happened a while ago to someone they don't know.

The kids resume eating breakfast. I want to apologize to Katie for Lucas bringing up a sore subject, even if he didn't know, but something stops me. I don't know what exactly. Instead, I kiss each of my children on the cheek, wish them a good day at school, and promise we'll figure something out for vacation week.

LUCAS STUDIED KATIE as she opened the refrigerator and pulled out a jug of orange juice. He still didn't trust her. She poured juice into a glass on the counter, returned the jug to the fridge, and took a sip. He was glad that their mom didn't make a big deal about them being up late. Blake didn't squeal, so that was good. The boys were up late discussing Katie. So far, Lucas and Blake had not been successful in their spying. Lucas got close one day when he was trying to find Katie's phone. He knew you could find a lot of information on phones, and he was hoping he could find out who Katie was always whispering to.

But she came back from the bathroom before he had a chance to find the phone in her purse. Blake didn't have any luck, either. And just now, Lucas didn't know what to make of Katie's dead sister, Molly. She never said she had a sister before. Lucas wasn't an expert on lying, but something deep inside him told him Katie *was* lying. Maybe it was a trick to find out what he and Blake had talked about. If only he could get his hands on her phone. Vacation was the perfect time to come up with another plan, he decided. He and Blake had a whole week to figure out what Katie was hiding.

CHAPTER 32

I ARRIVE AT the bookstore in Concord where Corinne and I agreed to meet. A large display of hardcover bestsellers and that new book smell make me yearn for the days when I read for pleasure. Not so much now. Most of my reading is confined to research and textbooks that are so heavy, they could double as lethal weapons. Customers are scattered throughout, riffling through books and magazines. Others form a short line at the register to pay for their purchases.

Corinne is a no-show. I've been sitting in the café section of the bookstore for twenty-five minutes, which leaves me wondering if she just flaked or changed her mind altogether. We exchanged phone numbers and email addresses. I checked my account multiple times in the past few minutes, hoping for a note, an explanation, something. I've called her cell phone three times, but she never picked up. The café's coffee grinder is in full operation, and the usually welcome sound exacerbates the unease building in my chest.

An idea occurs to me and I head for the register. An older man with a head full of platinum hair and hunched shoulders rings up the last customer. As the customer leaves, I approach him.

"Excuse me, sir. I was supposed to meet someone here, but

149

she's a no-show. I was wondering if you could tell me if she comes here often. Maybe I can hang around a little longer or come by later."

I pull out my phone and find the appropriate photo of Corinne I snapped from her online profile. The old man picks up his glasses from the side of the register and puts them on. He squints a bit and then recognition floods his face.

He says, "I sure do. Corinne comes in here at least once a week with her son, Brody. A little hyper if you ask me, but he loves books and that's good for business."

"Have you seen her at all this week?"

"Um, now that you mention it, she comes in here every Tuesday. I could set my clock to her, but she didn't show up yesterday. She could have had an emergency of some kind. Can't say for sure."

"Perhaps you're right," I say. "I'll check in with her again to make sure she's okay. Thank you."

"Harvey's the name, Harvey Miller. If you ever come in again, give me a holler."

I agree to look Harvey up the next time I come into the bookstore. An endless loop of questions takes over my brain as I head to my car. Did someone get to Corinne and order her to back off, and if so, was that person Jenna? Or did Corinne decide on her own that she didn't want to get involved?

I pull out my phone from my purse and open the app for the online platform on which we connected. Maybe she posted something that will provide a clue as to what's going on. I pop open the car door and slide into the driver's seat. With one hand on the steering wheel, I type her name into the search bar with the other. My eyes blink rapidly at the screen.

Corinne's profile has been deleted.

The temperature inside the car drops, despite the afternoon

sun glinting off the windshields of the other vehicles in the parking lot. Another strange episode to add to the growing list.

I tap my fingers on the steering wheel. My mind gallops without any predetermined destination. I pick up my phone again and text Corinne Beal, then wait.

When the response comes a couple minutes later, it's cold, curt and final.

Leave me alone or else…

CHAPTER 33

WHERE ARE YOU going?" Jenna asked.
"Quick trip to visit a client. I should be back tomorrow night."

"Where?" The skepticism on her face was unmistakable, but Charlie didn't have time to worry about that.

"Jersey. It's a start up."

"Don't you think it's weird that Abbie's father never got back to you?"

"What?"

"The night of the dinner. She said she would hook you up with her dad, but so far, we haven't heard a thing. Just wondering," she says, filing her fingernails.

Charlie placed his overnight bag on the kitchen floor. "What are you talking about?"

"I'm saying Abbie may be more cunning than we think."

Charlie took slow steps until he stood directly in front of Jenna. "Did Abbie say something to you?"

"She's too smart for that. But you, the so-called brains of this operation, missed it. I don't think she had any intention of introducing you to her father. It was a ruse, pure and simple."

"A ruse for what?"

"To gather information on us, stupid."

Charlie's head spun, but he wouldn't show Jenna he was concerned. He had all but forgotten that Abbie had made the offer, and he'd been excited about the prospect of meeting Jason Cooper. How could he have been so stupid and not see through Abbie's smokescreen? He knew from the beginning that she was clever, but he never thought she would pull one over on him, right in his own home. The chick was shrewd and gutsy. Now, here he was looking stupid in front of Jenna, who had been nothing but a pain since they got here. He couldn't wait to ditch her.

"It doesn't matter. We proceed as planned."

"You must be hard of hearing," Jenna said softly, splaying out her palm and admiring her fingernails. "We're on her radar now."

"Whose fault is that?" he asked, the contempt he'd been nursing rising to the surface and spilling out. "All you had to do was simple reconnaissance, keep a low profile. Instead, you had to go making a splash, running your mouth, raising suspicion."

She glared at him. "I did my job. Don't blame me because you're a failure, Charlie."

His anger flared. The large vein at the base of his neck pulsated. "One more careless mistake and this mission is sunk. Do I make myself clear? You screw up again, I'm calling the boss and telling him the deal is off, that you're out of control."

It was her turn to eye him with contempt. Then she returned to filing the nails on the other hand.

"You're welcome to do that. If you have a death wish," she said calmly.

She could pretend to be the one in control all she wanted, but Charlie was done and ready to move on. Start over fresh with the millions he was about to extort from someone who would be more than eager to pay up.

He couldn't stand to be in the same room with Jenna any longer, so he reached down for his bag, and picked it up.

"Bye, Jenna," he said. And never looked back.

CHAPTER 34

I T'S SEVEN THIRTY on Saturday morning. The Wheeler jet should be landing at Hanscom Airforce Base in Bedford within a half-hour, according to Christian's latest text. The kids are in for quite a surprise. At least, that's what we're telling them.

Ty sets up the breakfast table while I finish up the food preparation: fruit smoothies, western omelette, toast, and turkey bacon. Alexis glides into the kitchen first, followed by Blake. They're both still in pajamas.

"Smells yummy," Alexis says. "I can't wait to dig in."

"Me, neither," Blake echoes.

"Your mom and I have a surprise for you," Ty says as the kids each take a seat. "But we want to wait until Lucas comes down so we can tell all three of you at the same time."

"What is it, Daddy?" Alexis is impatient, her eyes bright and expectant.

"Patience, Pumpkin," Ty says.

"I'll get Lucas," Blake volunteers. "Thought he was already downstairs. Be right back."

He slides off his seat and disappears from view.

Ten minutes later, Blake still hasn't returned to the kitchen. That worries me, so I excuse myself to see what's going on.

I push the bedroom door wide open, expecting to see Blake and Lucas arm wrestling or just horsing around. Instead, Blake stands in the middle of the room, staring at Lucas' empty bed.

"What's going on, Blake. Where's your brother?"

"Gone."

"What?" I step further into the room. "What do you mean he's gone?"

Blake turns and looks me in the eye. "I can't find him anywhere. I came to the room and his bed was empty, so I thought he went to the bathroom and he wasn't there either. I checked everywhere, Mom. Lucas is gone."

Fear twists in my gut like a lethal, poisoned sword. My breathing comes out in short, rapid bursts.

"Nothing to worry about, sweetie." I pull Blake closer. "I'm sure Lucas is around here somewhere, just playing a trick on you. He'll turn up I'm sure. Do me a favor. Go downstairs and tell your dad I need to see him right away."

By the time Ty shows up seconds later, because he must have sprinted up the stairs, we're both in full-fledged panic mode, but pretend that we're not.

"Just help me look," I say. "He has to be in the house, Ty. Or maybe he went outside to the back yard."

"I'll check outside, you search in here," he says.

I search under every bed, in every room and in every closet, yelling for my son. His siblings join the search. We comb through the attic, then head downstairs where we rummage through the garage. Then the basement, which we practically rip apart, all the while yelling for Lucas. All the spots where the kids played hide and seek are turned upside down. The house comes up empty.

"Lucas, this isn't funny!" Alexis bellows as we stand in the hallway of the second floor of the house. Her lips are already quivering, the tears circling.

"Yeah, dude," Blake chimes in. "You're freaking us out. Mom and Dad have a surprise for us. You're going to miss out."

The resounding silence of our collective fears bounce off the walls and reverberate throughout the house. I hug my children and offer reassurances that their brother will turn up soon. All the while, the paralyzing fear that I'm about to live every parent's worst nightmare slowly rips through my chest.

Ty slogs his way up the stairs like a slow dripping leak, his face crestfallen. "I looked everywhere. The backyard, knocked on the neighbors' doors. Nobody has seen Lucas around. I even made it to the Paynes' house. No one was home."

"Maybe one of his friends heard from him. I'll call the McSweeneys. Liam might know something."

Ty offers to call the Anderssens to see if Caleb knows anything. After brief conversations of surprise and concern, neither Liam nor Caleb or their parents have either seen or heard from Lucas.

Just for a moment, time stands still. A surreal mist hovers around the edges of our reality. I swallow hard. The back of my throat hurts, raw with anguish. Ty repeatedly rubs the back of his neck. Neither one of us is willing to make *the* call. Because if we do, then the nightmare becomes real. It means Lucas won't walk through the door any minute, his filled eyes with mischief, telling us it was just a game he and Blake devised and he was determined to win. They're competitive like that.

Ty's phone vibrates and we both jump. He retrieves it from his pocket and stares at the screen.

"Is it Lucas?" I ask anxiously, attempting to grab the phone from his hands.

"It's a text from Christian. The jet landed. The pilot and crew are waiting on your mom and the kids."

I hiccup several times. The strength to pretend this isn't happening seeps out of my bones.

"Make the call," I say to Ty, my voice a decibel below a whisper.

CHAPTER 35

OUR HOME IS officially a crime scene. Police cruisers have taken over the driveway and the street. Uniformed officers are combing through the house. Their footsteps can be heard from every direction, and the sounds of hushed conversations and phone calls permeate the air. I sit on the living room sofa. Ty is next to me. He rubs my shoulders in an attempt to stop the shaking. It's useless. There's no comfort to be had. I blame myself. If only I had acted sooner, paid closer attention to the feeling in my gut that something was wrong, this wouldn't have happened.

A crushing tsunami of accusation and condemnation slams into me.

You should have done better. What kind of mother are you? An awful one. You deserve to suffer.

My tears are stunted by the guilt crippling me. Blake and Alexis sit next to their father, searching his face for some clue that the chaos that has erupted around them is a bad dream. And just as when they were younger, he would restore order, chase the boogey man and the monsters away. The only problem is, this time, it was their mother who allowed the monsters to get close.

As Alexis sobs and Blake sits trembling, silent tears streaming down his face, a tall man in a dark suit and commanding presence enters the room. He introduces himself as Detective Gabe Flores and takes up a seat in an armchair across from us.

He must be the detective in charge, I presume. Good. Someone has already been assigned to the case, so we know who to look to for answers. Detective Flores has a head full of thick, dark, wavy hair, sharp, intelligent brown eyes and an aura of confidence.

"Tell me what happened," he says gently.

I'm not sure if he's talking to Ty or me, which one of us he expects to give him the story. From the look on his face, he leaves that decision to us. I remain silent.

Ty explains how we all gathered in the kitchen, ready to spring the surprise trip to the Bahamas on the kids, but Lucas wasn't down yet. And how Blake went to get him.

"About what time did Blake go to look for Lucas?" he asks.

"A little after seven thirty," I say.

The detective nods in Blake's direction and asks us, "Do you mind?"

Ty nods. I lean over and reach for Blake's hand.

"Honey, the detective wants to ask you a couple of questions. He wants to help us find your brother. Just answer his questions as best as you can recall. And if you want to stop at any time, just let us know, okay?"

He nods, and the detective proceeds.

"What did you see when you went to fetch your brother?"

Blake doesn't say anything at first. He struggles to compose himself. I tell him to take his time to collect his thoughts.

"He wasn't there. When I went to his room to get him, so our dad could tell us what the surprise was, his bed was empty.

Then I looked in the bathroom and he wasn't there either. I waited for him to come back to the room, but he didn't. Then Mom came up."

"Thank you, Blake. Did you see Lucas at all this morning, before you came downstairs and then went back up to get him?"

I wince, flipping the question around in my head. Ty's stunned expression is frozen in place like an ice sculpture. *We didn't think to ask Blake.* When Blake volunteered to get his brother so Ty could tell them about the trip, we just assumed Lucas was sleeping late and Blake knew that. This scenario plays out in our household every day. One of the kids is always late getting the day started. But after Blake sounded the alarm, it never occurred to me to ask if he had seen his brother *at all* before he came downstairs.

"It's okay, sweetie," I say, in rasping breaths, fighting to control the nausea circling and the pain in the back of my throat. "You can answer the detective's question."

"No, I didn't see him. I thought he made it down to breakfast before me."

Fresh tears erupt. I pull him onto my knees and sooth his tears. "It's okay, sweetie. You couldn't have known he wasn't in the house. It's because of you that we knew something was wrong. You did good by telling us."

"We'll find out what happened and bring your brother home," Ty says. "In no time, the two of you will be back to bickering and getting on each other's nerves."

"You promise?" Blake asks through sniffles.

We look at the detective. It's his job to help us bring Lucas back. No pressure or anything.

"We'll do everything we can to bring your brother home, Blake."

That's not very comforting. It's so vague. We'll do everything we can is not the same as we'll find your son and bring him home safe and sound, is it?

Detective Flores turns his attention back to Ty and me.

"What was Lucas wearing?"

"Cotton pajamas, baby blue and white stripes, matching top and bottom," I explain.

"Do you have a photo of him in that outfit?"

"We do," Ty says. "We have a family snapshot of him wearing it around the holidays last year."

"Great. I'll borrow it on my way out."

"Now, has Lucas ever gone missing before today?"

Ty and I give the detective a bemused look.

He registers our confusion and explains, "For instance, has he ever gone missing during a trip to the supermarket or maybe he continued to stay hidden long after a game of hide and seek was over?"

"We know what you're asking, detective," I say. "The answer is no. Lucas is a sensitive child. He would never deliberately worry us."

He writes something down and then asks, "Who else knew about this trip the kids were about to take?"

Ty thought about it for a moment and starts ticking off fingers. "My in-laws. My mother-in-law was accompanying the kids. My parents, and Christian Wheeler. That's it. We told no one else, not even the kids or their nanny."

The detective rubs his jaw as if trying to make sense of what he's learned so far. Then he says, "Who's Christian Wheeler, and what does he have to do with the trip?"

Ty and I glance at each other again, uneasy, not sure how to explain Christian's involvement without exposing the complicated familial ties.

Ty jumps in, saving me from having to tell half-truths.

"He's a close friend of ours. He made his family jet available to us to take the kids down to the Bahamas."

Detective Flores purses his lips, a thoughtful expression flittering across his face. Then he says, "Any particular reason you decided to go that route? This is an affluent neighborhood, but not too many residents can afford to send their kids off to a tropical paradise via a private jet, especially young kids."

This is not the time to hold back. Everything matters now with crippling urgency. I made the mistake of dragging my feet before, and now my son is paying the price.

"There have been some strange occurrences over the past several weeks," I say to Flores. "We thought," I say, glancing at Ty, "it would be safer to have the kids go somewhere on their spring vacation. Ty's parents are in the Bahamas, and the kids were going to visit them. Christian's family owns Levitron-Blair, and I called in a favor to use the jet."

"Please fill me about these strange occurrences," the detective says, leaning forward, pen and notebook at the ready.

I explain what transpired over the past few weeks. Flores takes it all in, his body language revealing nothing, but his eyes say he's a man whose brain is working overtime to see how everything computes. Before he can lob another question, my phone dings. I stand up and pull it from the pocket of my jeans. It's Christian calling. I pick up.

His panicked voice comes down the line. The pilot and crew have been on the ground for a while. He hasn't been able to get in touch with me or Ty. And my mother hasn't arrived yet, either. He asks if everything is okay and what the holdup is.

I don't know how to answer him. My knees feel like they will buckle at any minute. A new wave of gut-wrenching sobs erupts, and I can't stop them. I barely register Christian's words of concern and the dread rising in his voice.

Ty is by my side in an instant and takes the phone from my clammy, trembling hand. He pulls me close with one hand and puts the phone to his ear with the other.

"It's bad, Christian," he says.

I hear Christian ask, his voice flat, "It happened, didn't it? Someone snatched Lucas."

"Yes. Someone did. The police are here. The trip is obviously canceled. We have calls to make to the family to let them know what's going on."

"How did this happen?" Christian asks.

"When we woke up this morning, Lucas was gone. We have no idea if he was taken at night while we all slept or what. Listen, I have to go."

"I'm on my way," Christian says.

After the call, I tell Flores that the kids are emotionally drained and I need to get them settled. I take Blake and Alexis by the hand and lead them to the family room.

"We're going to find your brother," I say softly. "Let's keep our thoughts positive."

They stare at me as if I'm speaking a foreign tongue.

I put on one of their favorite movies, which won't do a thing to distract them. "I'll be back in a little bit. Your dad and I need to finish up with the detective. Then we'll be right here with you. You need to eat something."

"We're not hungry," Alexis says, a grave look floating across her face.

"We just want Lucas to come home," Blake says. "Where did he go, Mom? He doesn't like strangers. Did a stranger take him?"

I grind my teeth to squash the wounded scream about to burst out of me. They're asking questions I don't have answers to, but somehow, I must keep it together for their sake. If they suspect their mother is unraveling, it will strike a crushing blow to their already fragile emotions.

They're seated on the sofa and I kneel before them. "Today is a sad day for our family. But we will find Lucas. And he needs the two of you to have good thoughts, positive vibes."

I turn away from my babies, for a moment, to gather what little strength I have left.

I turn to them once more and say, "It will help him. He will know how much we love him, and he won't be so scared. It will help him to be brave."

They both give me the glassy stare. I don't know if anything I've said has gotten through to them but I had to try. I get off my knees and hug them tight.

"I love you guys so much. But remember what I told all three of you, about when difficult situations come up?"

"We're Coopers," Alexis says. "Coopers don't run away from their problems."

"They wrestle with it, like a math problem, until they find the solution," Blake finishes.

"That's right," I say, proud of them for remembering. "Lucas' disappearance is a difficult math problem we have to solve. And we will."

CHAPTER 36

H AS YOUR FAMILY been threatened by anyone?" the detective asks.

I'm back in the living room, sitting next to Ty, who takes my hand in his and offers a gentle squeeze.

"No direct threats," Ty says.

A questioning frown blooms over Flores' face. "What do you mean by that? Was there an indirect threat?"

"Not really," I say. "Just gut instinct. No proof of anything."

He looks down thoughtfully at something he wrote and then asks, "How many times has either Charlie or Jenna Payne been in your home?"

Ty and I glance at each other. I tunnel through the fog in my brain to come up with the right answer. I mentally tick off the number of visits.

"Four times. They showed up twice together. Then Jenna dropped by alone twice. The day Liv didn't show and another day when she came by with pastries and pitched the idea that Katie Nicholson could be a possible replacement for Liv."

"I see," the detective says, looking at his notes.

He looks up once more and says, "What areas of the house did they visit?"

"Just the kitchen," I respond. "On the day Jenna came over to tell me about Katie, we briefly entered the family room."

"And how long did each visit last, to the best of your recollection?"

I let out a deep sigh. "Around ten to fifteen minutes, not even. The first visit lasted about twenty minutes."

What about your other neighbors, do you get along with them? Do you trust them?"

Ty answers swiftly. "No way any of our neighbors would kidnap Lucas."

"I've seen a lot of strange things in my day, Dr. Rambally," the detective says. "No neighborhood, no matter how affluent, is immune from crime. Our officers will canvass the area, and interview potential witnesses."

Shivers go up and down my spine. My mind races, as I try to recall any odd incidents with the neighbors, either recently or in the past. We've lived on this street for a decade. Have I said anything unkind to anyone in that time? Did I do anything that could have been viewed through a negative lens? The human mind can withstand just about anything. It can also be weak and fragile, especially in someone who's not all there to begin with. You can't tell just by looking at someone whether they are of sound mind or not.

Flores drags me out of my paranoid musings when he says, "Any ransom demand so far?"

"No, nothing like that," I say.

"If you get a call, we need to know immediately, understood?"

"Yes, we understand."

"Good. The clock started ticking before you discovered he was gone. So we're behind already."

CHAPTER 37

C HARLIE PAYNE HOPPED out of the car, tipped the driver and then hoisted the heavy backpack over his shoulder. Common sense would suggest that renting a hotel room in a town less than five miles from Lexington was beyond idiotic, but Charlie was no idiot. When he left the house yesterday and told Jenna he had a quick business trip to Jersey, he had told the truth. If anyone were to check, Charlie Payne purchased a ticket and boarded a flight for Newark International Airport.

He arrived in the lobby of a well-known three-star hotel chain and did a quick, visual sweep. Long, dark brown reception desk, plaques on the walls, a woman and a guy checking their reservations computer. Off to his right were two dark blue sofas with red throw pillows, and large bouquets of pretty plants on a table in the center. He would have preferred to go the cheap motel route. With enough cash at places like that, people were less inclined to ask a lot of questions. But he needed a room with Wi-Fi that wouldn't crap out on him. A place that didn't smell of stale, greasy food or cigarettes, had stained carpets and rickety, mismatched furniture. That would not do if he was going to have the relative of a billionaire holed

168

up in the space until the transaction was complete.

He approached the front desk and stood behind an old man who was giving the clerk a hard time. It was around four in the afternoon. There was barely anyone around, except for an older couple checking in with the male clerk. Charlie wanted the female clerk to check him in.

She finally got rid of the troublesome old man by pawning him off on a manager, a harassed looking man who didn't want to be bothered, either.

"Hi Rhonda," Charlie said with a smile. He had already picked up her name from her name tag a split second before. "I'd like a room with a double bed, please."

"Let me check our availability," she said. She tapped a few keys on her computer and then looked up at him. "Looks like we have a couple of rooms that will fit the bill."

"Great," Charlie said.

"Driver's license and credit card, please."

Charlie dug into the pocket of his windbreaker and pulled out his wallet. He leaned in close to Rhonda as if he were about to divulge highly classified information.

"Is there any way I can pay cash?" he asked. "I'm booking the room for myself and my son. His mom and I are going through a bitter divorce, and I don't want her knowing about this credit card. It's all I have left. She'll take me to the cleaners in the divorce. I just know it."

Rhonda gave him a sympathetic look. "I'm really sorry, sir, but we need to have a credit card on file. You don't have to charge your room on it if you don't want to, but we need it on file. Sorry. Those are the rules."

Charlie rubbed his eyes and the tears started brimming. "Please, Rhonda. I can tell you're a good person who follows the rules. But I'm just a father who wants to spend time with his son without some shark lawyer thinking I'm rolling in dough. My son is all I have left in this world." He lowered his voice to a whisper. "I don't have a ton of money but I'm willing to give you a huge tip if you would help me out. Two hundred dollars cash. It will tap me out, but it's only fair that I compensate you for you trouble."

Charlie could see her resolve crumbling. Her shoulders relaxed. She swallowed and gave him an understanding nod. She looked to her left and then to her right, as if scanning for potential busybodies who might bust her.

"It's okay," she said, softly. "You don't have to give me anything. I'll take care of it. I'll make up a story if anyone asks why there isn't a credit card on file for your room. Just make sure you pay the cash when you check out."

"I'm so grateful. My son and I thank you."

She handed him the key card. "You're in room 305. The elevator is off to your left and we have continental breakfast in the morning if you want to catch a bite to eat with your son."

He nodded at her, and sprinted to the elevator. Luckily, he was alone. He was in no mood to speak to anyone. He was too wound up. He hadn't heard from Katie yet, another reason he was nervous. For this to work, she had to execute her part flawlessly.

The room was clean and well kept, no stains on the carpet that he could see. His eyes landed on the desk and the chair. Perfect. It would be his command central. There were two neatly made beds, a large flat screen TV perched on the wall, and thick floor-length curtains at the windows.

He picked up the remote on the nightstand and flipped on the TV. The background noise would help him think. He put on a sports channel and got to work. He tossed the backpack on the bed and unzipped it, removing his laptop, the appropriate cables and chargers, and the other equipment he would need.

He called Katie Nicholson. The call went to voicemail, which irritated him. She was expecting his call, so why hadn't she picked up? What was she doing? Charlie shed his windbreaker and tossed it on the bed too. He would check the thermostat later. He might have to adjust the room temperature.

He tried her again. "Why aren't you picking up your phone? I'm waiting on the package. Call me for delivery instructions."

Once he hung up, he moved the equipment to the desk. When everything was set up to his liking, he took a seat, cleared his throat, and placed a call to New York. He asked for the appropriate name and was transferred. A pleasant female voice confirmed he had the right office. He left a cryptic, ominous message and then hung up, not bothering to wait for a response from her.

CHAPTER 38

I'M COMPLETELY SAPPED of energy and tears. I now operate in some inexplicable space in my universe where nothing makes sense and a strange fog blankets my mind in blocks of time. The kitchen has become a sort of nerve center for the investigation and everything and anything that has to do with bringing Lucas back. Blake and Alexis were sent to nap and they didn't protest at the odd request, given the time of day and the fact that they're way past the age for naps. My parents, my brothers, Lee and Miles are here, as well as Christian. No one knows what to do or say.

An exhaustive search of the house and backyard have yielded no clues. Officers combed the neighborhood and conducted interviews. No one saw or heard anything. A few have security cameras, but none of them were turned on last night. A press conference to plead for Lucas' return is in the works.

It's time to call Jenna," I say weakly.

I've been avoiding Jenna like a lethal case of Ebola ever since the incident in the café last week when Corinne Beal called her Maren Dinsdale. I used the too-busy card, and after a while, she gave up trying to communicate with me.

"I'll put her on speaker phone," I say to the room.

I take a deep breath and give everyone the here-goes-nothing look. I tap the speaker icon on the phone and dial. My gut twists into knots as the first ring yields nothing. Anxiety crawls up from my belly and lodges in my throat as the phone rings a second time and she doesn't pick up. On the third ring, I'm about to jump out of my skin. When the call heads into the fourth ring, she answers.

"Jenna, it's Abbie," I say, struggling to breathe.

"Abbie what's wrong?" she asks, her voice sharp and concerned. "You sound terrible."

"It's Lucas."

"What about him?"

"He's gone."

A short pause then, "What are you talking about? Gone where?"

"I don't know, Jenna. Someone took Lucas from the house while we were all asleep last night and we don't know where he is."

"What the hell?" she exclaims. "You're saying someone kidnapped Lucas?"

"That's exactly what I'm saying."

Another short pause, then, "What can I do? I'm so sorry, Abbie. I can't imagine what you and Ty must be going through."

"Did you see or hear anything last night, anything out of the ordinary, anybody hanging around our house when we weren't here during the day?"

"Well, no. I flew to Texas yesterday. Charlie went away on business, and I'm visiting friends."

Fresh tears roll down my cheeks. I don't know what I was expecting from her. "Well, if anything comes to mind, will you call me?"

"Of course, I will, Abbie. I'll come see you the minute I get back, and I'm hoping that Lucas will be home safe and sound long before that."

"When will you be back?"

"In a few days. Will you please call me and update me if anything changes? I can't imagine what the little guy must be feeling. Scared, alone with strangers, and no idea what they will do to him."

An intense hatred of Jenna Payne or whatever her real name is wells up inside me, striking at my very core. Reminding me that my child is alone and scared and I'm living every parent's worst nightmare is nothing short of cruel. I've tried to stifle the vicious thoughts as they attempt to break through my subconscious and grab a hold of me. Her words just ripped that door wide open, unleashing a flood of dangerous, agonizing theories.

What if Lucas was abducted by child traffickers? What if he's dead?

I hang up on Jenna and lean against the counter for support. My dad comes to stand next to me and pulls me into his arms while everyone else stays silent and solemn. A cell phone rings and everyone in the kitchen checks to see if it's theirs. It's Christian's. He excuses himself.

A minute later, he reappears in the kitchen, looking dazed.

"What is it?" I ask.

"I just got a call."

"We all know that," an impatient Miles says. "Who was the call from? Come on, man. Don't leave us hanging."

I level an admonishing glare at my baby brother, warning him to take it easy.

"That was my assistant, Courtney," Christian says. "She received a call from a woman with a British accent asking to speak to me. When she told the person I was unavailable, the caller said she had Lucas."

A collective gasp erupts around the kitchen. Anxious murmurs float in the air as various family members try to discern what it could all mean. My inner being is experiencing a calm that it hasn't since the nightmare began. *Lucas is alive.* That means a negotiation can take place for his release. The rest will work itself out.

"Did the caller say anything else to your assistant?" my father asks. Was there a ransom demand?"

"Yes. For five million dollars." The number rolls off Christian's tongue, smooth as silk.

No one says a word. We're all trying to digest the astronomical figure. I return to my seat. Ty and I certainly don't have that kind of money. We couldn't make a dent in it, even if we tried. But some invisible force compels my gaze to land on my parents. Then an obvious thought strikes me.

"Wait a minute. Why would the kidnapper call your office looking for you, instead of contacting Lucas' parents?"

Christian responds, "Isn't it obvious, Abbie? They know."

Slowly, I examine each face. The group of us in this kitchen, seven in all, plus Christian's parents, Ty's parents, and my best friend Callie are the only people in the world who know the truth about Lucas' paternity. That's a lot of people in on one little secret. Does it even matter how the kidnapper found out? We never had the chance to tell Lucas the truth. We were waiting for the right time and now, with this latest development, the decision regarding when and how has been ripped from us.

But the picture is becoming clearer. Whoever has Lucas has decided to parlay that knowledge into a lucrative payday.

"It doesn't matter what they know," Dad says. "We're getting our grandson back." He looks at me, and then Ty. "Your mother and I will pay the ransom."

"No disrespect intended, Mr. Cooper. But I can't let you and Mrs. Cooper do that," Christian asserts.

"Why not?" Dad's eyebrows arch up, his eyes wide.

A tense silence follows. We hold our collective breath. Christian plucks at the cuff of his shirt. The last time he and Dad tangoed was back in high school. Christian and I had just started dating, and I brought him to the house to introduce him to the family. Dad's interrogation was rough. So much so that Mom and I had to jump in to get Dad to chill out.

"Lucas is my relative, too, and I would like to help. Besides, the kidnapper specifically asked for me."

"So what? She doesn't care where the money comes from. Shelby and I have it handled."

A panicked expression flitters across Christian's handsome face. "I understand where you're coming from, Mr. Cooper, I really do. But can you raise that kind of cash in a matter of a few hours? Because I'm willing to bet my Levitron-Blair shares that the kidnapper will give us a very short window. And let's not forget, we don't know what the instructions are yet."

Dad is about to say something, but Mom tugs at his arm and gives him the look.

Christian is right, although Dad will never admit it, nor should he. While my parents are self-made millionaires, Christian has access to billions of dollars and could have those funds available with one snap of his perfectly manicured fingers. The kidnapper most likely knows this.

Ty rubs his fingers through his hair, as if trying to erase a painful bump. "Cooper, can I see you in private for a minute?"

We excuse ourselves and end up in the living room.

"Don't you find this strange?" he asks, pacing up and down the room.

"Care to be more specific?"

176

"How can we guarantee that whoever this woman is will release Lucas once she's paid? The whole thing could be some vendetta against the Wheelers, and Lucas is to be used as a pawn. She could come back for more and continue to hold Lucas."

"There are a million scenarios, Ty. The only thing we know for sure is that Lucas was taken and a ransom demand has been made."

Unease rolls through me like a dark mist. The living room walls look like they've shifted closer. Ty's reasoning makes some kind of sense. It could explain why Christian was contacted instead of us, Lucas' parents. Could the kidnapper or kidnappers have something against the Wheelers, and Lucas was a path to revenge? If that's the case, does that mean I've been dead wrong about Jenna Payne all along?

He stops pacing, takes a few steps to stand directly in front of me, and hugs me tight as if he never wants to let go. "We'll get our boy back," he says, his voice low, shaky. "The how may not be that important right now, but it bothers me that Christian is involved and our son's fate is in his hands."

I extract myself from his embrace and look him in the eye. "Why is that?"

His hands fall to his sides. "I know this may sound sexist or old fashioned or whatever, but this is my family crisis. Another man was called to handle it. It doesn't feel good, Cooper."

My stomach flops, despair almost choking me. My eyes burn. He feels helpless and guilty. Ty isn't the macho or controlling type, but he does have his pride, and his family is everything to him. He wants to be the one to bring Lucas home. Not to play hero or some vain attempt to feel important, but because of the promise he made to each of our children the day they were born. That he would do everything in his power to keep them safe and protected until they could fend for themselves as adults.

"You didn't let Lucas down, Ty. I know that's what you're thinking. Look at it from another perspective. There's hope. You and I may not be able to come up with five million dollars but there are people who love Lucas who can."

"You're right. It's just…I mean…"

He turns away from me. His gaze lands on a photo of him and Lucas on the mantel above the fireplace, professional day at the kids' school. A huge grin is plastered on both their faces with a chalkboard in the background. Poor Ty was pelted with questions from a bunch of fourth and fifth graders that day: Lucas' classmates and those of Blake and Alexis.

I take a few steps and wrap my arms around his waist, resting my face on his shoulder blade as he continues to gaze at the photo. His chest heaves and his shoulders sag. We stay that way a minute or two.

When he faces me once more, his countenance is that of a man haunted by what he perceives to be the biggest failure of his life. Failure to protect his child. A promise broken.

I start whimpering, wiping away errant tears. "We'll get him back."

"We'll get him back," Ty echoes.

CHAPTER 39

B RIAN ARCHIBALD ROGERS, a.k.a. Charlie Payne, clenched his fists as he paced the carpet of the hotel room, a desperate man at the end of his rope, about to plunge off a cliff. He warned her what would happen if she didn't do exactly as he said, but she didn't listen. He underestimated mousy, desperate-to-stay-out-of-jail Katie Nicholson. He left numerous messages, each more urgent than the one before, yet she spat in his eyes with her silence.

Where was she, and what did she do with the kid? he wondered.

Brian went to the windows and drew the curtains back. The blinding sunlight of the April afternoon encased the room. The windows overlooked the parking lot. Did she just pull in? The hotel only had four floors, and he was on the third. He could easily see what was going on from his vantage point. Sun beams ricocheted off the windshields and chrome wheels of the cluster of cars. A mother held her infant in his car seat with one hand and opened the car door with the other. Two rows back, a couple argued. The woman gestured like, well, a madwoman. She got into the passenger seat and slammed the door. The man went over to the driver seat and did the same, backed out slowly, and then stepped on the gas, leaving a cloud of smoke from burned rubber to drift in the air.

But no Katie with an uncooperative child at her side.

Then with no warning, thunder roared in the distance. The sky opened up and unleashed a punishing downpour of fat, angry raindrops. Then another clap of thunder, accompanied by lightning.

Brian suddenly felt dizzy, closed the curtains, and returned to the bed. He flopped down face first as his throat clogged up with disappointment and anxiety. Yet the more he thought about it, the angrier he became. He couldn't understand why Katie had double-crossed him. Something dramatic had taken place, he could feel it. She was no longer afraid he would sell her out to the cops, otherwise, she wouldn't have pulled a fast one.

He sat up and started flipping through channels on the TV to calm his racing thoughts. Everything had been meticulously planned. The best part of the plan? He would use his real name, his legitimate U.S. passport to leave the country, free and clear. It was still valid after four years in prison. He had renewed it two years prior to going in, and he still had a solid four years left before it expired. He wasn't convicted on a drug offense or had outstanding child support payments or anything like that, so there was no reason for the feds to flag his passport.

Four years for manslaughter he thought, as he scooted off the bed and returned to his makeshift workstation. He had been a drunk college kid who got into a stupid fight over a girl. Deacon Rivers and two of his friends were ready to beat him to a pulp, no matter how many times Brian explained there was nothing going on between him and Beth Whitman, Deacon's supposed girlfriend. They were making small talk at the party. That was it. But Deacon was beyond wasted and didn't want to hear any of it.

Brian defended himself against a savage attack. To this day, he couldn't recall all the details. All he knew was that there was punching and kicking, and at some point during the melee, he landed a fatal blow to Deacon's skull. He died two days later in the hospital. Brian was arrested, tried, and convicted. It took him the better part of a year to let go of the bitterness, the unfairness of it. Over time, he came to grips with the unvarnished truth. He took a man's life. The circumstances didn't matter. His parents had written him off and never once came to visit him.

He opened up the file he had compiled on Abbie and her family based on information he gathered from Iceman and his own research. As he scrolled absently through photos and notations, hoping for inspiration about his next move, his anger at Katie spiked once more. Why wasn't she afraid he would turn her in if she didn't deliver Lucas?

He should feel like a hypocrite for blackmailing her, but he didn't. What she did was far worse, leaving a man for dead after she ran him over like road kill, and keeping quiet about it.

Brian scrunched his nose. A photo of Christian Wheeler climbing into the back of an SUV flittered across the screen. A tall, muscular guy dressed in all black, most likely security, scanned the area for threats. The next photo was of Christian seated next to Abbie and her mother and daughter during New York Fashion Week. The next photo depicted him sandwiched between Abbie and world-famous fashion designer Callie Furi. They grinned for the camera as though the three of them were in on a joke that no one else was privy to.

An idea began to worm its way into Brian's head. A solution to his predicament. He didn't need Katie after all. If his plan fell into place quickly, as he thought it would, he could be out of the country within twenty-four hours.

CHAPTER 40

L UCAS HAS BEEN missing for less than twenty-four hours, yet it feels like someone sentenced me to a lifetime of torture. The police agree this is a straight, kidnapping-for-ransom case. Ty and I had no choice but to provide Detective Flores an abbreviated version of the familial connection Lucas has to the Wheelers. In light of that information, the idea of a press conference was nixed. No point in aggravating the kidnapper.

The question of how someone was able to walk into our home, bypass the alarm, head upstairs to Lucas' bedroom, grab him, and vanish into the night is still baffling. The window in his room hadn't been tampered with. No clues so far. No hair. No fiber. No prints.

Investigators confirmed that Jenna Payne did board a flight for Texas as she claimed. Charlie's whereabouts were verified, too. He booked a flight for New Jersey and went away on business as Jenna said. Yet, I can't help but ponder the strange coincidence that both of them happened to be out of town when Lucas was nabbed.

I sit in the family room with his baby album on my lap. Ty is next to me and Christian is seated across from us. My parents are with the twins. If I gaze at his pictures long enough, will Lucas, wherever he is, feel how much I love him through some weird telepathic channel?

When I turn the page and come to a photo of him in his high chair at fifteen months, with his spaghetti dinner all over his face, head and clothes, his blue eyes beaming with mischief, my breath hitches. My hands go limp as though the bones dissolved while I wasn't paying attention. The album slides off my lap, ending up at my feet.

Ty clasps my hand in his. "We'll get him back, Cooper. Hang on just a little bit longer."

I don't know if he's trying to convince me, or himself. Each passing hour without news pushes me closer to the edge of a breakdown. We're all sitting here, waiting for the kidnapper to call with instructions to make our world right again.

"Ty is right, Abbie," Christian says, his voice a hoarse whisper. "We will get Lucas back. In the meantime, we need you to do what you do best, hold it together. We can't get through this without you."

"I'm not indestructible, you know. But you're right—if I melt down, it's going to be epic."

A fleeting but disheartening thought flashes through my mind. *School.* My dissertation defense is next week. I'm in no state of mind to continue preparation. The bulk of the work has been completed, though. Dr. Ackerman, my advisor, already guided me through public research and private defense as a lead-up to the real thing. The day Liv didn't show up for work, the beginning of this seemingly endless nightmare, was my pre-defense meeting. Dr. Ackerman determined that the manuscript and PowerPoint slides were ready. He would have distributed the documents to the defense committee within a couple of weeks of that meeting. My defense date is still on the calendar. I should call Dr. Ackerman and tell him I won't make it. It's all but over. Another dream turned to dust.

Christian's cell phone rings, startling us. He picks up immediately.

"Yeah," he says in way of greeting.

"Yes, this is Christian," he says, irritated.

He signals for us to get closer.

"I think I have the right to know who's shaking me down for five million dollars, the nut job who's using Lucas for profit."

I note that Christian didn't use the term nephew when referring to Lucas. That was probably smart. No point in confirming anything for the extortionist.

A woman's voice is on the other end of the line. Christian pushes a side button on the phone to pump up the volume. We still have to strain a bit to hear.

"Do you have a pen?" the woman asks. "The money needs to be wired to this account."

"Hold on a minute."

I rush to the sofa and rummage through my purse to find a pen and my miniature notebook I carry around.

Christian signals to me to write down what she says and repeats the account number and instructions.

"I want to hear Lucas' voice. I need proof that you have him and he's safe."

Pause. As if she wasn't expecting that. What kind of amateur thinks that someone is just going to hand over millions of dollars without any proof the victim is alive? Ty and I look at each other. Panic boils in the pit of my stomach. What if this is a hoax and this person doesn't have Lucas? Christian squeezes the phone so hard his knuckles go white.

"No," she says coldly. "If you ever want to see your nephew

again, you'll do exactly as I say. You wire the funds. When I receive confirmation, I'll tell you where to pick him up. No police. You come alone. If you deviate in any way, you'll be collecting your nephew's dead body. And don't worry. I'll make sure he doesn't suffer too much."

We just stare at the phone in Christian's hand, hypnotized by the words. We know she hung up but each of us, in our own way, is wrestling with the implications of what we just heard.

Silent tears snake down my cheeks. The vile, horror-inducing words swirl around in my head. The faux-casual comment about him suffering was meant to twist the knife a little deeper. She had to know that we were listening, or at the very least, Christian would tell us everything. *She* wants us to suffer. Surprisingly, I pull myself together long enough to head to the sofa before I collapse. Ty and Christian follow my lead and take seats. Christian plays with his cell phone while Ty picks at an invisible piece of lint on his shirt.

"I have this gnawing feeling in the pit of my stomach that this woman, whoever she is, doesn't have Lucas."

Ty looks at me, flummoxed. "What makes you say that?"

I shrug. "I don't really know. Just a feeling. Call it mother's intuition or whatever. I can't shake it. It's all too neat."

"Are you saying I shouldn't pay the ransom?" Christian asks, fear and confusion blooming over his face.

"I don't know what I'm saying. It's possible that she does have Lucas and if we don't do as she says, she will do what she promised and take him out."

A primal ache works its way through my chest. Helplessness, fear, and black rage collide, threatening to stall my breathing. I can't afford another gigantic mistake. I ignored my gut when it told me I should have pressed Liv about what was bothering her. My hesitation had disastrous consequences. I can't make the same mistake again, not with my son's life at stake.

I say to Christian, "Give that vile, despicable woman what she wants. Pay the ransom."

CHAPTER 41

I T WAS TOO easy. Five million dollars wired into his account. Katie Nicholson had double-crossed him, but he was having the last laugh. He was now a millionaire, a millionaire who needed to get out of the country and never look back. Brian congratulated himself on his ingenuity. Hitting up Christian Wheeler for the ransom had been the plan all along. He was going to split the money with Katie, a cool million was her payout. But when she refused to return his calls and was a no-show with Lucas, the idea occurred to Brian that she had done him a favor.

He accomplished two things with that call to Wheeler. First, pretending that he had Lucas all but guaranteed Wheeler would come through with the funds. Second, he used voice altering software technology to sound like a woman. That part of the scheme would cast suspicion on Katie. She deserved it for backing out of their plan and leaving him hanging.

He had paid cash for his room at the hotel upon check out as he had previously arranged with Rhonda. A cab was waiting for him as he stepped out into the morning sunshine, decked out in sunglasses, a baseball cap and dark clothing. Last night, he had colored his hair, taking it back to its natural dark chocolate brown, not the dirty blond he was sporting as Charlie Payne. It matched the photo in his passport, so it just made sense.

He climbed into the cab and tossed his bag next to him.

"Logan Airport," he told the driver. "I'll pay extra if you step on it."

Brian was eager to put this whole mess behind him. As the cab ate up the miles on the highway, he thought about Iceman and how angry he would be once he found out what Brian had done. The fact that he was able to extract millions from Christian Wheeler without hurting a hair on the boy's head made Brian proud. Iceman was wrong. Katie was wrong. And Jenna had underestimated him for the last time. She would be left to explain his absence.

He chuckled to himself. How was she going to get out of that one? Would she proceed with Iceman's crazy revenge scheme, take out Lucas to rain down an avalanche of pain and misery on the Ramballys and Wheelers? Brian never fully understood why Iceman wanted to go to these lengths because he was always stingy with information. Iceman was a psychopath who was ruled by his sick brain, and Jenna was ruled by impulse and attitude. Brian felt sorry for them both.

The taxi pulled up behind a long line of cabs, cars, SUVs and shuttles at the curb of terminal E, the Swiss Air departure gate at Logan International Airport.

"Here you go," he said, handing the driver a wad of cash.

The driver nodded and said thank you. Brian grabbed his backpack off the seat and left the cab.

He approached the Swiss Air counter. Nervousness overtook him. There was only one person in front of him. He breathed in and out to calm himself, to stop any thoughts that would cause panic. He wasn't prone to panicking, but he was just hours away from making it out of here and beginning a new life.

The serious-looking man in the blue uniform asked him about his destination.

"I need to purchase a ticket to Zurich. Any flights available?"

The man looked at him curiously, then started typing on the computer keyboard.

"We have a flight leaving at nine-thirty this evening."

Brian's heart sank. He glanced at his watch. It was only ten thirty in the morning. What was he going to do at Logan Airport for almost ten hours? He needed to leave U.S. soil immediately.

"That's a long wait," he said. "Do you have flights to anywhere else that leaves sooner?"

"Anywhere in particular?" the man asked, sarcastically.

"I don't care. Somewhere that Swiss Air travels before this evening. I can hop a flight to Zurich any time. Let's just say I'm feeling adventurous. Escaping a bad breakup."

It was way more than he wanted to say, but the agent was beginning to look at him all weird. Brian needed to reassure him that he was just some poor slob who wanted to see where the wind would take him.

The trick worked. The agent's features relaxed. He continued typing, looking for a flight to anywhere that left before tonight.

An idea occurred to Brian. He pretended his phone had vibrated, took it out of his jacket pocket and excused himself. Once he was comfortably out of the line of sight of the agent, he hurried. He needed to leave international departure and head to the domestic departure terminals. It didn't matter which airline. He was sure he could hop a flight to New York within thirty minutes and from there, he could get a flight out of JFK, heading to Europe before nine-thirty tonight.

CHAPTER 42

W HERE'S LUCAS, WHERE'S my baby?" I shout at
Christian then push past him as he walks in the front
door. My eyes dart to the left and right of the driveway, across
the street up and down. No Lucas.

A gasp of bitter anguish escapes me. I stand still, my
mouth dry, disbelief and horror invading my chest, exacerbating
the tightness, that feeling that it's about to implode. A pair of
gentle hands rest on my shoulders. Christian wants to offer
encouragement, but I don't want to hear it. I shake off his
touch and refuse to turn around to look at him.

"Come inside, Abbie," he says, his voice blubbering. "We'll
figure out what to do next. This isn't over. We won't stop until
Lucas is home. I don't care what it takes or how long. We'll get
him back."

"I don't want to talk about it. Leave me alone, please."

"I'm sorry I came back empty-handed."

"Stop talking. Please."

"Abbie—"

Stop talking!" I shout.

I can't catch my breath or speak and the tightness in my
chest is getting worse…I can't breathe…I can't breathe.

I WAKE UP in our bedroom, feeling like I barely survived a vicious attack by an angry mob. I don't recall how I got here. One minute I'm screaming at Christian and the next, I wake up in my bed. What the heck happened and how long was I out?

I swing my legs off the bed and stand. A little wobbly, but I'll be fine. I head for the bedroom mirror and the image that stares back at me is frightening. Dark circles under red, bulging eyes. My hair looks like a gang of raccoons mistook it for a garbage bin and rummaged through it.

When Christian came back with no Lucas, something inside me broke. We were tense the whole time he was gone, but I knew something was wrong because he wouldn't call or text. Ty kept telling me it was because he didn't want to ruin the reunion by giving us a blow-by-blow account of his movements. But in that moment, which should have been filled with optimism and anticipation, I knew. When my fears were confirmed, I lost it. I've never fainted in my entire life, but it looks like that's exactly what happened.

After a long, hot shower, I change into jeans and a blue-lace, asymmetrical tunic top with three quarter sleeves. I brush my hair until it shines and let it hang past my shoulders. I throw on some powder foundation so my face doesn't look like death. Then I head downstairs to gear up for the next battle in the war to bring my son home.

CHAPTER 43

M Y BRAIN IS about to explode from a headache so intense, I would consider sticking my head into an active volcano if someone told me it would stop the pain.

Christian confirmed that I started hyperventilating when he returned without Lucas, lost my balance, and would have hit the ground had he not caught me in time. He brought me inside and once I had calmed down, Ty convinced me to take a mild sedative so I could sleep. Whatever temporary relief that provided evaporated when Christian told Ty and me what happened when he went to pick up Lucas at the appointed time and place, set by the kidnapper.

After that, the painful truth whispered harshly: we committed a tactical error. The only thing left to do was to call Detective Flores and confess our titanic screw up.

I sit in between Christian and Ty, with Detective Flores and his partner, Detective Corwin, across from us at the kitchen table. Corwin is of average build with a buzz cut, and joins us for the first time. I pop two extra strength Tylenol into my mouth and wash them down with bottled water, placing the almost-empty plastic bottle in the center of the table. I close my eyes for a few seconds to collect my bearings.

"Why don't you walk us through the drop?" Flores says to Christian. "What you did, not involving us, was dangerous. Not the smartest move. Now we're playing catch up."

"She said, 'No police!'" Christian's sharp words buzz through the kitchen, and then fall like dead leaves in autumn. He crosses his arms over his chest and blows out a noisy breath.

"She was very specific about the instructions. We had no way of knowing whether it was a bluff or not. It was a risk worth taking."

Flores ignores the outburst and plows ahead. "What were your precise instructions?"

Christian walks the detectives through the instructions we heard over the phone, the threat to Lucas' life if we involved the police and so on.

Then Ty jumps in and says, "We asked to hear Lucas' voice, proof that she had him, but she refused. We thought that was strange, but we figured she held all the cards and if we wanted to see Lucas again, we would play by her rules."

I add nothing to this discussion. It would take too much effort.

"What happened next?" Corwin asks.

Christian sits up straighter in his chair, places his hands on the table and leans in.

"I agreed to the terms, had the money wired so it could be verified by the timeline she set. Nine o'clock this morning."

"Did she provide any clue that could tell us where this account is set up?"

"No. Besides, the money may have already been moved around several times, making it difficult to track. The account number she provided was just the first stop. No way she's going to keep the funds there, waiting for the law to catch up with her."

"What else?" Flores probes.

"When she confirmed the money was in the account, she gave directions to an abandoned lot in Woburn, said Lucas would be there but she wouldn't. But I had to show up at exactly ten o'clock to pick him up, and not a second before."

"So you followed the instructions to the letter?" Corwin asks.

"Yes. But it was all a hoax. When I arrived, there was nothing but cracked pavement, trash and the sound of traffic whizzing by. I waited for an hour and ten minutes in the hope that she was just running late, but no sign of Lucas."

"She was stalling so she could make her escape and move the money around electronically," Ty says. "She was long gone by the time Christian showed up."

Flores nods and then says, "We will check to see if there are any cameras in the area that might have picked up something, although that's doubtful. Kidnappers usually pick a specific spot for a reason. No cameras, for example. Abandoned." He pinches his throat and then emits a dry cough.

I volunteer to get him some water from the cooler and place the glass next to him. He takes a long gulp and then places the half empty glass on the table. He continues, "What makes this case even more challenging is that we don't have a description. We're not sure the voice heard over the phone is the person's real voice or whether it was altered."

"In other words," Corwin adds, "without a description or any supporting information, we can't have airport, nor bus and train personnel be on the lookout."

"There's also another angle we need to consider," Flores adds. "We're twenty-four hours into this case. We have to consider the possibility that whoever took Lucas could be gone from the country."

A desperate gasp escapes me. Ty and Christian sit frozen, not even a slight blink of the eye to confirm they're human and not statues. My headache surges again, hammering away at my frontal lobe. I stand up slowly on shaky legs, excuse myself, and shuffle out of the kitchen and up the stairs.

Ty catches up to me. "Cooper, what's going on? Are you ill, do you need to lie down?"

Only after we both enter our bedroom and the door closes behind us am I able to speak.

"Our passports."

"Because of what the detective said, you want to see if Lucas' passport is still in the case."

Ty plops down on the bed like a sack of potatoes and drops his head into his hands. I lumber toward the large, walk-in closet, open the doors, and drag out the fireproof case containing our important documents that include the deed to the house, birth certificates for the kids, our taxes and other financial documents, and of course, our passports. Placing the container in the middle of the bedroom floor, I retrieve the keys from the bottom of one of the dresser drawers, then get down on my knees to open the case.

With trembling hands, I pull out the padded envelope that contains the passports, then stand up and empty the contents on the bed. Four, small blue books with an image of the Bald Eagle, and United States of America emblazoned in gold tumble out.

Four. Not five. Although the truth is staring me dead in the face, I go through each passport, matching the names and photos inside.

Fear trickles like ice water through my veins. If Lucas was whisked out of the country as this suggests, trying to find him has gotten ten times more difficult. Which means that something much more sinister than we could have ever imagined paid us a visit. If my suspicions are right, whoever took him has been in this house before. Enough to know where we keep our important documents. My muscles clench and I feel sick to my stomach.

CHAPTER 44

I VENTURE A GLANCE at Ty, whose face seems to have taken on a purple hue. He drags himself off the bed and begins to pace up and down the room. He returns to the bed, stands next to me and picks up the passports, one at a time, thumbing through the pages. When he's finished looking through each of them, he says nothing. Then in a slow, uneven amble, he makes it to the window. He doesn't draw the curtain aside to let in the sunlight, he just stands there, his back to me, not saying anything.

A few beats of raw, aching silence follow. "This is all on me," he says eventually. "There's no other way to look at it."

"How is this your fault, Ty? Tell me."

"I was too busy building my career to keep a close eye on my family. I spent all my time making sure other people and their families were okay, and neglected my own."

In a few steps, I make it to the window, take him by the arm and force him to turn around and look at me.

"It's normal to have parental guilt about something like this, but don't stand here and tell me that this tragedy could have been prevented if you had a nine-to-five-job."

A gust of anger trails across his face. "I don't have the

stomach for your snarky, know-it-all attitude, right now, Cooper. You don't get to tell me how to feel. You're not the only one who has been in hell since Lucas went missing."

He brushes past me and plops down on the bed once more, his head bent, staring at the floor.

Tears well up in my eyes. "I'm not that selfish." I aim a furious glare in his direction. "I know you're hurting, too. It's not your fault that Lucas is gone. I was just trying to reinforce that point. I wasn't trying to…"

I stop to catch my breath. "You know what? I'm sorry. I'll just take myself along with my snarky, know-it-all attitude and leave you alone."

I scurry past him and almost make it to the door when his words stop me cold.

"Don't! Don't go."

I turn around slowly. He looks up at me, broken, laid bare. I sit beside him.

He continues. "It's not only the fact that Lucas is missing. It's been eating away at me for a long time that I don't get to see my kids grow up, to be part of their daily lives."

His forehead creases with worry. "I'm missing out on those moments that create a lifetime of memories. It's not lost on me that you're raising them by yourself. I'm an absentee father, and I don't know how to fix it."

He slogs his way across the room to the large, cherry dresser and leans up against it. "I keep telling myself once cardiothoracic specialty training is over, it will get better. But that doesn't look promising. My patient load is increasing. Stevenson told me the other day that the department is getting calls from people outside the country who are specifically asking for me, to take on their cases."

Guilt and shame plunge through me like shards of ice. I've

been secretly fostering resentment against Ty for so long, and not once did I stop to consider things from his point of view. Because I was the one home with the kids, and had them in quick succession, I could only see my struggles.

The days when I felt like I was living in an alternate universe where nothing made sense. The times I didn't know what I was doing and it didn't matter because three little people were constantly demanding things from me, twenty-four hours a day, seven days a week.

In my way of thinking, he didn't have to deal with any of it. He was around adults, living his dream, and he was insulated from all the messiness and craziness of having young kids. He wasn't the one who slowly went out of his mind at times. On many occasions, when he did make it home, exhausted after working multiple shifts, I would give him the cold shoulder because I had a bad day or bad week. Ignoring him was my way of leveling the playing field. When he couldn't take it anymore, he would just go back to the hospital.

"I was wrong, earlier. I am selfish. I had no idea you were carrying around this burden. It was easier to focus on me and what I felt and thought and needed."

"You're not a mind reader, Cooper, and I'm not sharing this to make you feel guilty. We used to talk about everything. I know it's happened less and less because of our schedules, but I miss that. And I worry Lucas will think I let him down. He's probably wondering why we're not coming to get him. That's what bothers me most of all."

He returns to the bed. I rub his back in smooth, circular motions.

"We can't afford to turn on each other, Ty, or completely fall apart."

"So what's our next move?"

"We look for hidden cameras or recording devices. It's strangely coincidental that the kidnapper struck the night before the kids were to take off for the Bahamas and knew where the passports were kept. The police went over every inch of the house looking for forensic evidence, but they didn't sweep for cameras and bugs."

"What about Katie?"

"What about her? I told her the kids would be with their grandparents for spring break."

"She had full access to the house, keys to the cars, everything."

I rub my eyes and then let out a deep, exhausted sigh. "I'm sure the detectives have her on their list of potential witnesses. I didn't want to bring her up because it would mean I was duped once again by someone pretending to be sweet and caring."

"How do you mean?"

"I brought her into our lives. I let my guard slip, even when I had this feeling in my gut that something was off with the Paynes. I greedily accepted the carrot that was dangled before me because I was in a bind."

I smooth out my blouse with nervous strokes then continue. "When Jenna volunteered to take the kids to school the day Liv didn't show and they were delivered safely, I saw it as a good sign. A sign that I was dead wrong about her. When she took the initiative to bring Katie to my attention, I couldn't believe it."

"Don't beat yourself up, Cooper. We did our due diligence. Katie checked out."

"I'm not so sure she did, Ty."

"What do you mean?"

"What if Jenna set us up? What if everything about Katie is fake? Fake qualifications, fake references, fake identity."

He thinks about it for a minute and then slowly shakes his head. "That's a lot of what-ifs, Cooper."

"What if Katie kidnapped Lucas and took off with him and the five million dollars?" The words tumble from my lips like loose pebbles determined to create a disturbance.

A probing shadow takes over his face. "You think Katie knows, that this was an inside job and not some random stranger who wants revenge on the Wheelers?"

"Possibly."

Ty stands and resumes his pacing. "How does Charlie figure into the equation?"

"Perhaps all three of them are in on the kidnapping scheme."

"Right. So Jenna was here doing reconnaissance, learning our routines, about our family and such."

"Correct."

"I see where you're going with this, Cooper, but there's one flaw in your theory."

"Which is?"

"Jenna and Charlie had no way of knowing that Liv would wind up dead, so they could bring in Katie to replace her."

"I don't know how all the pieces fit yet."

"Jenna claims she'll be back in a few days."

"And you believe her, why?"

"Grasping at straws I guess," he says, shrugging. "But where would the kidnapper take Lucas that would require a passport, and why?"

CHAPTER 45

W HEN I SWING open the front door and see Jenna Payne standing there, I almost keel over from shock. Her long, ginger-red hair is cut shorter now, barely touching her shoulders. There are tired circles around her eyes, but otherwise she looks the same, decked out in jeans and a cream-colored University of Colorado sweatshirt.

"Hi, Abbie," she says, cautiously, as if she's not sure what kind of reception she will get from me.

"Jenna. What a surprise."

"Any news on Lucas?"

"No. Nothing yet."

We both stand there, eyeing each other awkwardly, neither one of us knowing what to say.

"Please come in," I say, breaking the silence. "I'm glad you stopped by. I want to ask you something."

Detectives Flores and Corwin left a while ago to pursue the missing passport and the Katie angle of the investigation. As Ty and I suspected, she was on their list of witnesses to interview, and they had no luck contacting her when they initially reached out.

Ty and Christian are both in the kitchen as I walk in with

Jenna. Neither one of them makes a move. I introduce Jenna to Christian. After she's seated, I busy myself brewing a fresh pot of coffee, not caring if anyone wants it or not. It's a way to collect my thoughts and occupy my hands. I need to approach Jenna carefully, without accusation or doubt. Whether or not I want to admit it, we need her help.

I place saucers and mugs on the table with cream and sugar, then the coffee canister in the center. I sit and send up a silent prayer that both Christian and Ty will pick up on my cues and follow my lead.

"What did you want to ask me?" Jenna says.

"Katie. How much do you really know about her?"

"Only what Muriel told me. Katie was new to Boston and looking for a job. She was a nanny to a Canadian couple who went back home. She thought Boston might be a good place to start over."

"What else?" I ask.

She cocks an eyebrow in surprise at the question.

"I'm not sure what you mean by, what else. You and Ty did your own background check on her, right?"

"We did. Master's degree in early childhood education, taught kindergarten and first grade until she was laid off, due to budget cuts in her district. Both parents and her sister Molly are dead. No criminal record, not even a speeding ticket. She volunteers at homeless shelters and nursing homes. Perfect. Nice and tidy."

"Okay, so…wait a minute," Jenna says. "You don't think Katie had anything to do with Lucas being taken, do you?"

"Anything is possible, Jenna," Ty says. "Katie had full access to the house, and she's not returning calls from the detectives. We're not saying she's guilty of anything. We just want to talk to her. Maybe she heard or saw something."

Her gaze hits the floor like someone just dropped a hundred-dollar bill.

"What is it?" I ask.

When Jenna looks up at me, guilt reigns supreme in her eyes. "I spoke to Katie yesterday."

The revelation gobsmacks me. Ty and Christian look at each other, stumped, and then all eyes return to Jenna.

"Explain," I demand.

"She called me, said she wanted to thank me for recommending her to your family. She said everything was working out great and went on and on about how wonderful you guys were. She offered to take me to dinner as a thank you. I told her it would have to wait until I got back from my trip."

"That is strange," Christian chimes in. "She had time to call you, but no time to return the phone calls from the detective. I'm sure they told her it's about Lucas."

I pick up the canister of coffee and pour myself a cup. I take a sip and then plead with Jenna. "If you know anything about Katie that we might have missed in her background check, now is the time to tell us. We got a ransom call that turned out to be a hoax. The person took the money and didn't produce Lucas. And Lucas' passport is missing."

I sound desperate, and everyone at the table knows it. Did I reveal too much information to a woman I don't trust? *Sure.* But if she thinks our attention is focused on Katie, she'll be less likely to think we suspect her involvement in Lucas' kidnapping.

"Are you serious?" she asks, cloaked in disbelief.

"My son is missing. I don't joke," I say.

"First Lucas, now Charlie," she says. It was almost a whisper, but I caught it.

"What do you mean by that?"

"Charlie isn't returning any of my calls. I don't know where he is. He left for a business trip that was only supposed to be a couple of days. My calls keep going to voicemail. My text messages go unanswered."

It's my turn to fix Jenna with a disbelieving stare. "Is that unusual for him?"

"Yes," she says without hesitation.

"What do you think is going on?" Ty asks.

Jenna shrugs. "I don't know."

"Did you guys have a fight? Are you having trouble in your relationship?" Ty asks.

"No."

"So, Katie won't answer calls from the police, and Charlie isn't answering your calls," Ty says. "Isn't that interesting?"

A brief stillness hovers awkwardly over the room. Then turning to Jenna, I switch gears and ask, "What do you know about the Wheelers?"

"Him?" Jenna asks, looking in Christian's direction.

"Not just him, his family."

"Um, well, I just met the man."

"Are you sure?" I implore. "You don't know anything about Levitron-Blair or the family who owns it? You've never seen Christian before, nor know of him?"

Jenna squints as if she's accessing her memory bank. "Yes, I've heard of Levitron-Blair. Who hasn't? But no, I've never met or seen Christian before. I would have remembered. It's hard to forget a face that gorgeous. But what does that have to do with Lucas missing or the fact that I don't know where Charlie is?"

"Nothing," I say, then take a sip of my coffee. "Have you reached out to Charlie's family to find out if they've heard from him? Friends maybe?"

"Charlie doesn't have a lot of friends. There were a couple of guys he hung out with in Colorado, but the friendship faded since we moved here."

"What about your family?" Ty asks. "Any members of your family he may have contacted?"

She shakes her head. "My mother is dead and I don't know where my father is. I haven't seen him since I was a senior in high school, and he pretended not to know me when I ran into him and what looked like his new family at the airport for a senior class trip to Montreal. I've written him off since. No big loss."

Christian reaches for the coffee canister and pours a drink for himself and then for Ty, who's holding up his mug. Jenna has quite a story. She seems to be telling the truth. I didn't detect any weird shifts in body language or wandering gazes or attempts to evade answering questions. So far, the only thing she said that piqued my interest was the fact that Charlie is also missing.

"Do you think Charlie might be involved with the wrong crowd?" I ask.

"I'm not sure what you mean," she says.

Ty jumps in. "I think what Cooper is asking is whether he could have gotten involved with people who do questionable things and kept it from you. Things like run a kidnapping scam."

"I wouldn't be the first wife to be left in the dark," she says, miserably. "The simple answer is, I don't know. It may sound pathetic, but I couldn't tell you for sure one way or the other."

"Maybe he's having an affair with Katie and they kidnapped Lucas together," Christian says, angry darts shooting from his eyes. "Have you thought of that? You're here and he's not, and neither is Katie, who's not responding to the police. The two of them were in on it and cut you out of the loop. Five million dollars. That's how much the kidnapper asked for and received."

Jenna's jaw drops, her mouth forming the word "Wow" on mute. When she closes her mouth, she looks like someone whose spirit was just trampled on by a herd of angry hippos. But then something sparks behind her eyes, an electrical charge of determination, as if she just decided she would get to the bottom of the disappearance of Charlie and Katie and make them pay.

"I can't even wrap my head around that. Someone said they had Lucas, and in exchange for five million dollars, they would give him back?"

"That's correct," Christian says.

"I'm sorry. That couldn't have been easy, to have hope and then have it ripped away by a conman."

I perk up. "How do you know it's a man? We never said whether the fake kidnapper was male or female."

"I just assumed," she says. "Are you saying it was a woman?"

Her gaze pans around the table. No one responds to the question.

"I'll take that as a 'Yes'," Jenna says. "You think it's Katie, don't you?"

"We didn't say that," Ty interjects. "The person had a British accent."

Jenna frowns. "British, huh? What would a Brit know about Lucas?"

"Don't be naïve, Jenna," Christian says. "Who said the person was British? Anybody can mimic any accent when it suits their purpose. It was just a ruse to throw us off."

"How can you be so sure?"

"What do you mean?" Ty asks.

Jenna reaches for the coffee canister and pours a cup. She takes a sip and places the cup onto a saucer. "Do you know for a fact that the kidnapper isn't a British woman?"

I look at Ty and Christian. "Well, we don't know much about the kidnapper. What little we do know doesn't inspire confidence. It could be a lone wolf who pulled this off, or it could be a crime ring. We just don't know."

A platoon of terrible thoughts hijacks my brain. If Lucas was whisked out of the country, does that point to human traffickers, people who sell kids on the black market for... I force the thoughts to dissolve, like the dawn giving way to the sunrise. Lucas is out there somewhere. We'll find him. And when we do, it won't be enough that he came back to us. The guilty party or parties will pay, and I don't much care when or how.

"I don't mean to add to your pain," Jenna says. "It must be heart-wrenching not having a clue where your child is, the constant worry. It's hard not to have bad thoughts, with all the terrible things that happen in this world. Unfortunately, kids are not exempt. Evil doesn't discriminate."

I look her square in the eyes. "You're right, Jenna. Evil doesn't. But vengeance does."

She doesn't flinch and holds my stare. Either she's telling the truth and she has no clue regarding Lucas' whereabouts, or she's a heartless, diabolical liar.

living a nightmare. The boogeyman comes to life and grabs them while they sleep, taking them away from you and everyone who loves them."

I hear a roaring in my ears and temporarily lose track of what I want to say. I don't have a prepared statement, preferring to speak from the heart. I pause to catch my breath. Tears circle. I can feel them slowly seeping out of my eyes, but I swipe them away with my arm. I want the coward who took Lucas, be it Katie or someone else, to know that they can't break me, they can't break our family, and we will find them no matter what hole they've crawled into. But my emotions have other ideas.

"You wake up in the morning expecting to see your child's smiling, mischievous face, ready to pull some prank on his siblings or get into some silly argument. But he doesn't come down to breakfast. He's not in his room. You search everywhere but you can't find him. Then you have to accept the truth. The nightmare that every parent dreads has visited your family. He's gone. That's what our family has been going through for the past two days."

I sniffle and wipe my tears. I have to finish this and get it over with. The sooner I do, the sooner the tip line can light up. "We need your help to get Lucas back. If anyone out there has seen or heard anything, even if you think it's insignificant, please call the tip line."

My heart thunders in my chest like a caged tigress raging against her imprisonment. I want the person or persons who took Lucas to suffer in the worst way possible. I can't say that in a public forum, though. My public face must be the devastated and terrified mother I am.

"Katie, if you have Lucas, we know you're taking good care of him. I don't know why you took him. I don't care why you did it. We just want him back. Please let him go. He's just a little boy who doesn't understand why he is separated from his family and why somebody he trusted would do this to him. Do the right thing, Katie. Return Lucas to his family."

CHAPTER 47

B RIAN ROGERS STEPPED into the Air France lounge at JFK International Airport in New York. The cacophony of sights and sounds of the busy airport extended to the lounge. Men and women could be heard speaking on their cell phones in rapid French, a young man pushed his father in a wheelchair, while a five-year old girl insisted that her father buy her ice-cream. Off to the right, a row of red and beige crescent chairs lined the space, occupied by individuals conducting calls with wireless ear buds or banging away on the keys of their laptops. A cleaner mopped up a spilled drink less than three feet from Brian, while a little boy, hoisted on his dad's shoulder, pointed to the jets on the tarmac he could see through the large windows. The PA system was in overdrive, announcing the thousands of flights that arrive and depart from JFK daily.

The noisiness and bustle made him feel safe. The more activity around him, the easier it would be to get lost in the crowd. He nabbed an empty seat amongst the cluster of chairs at the center of the lounge. In a couple of hours, he would be airborne, heading to Charles de Galle Airport in Paris. He wasn't sure how long he would stay in the city of lights, but his key destination would be Zurich, Switzerland.

When his attention shifted to the flat screen TV in the lounge, he couldn't believe what he was witnessing. He rubbed his eyes a few times, blinked and refocused. The image hadn't changed.

Abbie Rambally stood at a podium that displayed multiple microphones, many of them emblazoned with the insignia of well-known TV networks. Her house on Cherry Blossom Lane stood in the background, although he couldn't see the house clearly. She was dressed in a simple, navy blue sheath dress, her hair pulled back in a casual ponytail, no jewelry. The caption on the screen read Rambally Kidnapping Press Conference.

Brian sprang to his feet, made his way to the customer desk, and asked the attendant if he could borrow the remote control to increase the volume on the TV. She scowled at him but obliged after he assured her it was only for a couple of minutes, as he didn't want to disturb other passengers. He walked closer to the screen and pumped up the volume.

The room spun around him. Passengers appeared in a giant blur. The words rang through his head like a cymbal crash. Abbie was making a plea for Lucas' return. Even more shocking to Brian, was that she was asking Katie Nicholson to return her son. Abbie had tears in her eyes, her face fragile and grief-stricken, as though a gentle breeze would topple her. Yet, the body language she exuded was in direct contrast to the anguished mom. The look in her tear-filled eyes was unmistakable. He knew that look well. It was seared into his memory. That was the same look Iceman had when he asked Brian to take out Lucas to make Abbie pay: pure, unadulterated rage.

If Katie Nicholson took Abbie's child, Katie was going to wish she hadn't. Abbie had unlimited resources at her disposal, thanks to the kid's relation to the Wheelers. His overflowing bank account was proof of that. Christian Wheeler forked over five million dollars without blinking. All he needed was the belief that his nephew would be returned once the transaction was completed.

Brian lowered the volume, retuned the remote to the customer desk, and headed for the bar. He pulled up the only unoccupied stool. When the bartender asked him what he was drinking, he ordered a glass of champagne.

"Celebrating, huh?" The guy next to him said. He was wearing a Yankees baseball cap, a long-sleeved denim shirt and chinos.

"I guess you could say that."

"Got good news?" the guy asks.

"You know, sometimes everything comes together just the way you wanted. The big payoff, you know what I mean?"

"Yeah. I'm Brian, by the way," he said, extending his hand.

"Same here," Brian responded, taking the hand.

"Whoa, two Brians sitting at the same bar heading to France on the same day. What are the chances?" He chuckled then said, "Wait, don't tell me you're on the 4:30 flight, too?"

"I might be," Brian responded, taking a sip of his champagne.

"You know what, a glass of champagne sounds good," Baseball Cap Brian said. He asked the bartender to bring him a glass and one for his friend. When the drinks arrived, the two men clinked their glasses.

"To things working out," Brian Rogers said. He took another sip of the champagne. Yes, things would work out quite well.

An unpleasant thought suddenly punched him in the head. How could he have been so careless? What if Baseball Cap Brian wasn't who he said he was? He was still in the U.S., for crying out loud. Just because Abbie Rambally had Katie in her sights didn't mean he was one hundred percent in the clear.

As long as he was on American soil, there was always a risk. He plunked down a ten-dollar tip on the counter, told Yankees Baseball Cap Brian he had to go, and bolted off the stool.

When his Air France flight was called, forty-five minutes before departure, a tranquil breeze of relief swept over Brian. Soon, he would put his home country in his rearview mirror. It wasn't that he was unpatriotic, he just didn't like being locked up. Did that for four years and had zero desire to head back to that place. It was time for a new beginning. Assuming the identity of Charlie Payne, a dying homeless man eight years Brian's senior, was the beginning of the do-over for him.

Call it chance, luck or whatever. Not long after he was released from prison, he ran into Charlie on the streets of Denver and struck up a conversation. He knew what it was like to be down on his luck. The man looked and smelled like death. All Brian had to do was befriend the man and pay him a few hundred dollars to make his last days tolerable. Brian decided to wait him out. It only took six weeks. He had been handed a chance at a new life, and he wasn't about to blow that opportunity for anybody, not Jenna, not Katie Nicholson, and certainly not for a psycho like Iceman.

Brian would fly to France first-class all the way. He had pulled it off. Spared Lucas, and made enough money to begin his new life. He had purchased the ticket cash and had only his backpack for luggage.

When it was his turn to board, he handed the boarding pass to the agent at the gate and held his breath. A green light popped up on the machine and it beeped once it scanned the boarding pass.

His muscles were still tense, as if in fight or flight response mode. He followed the other first-class passengers up the gangway to the plane's entrance. He was welcomed to the first-class cabin, where he placed his carry-on in the overhead bin, sat in the plush leather seat, and stretched out.

He refused an offer of champagne, and kept his eyes closed during the entire boarding process. He didn't want to talk to anyone. Mostly, he wanted to get his emotions under control and banish the paranoid thoughts. What if the police showed up, hauled him out of the expensive seat, and dragged him off to jail? What if Jenna discovered his duplicity and decided to rat him out?

He ignored the noise surrounding him: passengers searching for their assigned seats, overhead bins being open and shut, and general chatter. When it was all done, and the pilot told the flight attendants to prepare for takeoff in both French and English, his anxiety came down a notch. But it wasn't until he felt the plane taxi, gain speed, and lift off the ground that he breathed calmly and opened his eyes. He had done it.

He, Brian Rogers, had executed the perfect con and gotten away with it.

CHAPTER 48

J ENNA PAYNE PULLED into the parking lot of the Walmart Super Center in North Reading, Massachusetts. At nine o'clock at night, the onslaught of shoppers had thinned out, although there was a smattering of people pushing grocery carts or heading into the massive store. She debated whether she should head in to stock up on water, snacks and a few other items, but decided against it. Cameras might capture her in the store. She was almost certain there were cameras in the parking lot, too, but that was easier to manage. With her now short, dark hair under a baseball cap, and dark clothes, as long as she kept her head down, there was little chance of her full face being captured.

She killed the engine but left the keys in the ignition, picked up the large flask filled with coffee, and reached for the gym bag from the back seat. She hurried out of the car and slung the bag over her slender shoulders, clasping the flask. Jenna walked four cars down to the black Chevy Malibu, which thankfully wasn't parked near a lamppost where it could be illuminated by light. She fished the key out of her jeans pocket, popped the lock, and tossed the bag in the back seat. She then slid into the driver's seat and jammed the coffee flask into the large cup holder.

It would take her three and a half hours to reach Derby, Vermont. By tomorrow morning, it would all be over. Returning to Lexington one last time had been risky, but well worth it. Her unexpected visit had thrown Abbie off balance. Jenna got that impression when Abbie opened the front door and saw her there. She couldn't hide how stunned she was to see Jenna. Her eyes revealed that she wasn't quite trusting, as Jenna had suspected all along. But after Jenna was invited in, and the conversation grew more intense, she could see Abbie easing up on her distrust, especially since Jenna sneakily handed Katie over as the culprit, the one who had most likely abducted Lucas.

Now, Jenna had every reason to believe she was in the clear. Only the border crossing was left now. According to her calculation, she would arrive in Derby after midnight. She had insisted on renting a car without a GPS installed, no matter how much the agent at the car rental counter tried to convince her she should. The town was just under two hours from the Montreal border. She had timed it perfectly. She couldn't arrive at the border too early or too late. It had to be smack in the middle of morning rush hour. Derby was one of the busiest border ports between the U.S. and Canada, and she would use that to her advantage.

Once safely inside Canada, Jenna would breathe easier, but not for long. Phase two of her plan would kick into high gear right away. There were a few bumps in the road, circumstances that demanded that she improvise, but she was a quick thinker and could handle stressful situations with a calm, rational mind.

That's not what Charlie thought, though. *The idiot.* He thought she was a loose cannon he had to control. Well, that's what she wanted him to think, and it worked brilliantly. He panicked and made a stupid move.

He thought he was so clever, thought he was the one calling the shots. Jenna didn't even care where he was. She had toyed with the idea of teaching him a lesson, but in the end, decided against it. It was too risky. She couldn't predict what he would do or say, so it was best to leave well enough alone. Wherever he was, she would never see him again, and that was fine with her. She had no more use for him, anyway.

As the car ate up the miles, and with nothing but trees, darkness and miles of road ahead for company, Jenna allowed her thoughts to wander freely. She had spent too many years of her life being ignored or abandoned. First by her loser father who left, and then her brothers died, followed by her mother, leaving her all alone in the world. Despite the deck being stacked against her, she had made her own luck.

Now, finally, she had it all. She was no longer alone.

CHAPTER 49

JENNA PULLED INTO the dark driveway and killed the headlights and engine. Again, not wanting to take chances that someone might drive by. The nearest house was miles away, but she had learned that one can never be too careful.

She pulled out the burner phone from the gym bag and typed a text message: *I'm here.*

A minute later, she exited the car, trudged down the gravel pathway to the house, and turned the front door knob. It was open. She stepped inside and quickly assessed the dimly lit living room.

"Where are you?" she asked. "The door was open."

He appeared from the direction of the kitchen in a long-sleeved, red dress shirt and black jeans. She flung herself into his arms and he hugged her tightly. Jenna was so relieved she wanted to cry. She had missed him terribly, the smell of him, the feel of him. His way of always making her feel calm when things got crazy. He kissed her hard on the mouth. She responded eagerly.

After they separated and caught their collective breath, he took her by the hand and led her into the kitchen. The space was small, with pale yellow walls, a refrigerator, microwave, and small table with chairs. He poured her a cup of tea he had prepared in advance and placed it on the table in front of her. He took the seat across from her.

"How is he?" Jenna asked, taking a sip of tea.

"Upset. Scared. Rebellious. But he's talking to me now. That's progress."

"He'll come around eventually. Once he gets his anger out, he'll calm down and accept his new reality, that he has a new family now."

"I hope you're right."

Jenna scrutinized her husband's face, his trepidation as transparent as glass. For a straight-laced, by-the-book guy like him, this was probably the scariest and most uncomfortable thing he'd ever done in his life.

Adrian Harper was a top mergers and acquisitions attorney for a major East Coast law firm. The two met in college. They dated briefly, but then decided to be just friends. Like so many, they drifted apart after graduation. Adrian went off to law school at Emory University in Atlanta, and Jenna pursed her masters in Fine Arts at the University of Michigan.

Fate intervened and they met up again years later, at the wedding of a mutual friend, and picked up where they'd left off, as if they were never separated by time and distance. They were married in Central Park after Adrian graduated from law school and landed the job in New York. It was the perfect place to begin their lives together. New York was the publishing capital of the world, and Jenna was lucky to get hired as a junior illustrator for an imprint of one of the major publishing houses.

When the idea of how they were going to become a family landed in their lap, there was no going back. After trying for three years to get pregnant and one miscarriage too many, they received the devastating news that their chances of becoming parents were slim to none. But Iceman had inadvertently given Jenna a gift, one she couldn't ignore.

"I know this hasn't been easy for you," she told him. "But you pushed through, and now we're about to have everything we want, a new life with our new family. Just a few more hours."

He reached out and touched her arm. "I would do anything for you. But I worry. Not about myself. I worry about you. I worry about the boy. And what about her? How is this playing out?"

She gave him a half smile. Adrian was the kindest man she'd ever known, always putting the feelings and needs of others ahead of his own.

"Don't worry about her. We're not doing this to be cruel, Adrian. We saved Lucas. You know Iceman would have found another way to get at him, take his revenge on the mother if Charlie and I didn't execute his plan. Don't go soft on me now. He's going to be fine. We're going to be fine."

"What about the mother?" Adrian insisted.

Jenna figured she should tell him the truth. "She's devastated and fragile. Also determined. She will not stop until she figures out what happened. And then..."

"And then what?" he asked, leaning closer.

"She's going to come after whoever she thinks took her kid. She's focused on Katie. Saw the press conference pleading for Lucas' return."

"How did you feel?"

"Fine. Just fine. Do you honestly think Iceman would have let things go?"

"He has for years."

"He was just biding his time. Whenever I visited him and the subject came up, I knew he was planning something bad. When he told me of his plan, I went along with it because I saw a better way out. I saw an opportunity for us to have the family we deserved, and that's what kept me going all this time. That's why I was able to look Abbie Rambally in the face and pretend to be her friend. I had to keep my focus on the end goal. We're almost there."

Adrian covered his face with his big brown hands, and then placed them on the table.

"I'm glad this will all be behind us soon. I almost blew it that night. I was terrified someone would see me leaving the house with the kid hoisted over my shoulder or worse, call the police. I still can't believe how easy it was."

That's why we took precautions. If anyone saw you, all they would have seen was Dr. Rambally leaving the house with his son. Besides, it was in the dead of night. Nobody would have been able to make a positive ID."

"Well, that custom-made mask did come in handy."

"Success in life is seventy percent planning and thirty percent skill."

"Is that a real statistic?"

"It could be."

Adrian went silent and steepled his hands together. From the pained look scrawled across his face, Jenna knew what he was thinking.

"Look at it this way. Lucas will be eighteen in eight years, then off to college. If he wants to go back to them, he can. I just want a little bit of time with him. We're going to be great parents. We'll give him a happy, healthy, safe upbringing, just like he's used to."

"And what about Iceman? What happens once he finds out you double-crossed him?"

Jenna shrugged. "I'm not in the least bit worried. We'll be long gone, never to be heard from again. Besides, he may have seen the press conference. It will only convince him that we did what he asked. I have no intention of calling him to confirm anything."

Adrian let out a deep sigh.

"What? Jenna asked.

"Tomorrow morning, crossing the border."

"What about it? I don't anticipate any issues."

"Lucas. What if they ask to see the note?"

"So what? It's perfect."

"What if they call? That worries me."

"I told you I would take care of all that. I've left nothing to chance. Stop worrying. It's why I suggested we travel separately. Lucas and I can pass as relatives and we both have American passports. If you came with us, it might raise questions."

Jenna's patience was wearing thin. Adrian was a highly intelligent man, but his fear and paranoia were clouding his judgment, making him ask dumbass questions.

"Pull yourself together, otherwise this whole plan falls apart. You are a Canadian citizen returning home to attend a legal conference. You will be dressed appropriately. A suit is like a uniform to you. I will take care of things on my end. You leave first. Lucas and I won't be far behind."

He nodded.

"Stop making it complicated. I know you're nervous, but we've done okay so far. The hard part is over. Crossing the border with legal documents is the easiest part of this whole thing, so relax. Okay?"

Adrian opened his mouth to say something but Jenna glared at him, that special look of hers that told him he better quit while he was ahead.

"Let's get some sleep," Adrian said, yawning. "The little guy is knocked out. Went to bed at nine o'clock. We have to watch him like a hawk once we get to Montreal."

"What do you mean?" Jenna asked.

"We don't want him using a device to communicate with his parents, do we?"

"I thought you kept him clear of electronic devices."

"I did. But they're everywhere these days. And he's a smart kid."

"Did he try to escape since he's been here?"

"Nope. But why risk the chance he might try to find help?"

"Don't worry about it. He will be sleeping when we cross the border. By the time he wakes up, we'll be at the apartment. We'll take turns keeping a close eye on him at all times. We just need to do it for twenty-four hours."

CHAPTER 50

L UCAS CREPT BACK to his room in the nick of time. The man called Adrian was talking to a woman in the kitchen he couldn't see, but she sounded like Mrs. Payne. He was glad he decided to stay up late, pretending to be asleep. Adrian checked in on him a couple of times. Lucas had one eye open in the semi-darkness. He told Adrian he was afraid of the dark and needed a night light. He wasn't, but he wanted to be alert and the light helped him stay awake.

Lucas wasn't sure what day it was. He recalled that his dad put him in a car in the middle of the night. He remembered it was dark. He'd said "Hi" to his dad, and Dad had told him to go back to sleep, so he had. But when he woke up, he was in the back of a car he didn't recognize. It wasn't the car either his mom or dad drove. The person driving the car wasn't his dad. He thought he was having a bad dream, so he started screaming for his father. Dad always knew how to chase away bad dreams, even though sometimes his mom did because Dad worked a lot.

Soon, Lucas realized it wasn't a bad dream. The stranger driving the car pulled over to the side of the road and stopped the car. Lucas had no idea where they were. It was still dark out, but he sensed daylight would soon come. There were mostly trees around. The road was narrow, like they were in the woods or something. Lucas didn't see any houses around, either. The place gave him the creeps. Then the stranger came into the back seat with him.

"It's okay, Lucas," he said in a quiet voice. "I won't let anything happen to you. We're just going on a little trip, that's all. No need to panic. It's a short trip, only for a couple of days."

Lucas wanted to believe the man, that nothing was going to happen to him, but he wanted to cry because he knew something was terribly wrong. The man knew his name and he was in an unfamiliar place, away from his family. Lucas wanted to be brave, but he was scared. The man seemed nice, but Lucas didn't trust him. He had on a dark blue jacket and white shirt and a fancy watch. He was African-American and had really white teeth with a space in between the two front teeth. He also had a dimple in his chin. He seemed a little scared too. His knee kept bouncing up and down.

"I want to go home," Lucas said. "Where are my parents?"

"They're home. They're fine. They'll come to get you in a couple of days."

"Who are you? What's your name? What about Blake and Alexis? Did something happen to them?"

The thought was more than Lucas could bear. He had to do something, get out of this car, make some noise, anything. Maybe another car would come down the road and stop to find out what was going on.

Lucas started screaming and kicking and punching. At one point, he tried to bite the man, and that's where the stranger drew the line. He pinned Lucas' arms down and told him to stop screaming and hitting him. It took a while, but Lucas eventually calmed down.

"Where are my parents?" Lucas asked through hiccups. "Take me home. Now! My parents didn't say it was okay for me to go with you because you're a stranger. Strangers are bad. They hurt people."

"Not all strangers are bad, Lucas," the stranger said. "I promise, I won't hurt you, but I need you to be a good boy."

"Why should I?" Lucas challenged. "I think you're lying. I think you want to do something bad to me. Otherwise, you would tell me your name and where my family is and why I'm in this car and where we're going and why..."

Lucas stopped to catch his breath. His head hurt. His heart wouldn't stop racing. He didn't know what to do. He was trapped. He started wailing again, the tears streaming down his face. He was sad and afraid he would never see his family again. He didn't know why the stranger took him, and he didn't know if his family was okay or not.

The man touched his shoulders and Lucas flinched. He didn't like being touched, especially by strangers. The man didn't try to touch him again after that.

"Okay, Lucas," the man said. "I'll tell you my name and where we're going if you promise not to scream or hit me or try anything stupid. Deal?"

Lucas didn't know if he should agree, but he was desperate for information. Maybe he could pretend to be sick and the man would have to let him go to the bathroom. Once there, Lucas could borrow a phone from another stranger, but this time, he wouldn't be scared. He would ask for help and he would have to get over his dislike of strangers.

Lucas nodded slowly but he didn't look at the man. He stared straight ahead. He noticed there were no signs on the road that he could see. He shivered.

"Okay, good," the man said. "My name is Adrian. We're

taking this trip to visit someone. Someone who really wants to meet you. They live in a little town a couple of hours away from home."

"Where are my parents and my brother and sister? Why aren't they on this trip, too?"

"Well, Lucas, your parents don't like this person very much because the person hurt your mom a long time ago, but the person is really very sorry about that. They're sick and just wanted to see you. Once they see you, I will drive you back home. The person wants to give you a special letter to take to your mom. I think it's an apology letter."

Lucas squinted at the man. Was he telling the truth? It would make sense why his parents weren't around if he was sneaking a visit to this person. But it struck him that something was still off about this whole trip.

"My parents will be looking for me since they don't know about this secret visit."

"I called your parents after we left to let them know. I didn't tell them where exactly we're going, but I told them the person wanted to see you. They were angry at first, but then they said I better have you back in a couple of days."

Lucas pondered that for a minute. Still didn't make sense. "My parents don't know you. Why would they let me go with you to meet this person?"

Adrian scrunched his nose. "Actually Lucas, I'm just helping out a friend. Mrs. Payne. You know her, right?"

Lucas nodded. "What does Mrs. Payne have to do with anything?"

"Your mother and Mrs. Payne are friends, and they both know this person we're taking you to see. Mrs. Payne didn't want to upset your mom by telling her the person wanted to see you, so she just asked me to drive you and we would meet up there."

"What happened to my dad?" Lucas asked.

"What do you mean?"

"My dad put me in the car. But when I woke up, he was gone and you were driving."

Adrian let out a deep sigh. Then he said in a mean voice, "Enough with the questions. You're giving me a headache. It's only for a couple of days, and then Mrs. Payne will drive you back home after you see this person."

Then he opened the door, went back to the driver's seat, and drove off.

Lucas decided Adrian was lying. He also decided he would figure out a way to call his parents or Blake. Lucas didn't care about this mystery person they were going to see. He thought Adrian, if that was his real name, made up a story so Lucas would stop yelling and screaming. For now, he would behave and observe everything and wait for the perfect opportunity. Adrian didn't like it when he screamed. But if Lucas was a good boy, pretended to do whatever Adrian wanted, he would learn more information about where they were going. This time, he wouldn't get caught, not like when he was sneaking in Katie's purse to find out why she was secretly talking to someone on the phone.

The sign said they had arrived in Derby, Vermont. Lucas didn't know anybody from Vermont. He just knew the capital was Montpelier since third grade when he memorized all the state capitals. But this place didn't look like a city. It was way in the boondocks. Soon, they pulled up to a little farmhouse with nothing around but grass and trees. Lucas didn't even see cows. The place looked like no one lived there.

Adrian opened the back seat of the car so Lucas could get out. He hesitated. This place was far away from everything, even strangers who could help him. But what would happen to him if he told Adrian he didn't want to go inside with him? Would he get mad and do something terrible to Lucas?

"Come on, Lucas. We don't have all day."

"I want to go home. It's creepy out here."

Adrian sighed, loudly. Lucas knew he was getting on his nerves. Adults did that a lot when they were upset or irritated. Lucas couldn't help it, even though he promised himself he would behave so he could learn more about Adrian's plans.

Adrian tapped his foot, his face angry. Lucas thought about it some more and then decided it was best to get out of the car. He didn't want to find out what Adrian would do if he got angry and really lost it. He had to remember they were in the middle of nowhere with no neighbors around to help him if something happened.

Lucas' foot hit something soft as he was about to step out of the car. He looked down and picked up Mr. Snoopy, his favorite childhood bear. What was he doing here? Alexis played with the bear now because Lucas thought he was too old for stuffed animals. Alexis still had tons of them. He picked up the brown bear with the ribbon tied around his neck and the red and green checkered hat on his head. At least Mr. Snoopy would keep him company. He was a friendly welcome face.

"Mrs. Payne will be here soon to take you to see that person," Adrian said after they stepped inside the house. "For now, it's just me and you, two guys hanging out. There's plenty of food, so anytime you're hungry, just let me know. But there are no phones here or electronics, no TV, radio, nothing. And don't even think about trying to run away." Adrian reached into his jacket pocket and pulled out a syringe with some strange liquid inside.

"If you don't do exactly as I say, I will plunge this syringe into your skin. You don't want to know what it's going to do to you. Are we clear?"

A terrified Lucas clutched Mr. Snoopy close to his chest and took a few steps backward. He didn't want to die. Whatever was in that syringe looked like it could cause death. He would do whatever Adrian said. But he would also look for a way out. He would try to figure out their plan while pretending to be good.

From what he'd overheard, they planned to take him to Canada, and the town was right on the border. Lucas decided the border might be a good place to try to escape.

CHAPTER 51

I T'S CLOSING IN on midnight. Ty and I are wide awake, drinking coffee by the gallon and plotting our next moves. The police received over a hundred phone calls after the press conference pleading for Lucas' return. Not a single call yielded any useful information. My son has vanished, and no one saw or heard anything. It's up to us to bring him home where he belongs. I've asked myself why me, why does life insist on tossing me from storm to storm? Then I remembered my father's mantra: *You were made to do hard things.*

After the press conference, the storm continued to rage inside of me. Anger, regret, bitterness. I haven't held my other two children in days. My parents stepped up to care for them. They're with Mom and Dad in Castleview, an hour away, until Lucas returns. We've video chatted, which is not the same as having them home. As much as I miss them, and this situation has taken a toll on them, they would give anything to have their brother home. So that's what Ty and I are going to do. We're going to make our family whole again.

The doorbell rings. The late hour doesn't even bother me, given the circumstances. I gulp down the last of my coffee, set the cup down on the counter, and leave to answer the door. I ask who it is and almost can't believe my ears. I yank the door knob so hard I'm surprised it didn't come off in my hands.

We just stand there in silence, staring at each other. Then we move in for a giant embrace, extending the silence. I can't help it; the tears flow of their own will.

"I came as soon as I could," she says.

We break apart and I nod. She places her bags at the foot of the stairs and follows me to the kitchen.

"Callie!" Ty shoots up from his seat, and comes around to embrace her. They both have a seat.

"Coffee?" I ask Callie.

"Please," she says as she sheds her red, stylish trench coat and hangs it on the back of the chair.

I head to the cabinet, grab an extra cup, and return to the table.

"I'm mad at you and Ty," she says, reaching for the coffee canister at the center of the table and pouring herself a cup. "If Christian hadn't called me, I never would have known that Lucas was missing."

"It wasn't intentional," I say. "Once we discovered he was gone, it was chaos, both emotionally and physically. We would have called you eventually. It was just taking a while."

"What's the latest?" she asks, sipping her drink.

I fill her in on the what's been happening, including the ransom scam, the press conference that yielded nothing, and the fact that nobody saw or knows anything.

"Christian told me about the Paynes," she says. "I want to hear it in your own words."

The steel in her voice isn't lost on me. To the casual observer, Callie appears to be a delicate porcelain doll, who would shatter at the lightest of touches. Her petite frame, glossy, raven hair, and light olive skin reinforce that delicate flower narrative. But the casual observer would be fooled. Though she can be sweet, selfless, and loving, Callie Furi also possesses a boldness and iron will that has served her well in both business and her personal life. Of all the friendships I've had over the years, my relationship with her has survived the longest because we're most alike in that way.

Callie and I have been best friends since we attended the same high school, St. Matthews Academy, an hour away from here. It was she who encouraged me to give Christian a chance when he started asking me out like a song stuck on repeat. I wanted no part of him at first. In high school, he had a firmly established player reputation and I was an uptight, no-nonsense academic overachiever who had her entire life mapped out at seventeen. Christian and I never would have entered each other's lives, had it not been for Callie.

"What do you want to know about the Paynes?" I ask.

"Everything."

I tell her everything we know, what we've experienced, ending with Jenna's visit earlier in the day.

She takes it all in, never interrupting me. When I'm done she says, "It sounds like this woman and her husband were targeting Lucas from the get go, got you and Ty to trust her, and then snatched him. Devious if you ask me."

"We've gone over that scenario a million times, Callie," Ty says. "We didn't expect to see her at all, but she showed up today as Cooper said. She was out of town when we told her what happened to Lucas. The next day, she showed up. Why would she do that if she had taken him?"

Callie taps a bright red fingernail on the table. "If she had help kidnapping Lucas, which I'm willing to bet she did, then it was easy to show up here and pretend to be innocent while her partner in crime did all the heavy lifting."

"We thought of that," I say. "But we haven't been able to pin anything on them. The evidence just isn't there to pursue them as our number one suspect. The police interviewed Jenna. And don't forget about Katie Nicholson. She's been dodging the police and nobody knows where she is. Her apartment was cleared out."

"So, what do we do now?" she asks. "What's the plan to bring Lucas home?"

I stay silent. My body relaxes into the chair of its own will. A memory of some kind is struggling to work its way to the front of my mind. Ty and I were figuring out what to do next when Callie arrived. Now, her question, put so bluntly, is forcing my brain to come up with a solution. There's someone out there who's supposed to help us find Lucas. Callie's arrival has triggered my memory bank. This person has helped me before. She knows who he is.

"Oh, my goodness, it was right there in front of me all along." I reach over and hug Callie so tightly, I feel like I'm about to crush her tiny frame. "Thank you, Callie."

When I release her, she looks at me as if I'm bonkers. But I've never been more clear-headed than I am right now. My heart soars with a lightness and optimism I haven't felt since the ransom exchange was a bust.

I look at my husband and my best friend and say, "I got it. I know what our next move should be."

"Now, would be the time to tell us," Ty says. "What's on your mind, Cooper?"

"Not what. Who."

They exchange matching looks of confusion. Then I blurt out, "Lance Carter. He can help us get Lucas back."

My gaze pings back and forth between Ty and Callie. Recognition comes into focus for them both.

Ty says, "I haven't heard that name in over twelve years. What made you think of him?"

"Callie."

Lance Carter attended the same high school as Callie and I. He was a tech genius who used his skills to help me out of a difficult situation. He exposed the person who was using a terrible secret I was keeping from extorting and blackmailing me. After graduation, Lance went on to study computer science and engineering at Carnegie Mellon University. We lost touch over the years, and I have no idea what he's up to these days.

A pensive gaze sails across Callie's face. Then she says, "I know someone who can look him up, find out where he is and how we can get in touch."

"You do?" I ask, excitement swishing through my veins.

She pushes her chair away from the table and stands up. "Let me make a quick call. It's late, but she'll pick up and get right on it."

"Thanks, Callie," Ty says. "I remember how Lance came through for Cooper. He definitely has the skills to help us find out more about the Paynes, and perhaps even locate Katie."

"We need to get Lucas back, ASAP," she says. "We can't sit around waiting for somebody, anybody to do something. We have to do it ourselves."

For the first time since our boy went missing, Ty shows a hint of a smile. I think we all feel that we've turned a corner. We followed the rules and got nowhere. It's time to stir things up.

CHAPTER 52

W HEN MY MOTHER shows up the next morning
unannounced, I know right away something serious
is on her mind.

"Is everything okay with Alexis and Blake?" I ask, ushering
her inside.

"They're fine. Your father is trying to convince them that
Go-Kart racing will be fun and they should give it a shot. They
just want to know if their brother will be home by the time
school resumes next week."

Mom heads to the patio at the back of the house, and
I follow with a serving tray loaded with coffee and pastries.
Once out back, I place the tray at the center of the table and sit
under the canopy across from her. Sunlight filters through the
trees. The air carries a light, musky scent mingled with fresh
pine as we head into late April.

"What's going on, Mom?"

"Something Blake told me last night. It's a clue that could
help find Lucas."

A hundred questions burn at the tip of my tongue, but
I beat them back for fear I will miss something crucial she's
about to say. I lean in closer, my throat tightening. "Go on.

What did Blake say?"

"The poor baby," she says, choking up. "I could tell this has been eating at him since his brother disappeared. He was so afraid you would be mad at him, I had to promise I would talk to you and he shouldn't worry."

I frown. "That sounds ominous. Blake has never been afraid to talk to me about anything."

"Well, these are not ordinary circumstances, sweetie. This is heavy stuff my grandbabies are dealing with. First Liv's death and now Lucas is missing."

"Tell me, please. What did Blake say?"

"It's two separate incidents. First, he said Liv asked him and his siblings if they had a classmate by the name of Kaley Witherby. Does that name ring any bells with you?"

"No, nothing."

"Anyway, Liv kept asking them if they were sure, like it was important. All three gave her a firm no."

"Why would Liv be interested in whether some random kid was a classmate of theirs or not? It doesn't make sense."

"I know. But it gets even more peculiar. Blake told me that he and Lucas decided to spy on Katie because they didn't trust her. Apparently, Blake caught her on the phone a couple of times, whispering. He told Lucas about it. You know how he is about strangers."

Mom swallows hard and then lets out a deep, long breath before she continues. "Lucas didn't like that scenario, so he and Blake came up with the brilliant idea to steal Katie's phone to see if they could find out who she'd been talking to, why she was whispering and so secretive about it. Lucas volunteered for the assignment of searching her bag for the phone. It seems Katie caught him as he was putting it back. He didn't get to see anything."

I turn the information over in my head, trying to decipher what it could mean. My children are smarter than me. That's what it means. They immediately detected a threat and tried to neutralize it. That was my job. I failed them. Now, Lucas is paying the price for my failure. My voice is barely above a whisper when I say, "I messed up, Mom. I really stepped in it this time."

"Abbie, what are you talking about? You can't blame yourself for this."

"Why not?" I ask through the tears trickling down my face. "I saw what I wanted to see. Katie's background check came back clean. All her references checked out. I was desperate for help with the kids because I was so focused on wrapping up my Ph.D. I didn't question why Jenna was so eager to help me. But Blake and Lucas, they knew something was wrong about Katie."

People see what they want to see.

That's what Jenna had said to me that day at the café when Corinne Beal called her Maren Dinsdale. A threat was right under my nose and I didn't see it. Instead, I saw a caring, qualified, temporary caregiver for my children. So, while I was busy seeing only what I wanted to, I missed a lot.

A thousand thoughts ignite in my head at once. I must connect the dots and soon: Liv, Jenna, Katie, Corinne. It all fits somehow.

"What are you thinking, sweetie?" Mom asks. "You weren't here just now."

"I was being set up long before I ever heard of these people. Jenna played me. That miserable wretch sat in my house and lied to my face, pretended to be my friend all the while plotting to snatch my child. I don't care if the police have no evidence pointing to her. She knows something about Lucas' disappearance. Did you know Charlie has disappeared too? Nobody has seen or heard from him for days."

Mom rises from her seat, comes to stand behind my chair and wraps her arms around me. "The whole family is distraught, sick with worry," she says, her voice trembling with grief. "Your brother, Miles, has been over at the house every day since the twins were dropped off. It helps. They're afraid someone else they love and care for might disappear or die on them. They follow each other everywhere. Blake won't let his sister out of his sight and vice versa. It just breaks my heart."

A strangled sob escapes me. Mom offers soothing words and strokes my hair. I pray Blake and Alexis don't feel abandoned by their parents. At the time, it made sense that Mom and Dad should take care of them. They could keep them safe and lavish attention on them. Finding Lucas takes up every minute of every day. It wouldn't have been fair to the twins to be caught up in the middle of that.

"They can't handle any more losses," Mom says, her voice weak. "But our sorrow will soon come to an end. We'll find Lucas. Whoever took him won't get away with it."

"No. They won't. I'm going to find out who Jenna Payne really is. Her true identity is the key that unlocks the mystery."

Mom kisses me on the top of my head and returns to sitting across from me. She pours herself a cup of coffee, and one for me, too.

"Callie's here," I say. "She came in last night. Her being here sparked something. Someone from my past who could help us."

"Tell me."

"Remember Lance Carter?"

"Of course. He was that nice guy who helped you catch your high school tormentor. What does he have to do with Lucas' case?"

"He just popped into my head last night after Callie arrived. I don't know why I didn't think of him before then. The brain is a funny thing." I bite into a pastry and continue. "Anyway, Callie used her contacts to find out where Lance ended up. After Carnegie Mellon, he attended graduate school at MIT and then went to work for the Defense Intelligence Agency, Cyber Division. He now runs his own cyber security firm in Virginia."

"Wow, that's impressive," Mom says.

"Even more impressive is the fact that Callie was able to get in touch with him early this morning. She explained the situation to him and he's eager to help us, because of you and Dad."

"What do you mean?"

"He never forgot what you guys did for him, as a thank you for helping me out in high school. You know, paying his tuition for all four years he attended Carnegie Mellon."

"The stakes were pretty high in that situation, sweetie. You could have been kicked out of high school and not made it to college at all if Lance hadn't stepped in and exposed your blackmailer, and what they were up to. Paying his tuition was the least your dad and I could have done for him. I'm glad he's back in the picture."

"I also have another idea."

"Which is?"

"I want to search the Paynes' home. There might be a clue in there. Something not obvious that maybe they didn't give a second thought to."

"How are you going to get inside?" A worried shadow crosses her face.

"I don't know, yet. Maybe there's a key under a potted plant or something."

Mom gives me a skeptical gaze.

"I have no idea, but if I get caught, I'll say Jenna asked me to pick up something for her because she's stuck somewhere. I have her cell number in my phone still."

"Be extra careful, sweetie. You don't want to get caught and have the police involved. They will accuse you of hindering an investigation."

"Well, they should have thought of it first, although I can't blame them. Jenna isn't an official suspect and they have no probable cause to search her house. So, I'm just helping them out, that's all."

"You've always been a go-getter. Please be careful."

"I will."

"Oh, by the way, Grandma Naomi cut her cruise short. I had to tell her about Lucas."

"It's fine, Mom. Ty's parents will be here soon, too. I hope Lucas can feel how much we love him. He's coming back to us. I can feel it."

"I know sweetie. I know."

CHAPTER 53

TRAFFIC STRETCHED OUT for miles before them on either side of the border. Sunlight gleamed off the rear windshield of the cars in front of her, the glare making it almost impossible to see, even after she pulled down the visor to shield her eyes.

Lucas sat in the back seat, quiet as a mouse. Jenna had instructed him to behave himself, otherwise, the syringe Adrian showed him would make an appearance. It worked before and worked again this morning. Adrian sent her a text thirty minutes ago saying he had arrived in Montreal and he was waiting for her to arrive with the package. Now, all she had to do was make sure that nothing was done or said to arouse suspicion.

Lucas was her nephew and they were heading to Montreal for a wedding. She was ready with the invitation if needed, as well as a signed letter from Lucas' mother granting Jenna permission to take her son out of the country. All would be well. In a matter of minutes, they would cross into Canada.

"Why do you look so different?" she heard Lucas ask from the back seat. "You had long red hair before. Now it's short and dark. You're hiding from somebody, aren't you?"

That was the thing about Lucas, she was discovering. He

asked a lot of questions and he was getting on her nerves. Jenna thought he was doing it on purpose, but she also conceded that he was trying to make sense of what was happening. She would be understanding. Up to a point.

"I like to switch up my look, okay? Having the same style all the time is boring."

"If Adrian is your friend, why were you kissing him? Are you and Mr. Payne getting a divorce? Is Adrian going to be your new husband?"

Jenna went completely still. She held the steering wheel in a death grip, her knuckles white. Was this what she was in for? Relentless questioning from a kid who was too smart for his own good?

"Something like that," she mumbled, and let the sentence hang vague.

"When are we going back home? I miss my family."

Her patience was wearing so thin, she almost blurted out that he was never going back. But she caught herself in time. She had no way of predicting what would happen if he realized that he wouldn't be seeing the United States again for a really long time.

She fiddled with the radio until she found a station she liked. She pumped up the music in the hopes he would take the hint. They started moving again. She could see the welcome to Canada sign in the distance. They were so close.

"What's your real name?" Lucas yelled over the music.

"You know my name." She took in a deep breath and then exhaled.

"Then why did Adrian call you Mrs. Harper? I thought you were Mrs. Payne."

Jenna felt panic rising up from her chest and leaving an acidic taste in her mouth. Lucas must have eavesdropped on their conversation last night. Adrian had believed Lucas was fast asleep by nine o'clock.

He had them both fooled. This line of questioning was proof he knew way too much. She would have to power through. Keep a cool head. She couldn't afford to flip out and confirm any of his suspicions.

Only three cars were ahead of them now. Jenna was worried about Lucas. With all these questions, was he going to cause a problem, in spite of his fear of the syringe? She double-checked to make sure the car doors were locked.

"Remember what I said, Lucas." She kept her eyes peeled on the road. "You just sit back and relax when we see the border agent. If you make any trouble, you know what will happen."

He remained silent. She took it as a sign that he understood the threat. The two passports were on the passenger seat. Only one car now stood between her and the new life she envisioned.

LUCAS KNEW SHE was mad at him. He hoped if he kept asking questions that annoyed her, she would get sick of him and take him back to his family. He had no idea what she wanted to do in Canada or who he was supposed to be visiting, but he thought a long time about this. He didn't think there was any person to visit. It was just a story Adrian made up. And then the fake Mrs. Payne was kissing Adrian, even though he said they were just friends. And then there was the syringe.

Adrian said not all strangers were bad, but Lucas now believed *they* were bad strangers. Good strangers wouldn't threaten to do bad things to him to keep him quiet. They lied a lot. Lucas hated liars, too.

But he had a plan. He thought about it last night. At first, he thought he would draw a sad face emoji on the glass with his fingers or that he would write the word *help!* But that wouldn't work because it was bright and sunny outside, and warm. He would need it to be cold outside and warm inside the car. He learned about evaporation and condensation last year in fourth grade. That's when another idea popped into his head. It was something he learned when he was in kindergarten. Mrs. Payne wouldn't know what it meant, and he would have to do it fast.

Lucas positioned himself as close to the window as possible. Luckily, she didn't make a big deal about it when he decided to sit behind her. He did it on purpose. With her eyes on the road, she wouldn't be able to see him unless she looked into the rearview mirror. When she provided the passports, she would need to keep her focus on the border agent.

Mrs. Payne handed the passports to the agent. He asked her why she was heading into Montreal, and she said a wedding.

"Who is the child in the back seat?" the agent asked.

"My nephew. He's part of the wedding."

It was time for Lucas to make his move. He waved wildly at the agent and when the man transferred his attention to Lucas, he closed his hand into an "A." He placed the outstretched palm of his right hand under the left "A" hand, raised both hands and pointed to himself. The agent looked at him curiously, then shifted his gaze from Lucas to Mrs. Payne.

Lucas heard him say, "Is your nephew okay?"

Lucas placed both hands in his lap quickly. Mrs. Payne adjusted the rearview mirror. All she saw was a stone-faced Lucas.

"Yes, he's fine."

"Then why was he making weird hand gestures?"

"He's a kidder. He's always playing pranks on his siblings. I'm surprised he didn't stick out his tongue at you and make funny faces."

The agent studied the passports. Then he said, "Do you

have permission from the parents to leave the country with your nephew?"

"Of course. How could I forget the letter?" She leaned over and picked up the letter on the passenger seat.

Lucas repeated the gesture again. The agent looked at him and then just shook his head. Mrs. Payne handed the agent the letter. He looked at it briefly then returned it to her.

"Everything seems to be in order. Welcome to Montreal. Enjoy your stay."

Lucas leaned back into the seat. Tears streamed down his face. He buried his face into Mr. Snoopy, who'd been sitting beside him the whole time. The more he didn't want to cry, the sadder he felt and the more the tears came until he couldn't stop them because they were big and just poured out of his body. The border agent didn't understand sign language. Lucas was asking for help in sign language. He didn't remember everything he had learned about signing, but he remembered the important things like the sign for 'help me', saying 'hello', 'thank you', stuff like that.

"What were you trying to pull back there?" she demanded.

Lucas ignored her and just continued to weep into the bear. He missed his family, terribly. Now they were in another country and it would be harder for him to get away from Jenna and Adrian. He didn't even speak French. All the signs were in French and English. He missed talking to Blake and sharing secrets. He missed Alexis teasing him, even if she made him mad sometimes. He missed his dad always defending him. And his mom. His mom was everything. The thought that he would never see any of them again was too much. Lucas broke down into what his mother would call an epic meltdown.

CHAPTER 54

C ALLIE, TY, AND I take seats in the Mezzanine Conference room of the Boston Public Library's main branch in Copley. It's a simple space with a white conference table at the center and hard plastic swivel chairs in bright blue, green, and orange. An LCD projector screen is at the front of the room.

Nervous energy envelops the space like a dense fog. Each of us knows that this could be our last play to find Lucas. Lance Carter suggested this meeting place. He reasoned it would afford us more privacy than a café or restaurant, and an opportunity to escape the scene of the crime for a while.

When Lance steps into the room and locks the door behind him, I'm flooded with gratitude and optimism. I saunter over to welcome him with wide, open arms. He hasn't changed much since high school. He's well over six feet tall, and sports a dress shirt, and slacks. His espresso-brown skin and cognac brown eyes produce an electric presence.

I introduce him to Ty. He gives Callie a hug afterward.

"We gotta break this habit Lance," I say, taking a seat. "You coming to my rescue."

"Yeah, Lance. You're making me look bad. I'm supposed to

be the hero," Ty jokes.

"It's all good," he says, his voice smooth and composed. "I'm glad Callie called and told me what was going on. I didn't need to think twice about helping."

We're all seated and Lance doesn't waste any time tackling the problem. A good thing. Time is not on our side. He pops open his laptop and types in the password.

"Callie filled me in on some of the details," he says. "How Lucas was taken in the dead of night and disappeared without a trace, and your suspicions about Jenna and Charlie Payne. But I'd like to come at it from a different angle."

"What do you mean?" I ask.

"Let's take a run at what we don't know and start from there."

"At first we thought that someone had a grudge against the Wheelers and was using Lucas as a pawn to extort money from them," Ty says. "Then that scenario blew up in our faces when the supposed kidnapper didn't produce Lucas but took the money, anyway. Then there are custody disputes—another popular reason for kidnappings but that doesn't apply to us."

"Which leaves the really bad stuff," Callie says.

The room goes mute. We all know what she means by the *really bad stuff*. Over the past two days, my head had been swimming with disastrous possibilities. I keep them in check by sheer force of will. It will break me if I allow those thoughts to take root.

"Not necessarily," Lance says, typing something into his computer. "You suspect the Paynes aren't who they say they are. That tells me there's a possibility you would recognize their real names or something about them if they didn't assume alternative identities."

"Good point," Ty says.

"Who would want revenge on you and take your kid to

make you pay?" Lance inquires. "Because based on what I've learned so far, somebody went through a lot of trouble to set up a very elaborate plan. And these folks are patient and determined."

Callie, Ty, and I exchange uneasy glances. There's only one person we know who fits the profile Lance described. But there's a letter from the State of Connecticut collecting dust in my bedroom closet. A letter that proves this person went to his grave, years ago.

Lance continues, "This scheme was set up a year or more in advance and took meticulous planning. They found out where you live, where your kids go to school, bought a house on the same street, and got IDs that turned up legit if anyone went poking around. We're dealing with pros."

Inky, black butterflies circle the edges of my psyche, threatening to rob me of my waning sanity. Lance's computer beeps as he gazes intently at the screen. Ty slumps in his chair. A bleak shadow rolls across Callie's face. I have no rational thought or clever analysis to help me make sense of this.

Lance clears his throat. "I hate to keep piling on the troubles, but I don't think Katie Nicholson took Lucas. She was working for the person or persons who did. The real mastermind behind the plot."

"That would explain why she took off," Callie says. "She did the dirty deed and ran like hell before the cops could catch up with her."

"Which brings us back to why you're here, Lance," I interject. "The key to bringing Lucas home is to find out who Charlie and Jenna Payne are. And Katie, too. Can't you do something with facial recognition software?"

"Not if they changed their appearance in any way. There would be problems with getting an accurate match. Facial recognition technology relies on very little variance in the image to capture a match against a database. Say someone lost a lot of weight or had plastic surgery to change their nose or jawline, for example. It would make a match difficult."

"But not impossible," Ty says.

"Do you have a picture of Jenna and Charlie?"

"Just Jenna," I say. I remove my phone from my purse and scroll through the photos to find the right one and hand it to Lance. "It's not a very good photo. It's her driver's license. I took it the day Liv failed to show up for work and Jenna took the kids to school."

Lance glances at it and says, "This won't do. It's a picture of a picture, so the image quality is a problem. Plus, there's a lot going on. Check out the Rocky Mountains ghosted in the background. This will reduce the effectiveness of the technology, but I'll see what I can do."

"What other tricks do you have up your sleeve?" Ty asks. "We're running out of time. The fact that Lucas' passport was stolen is another bad sign."

"Leave it to me and my team. Charlie and Jenna Payne are the ones running out of time. They can't hide from me."

CHAPTER 55

"I WISH YOU could stay longer," I moan.

"Fashion empires don't run themselves, or so I've heard. But I'll be in New York soon and you guys can come visit me. *All* of you."

Callie is saying her goodbyes. The sleek, black luxury sedan waiting to take her to Logan Airport is parked at the curb outside the library, lights blinking, a uniformed chauffeur at the ready to open the door. Lance has already taken off, and Ty and I are about to head home.

I look up suddenly, not sure why. A thick, fluffy cloud shuttles across the clear, blue sky. I cast a lengthy gaze before redirecting my focus to Callie. A warm, gentle breeze blows, stirring stands of hair across my cheeks.

"Thank you, my friend. I can never repay you."

"Will you stop it," she admonishes.

"I mean it, Callie. For the first time since this nightmare began, I'm truly hopeful. Helping us get in touch with Lance got us to this point. He plays by a different set of rules than the investigators do, and that's a good thing in this case."

"I love you guys. Besides my parents, you and Ty and the kids are the closest thing I have to family."

"Bring it in here," Ty says, his arms open wide. We obey, not caring if we look silly to pedestrians on the busy street who may wonder why three people are huddled in a group hug in the middle of the morning on the sidewalk.

After we separate, Callie wipes a stray tear, winks at us, and finally climbs into the car. The driver shuts the door and takes his position behind the wheel. We wave as the sedan pulls away from the curb.

GRANDMA NAOMI COOPER rises to her feet and embraces me, and then Ty. At almost eighty years old, my paternal grandmother possesses the energy and *joie de vivre* of a woman thirty years younger. Her blue-gray hair is styled in a coiffed bob, highlighting her raw sienna complexion.

"How soon is my great-grandbaby coming back to us? Shelby says this Lance Carter guy is some kind of tech guru and he can track down these shady people, this Jenna woman and her husband."

"Lance is not a magician, Grandma, but we believe he can help us bring Lucas home."

She shakes her head as if searching for clarity about her great-grandson's disappearance. Grandma has a special bond with all of my kids, but it started with Lucas. She was in the hospital the day he was born and moved in with us to help me take care of him. If it weren't for her, I would have lost my mind. When Lucas arrived, I was still grappling with the aftermath of the brutal beating and horrific sexual assault that led to his conception. Combined with the stress of parenting a newborn—a role for which I was ill-prepared four months after my twentieth birthday—Grandma understood the gravity of my situation. Her patience, love, and guidance helped get me through the first few months as a new mother.

"Well, somebody better do something, and quick." Her voice spikes upward, fear and frustration wrapped in her words.

She returns to the seat she occupied when we first walked in. Ty pulls out a chair opposite her. I attempt to busy myself so I won't have to acknowledge the haunted expression on Grandma's face, nor the dread engulfing me like greedy, destructive flames.

What if Lucas comes back to us, but he's not the same? What if his ordeal leaves deep, permanent scars that cannot be overcome?

But there's nothing to occupy my hands or squash the harrowing thoughts. The kitchen is pristine, countertops gleaming, aluminum sinks clear of dishes. The tiled floor so fresh and sparkling, I could eat off it. I give up and sit next to Ty.

I draw in a long breath. "We're optimistic, Grandma. If we're right and Jenna took Lucas, we *will* find him. Once we uncover her identity and motive, he will come home."

Ty clasps my arm but says nothing.

Grandma fiddles with her multi-colored Tahitian pearl necklace. After a long pause, she says, "I pray you're right. That Jenna has him and he's being treated well."

She shifts her gaze to a drawing on the refrigerator door. Five snowmen, each one a different height with a different color scarf around its neck. Our family. Lucas painted it last Christmas. Grandma leaves her seat once more and approaches the refrigerator with reverence in her steps. She stands in front of the image and runs her fingers up, down, and across the painting, her eyelids fluttering shut as she does so.

My head spins like a top. I'm about to start sobbing.

Ty picks up on my distress and rescues me. "Grandma, Abbie and I have something we need to do. It won't take long, but if my parents come back from visiting the twins before we do, tell them we'll be home soon."

We rush to our feet, land kisses on her cheek, and express our gratitude to her. Then we bolt from the kitchen as if we were facing mortal danger.

CHAPTER 56

W E BREAK IN from the back, not the front where anyone passing by could see us. We're taking a gamble that Jenna wouldn't have bothered to set the alarm. She hadn't.

"You search downstairs and I'll head upstairs," I say to Ty, slipping on the latex gloves I had hidden in my pocket. Ty does the same. "Meet back in the kitchen to compare notes."

The layout is similar to our house. I waste no time heading upstairs to the master bedroom. I scan the room first. Pretty simple, nothing to indicate a married couple inhabited the space. The bed is neatly made up. I head for the walk-in closet and it's empty. No clothes, male or female. There's a shoebox at the top. I pull it toward me and take a peek inside. Empty. I go through every inch of the closet and find nothing, but empty space and corners.

I move to the dresser drawers, opening them one by one. Empty. It's as if no one ever occupied this room. I look under the bed in case something rolled under there, and come up empty. I head to the bathroom in the hopes that a sliver of DNA was left behind. A strand of hair in the sink, or sticking out of a hairbrush. The sink stares back at me—dry, white, flawless porcelain. The shower—dry as tree leaves in a drought—hasn't been used in a while, either.

I scurry to the remaining bedrooms, and with the exception of the first room down the hall from the master, they are empty with the same unlived-in look.

In the bedroom down from the master, a T-shirt and a pair of jeans hang in the closet. There's no dresser in this room, just a slightly messy bed and a bean bag in the corner. There are no curtains in the window.

There's no doubt in my mind that a female occupied the third room. Not because I have great powers of deductive reasoning, but because there's a perfumed lotion on the nightstand. The small dresser beckons me. I poke around inside and come up with a black sleep mask.

I amble down the stairs and enter the kitchen to find Ty seated at the table with tiny pieces of paper spread out before him.

"What's that?" I ask.

"The key to the puzzle. If we can figure out who's in this photo, we can uncover Jenna and Charlie's true identity."

I grab a chair and sidle up next to him. "It can't be that easy, Ty. For over a year, these people planned how they were going to snatch our son. Do you think they're just going to leave a big, fat clue behind so they can get caught?"

"People get careless when they're under extreme duress. They make mistakes. Mistakes that seem inconsequential at the time. But the details—that's where they mess up."

"Where did you find it?"

"In the trash. That was the only thing left in the bin."

"I found nothing upstairs. But you know what's strange?"

He looks up from his task. "We're way past strange. What is it?"

"Jenna and Charlie aren't really husband and wife. They

were just pretending to be a couple."

Shifting a piece of the ripped image into place, he says, "How do you figure?"

"They slept in separate rooms, not the master."

"Maybe they had problems in the marriage and decided to vacate the master."

"I don't think so. In such cases, one half of the couple would remain in the master. The other would move to a guest bedroom or the basement or something."

"That is strange. Yet it fits with the theory that they were sent to do a job. But by whom, and why?"

"Once we put this photo together, it may tell us," I say, picking up a small piece that looks like part of the sky.

Six painstaking minutes later, a picture emerges that sends shockwaves through my veins.

My husband and I stare at the image in stunned silence. The photo depicts a woman in her late twenties or early thirties with her arms around two little boys, identical twins who look like Lucas: Spencer and Zachary Rossdale.

CHAPTER 57

I DON'T KNOW HOW I made it home. My legs can barely support me. Somehow, I find the strength to take the stairs two at a time with Ty on my heels. Maybe it's adrenaline. I fling open our bedroom door and head straight for the walk-in closet. I pull the heavy container with our important documents inside, dumping the contents in the middle of the bed.

"I'll help you look," a slightly breathless Ty says.

After going through multiple documents, he yells, "I got it." He holds up a white envelope with a state seal and address at the top left corner.

With trembling hands, he opens it. We sit next to each other at the edge of the bed and read the letter together.

"Says the same thing it did when we first read it four years ago," Ty exclaims.

"Okay. So what does that photo mean? Why did Charlie and Jenna have it in their possession?"

"I would speculate that they're working for him, but he's dead. It says so right here." He waves the letter in the air. "Zach Rossdale was murdered by another inmate. Given his violent nature, this shouldn't have surprised us. You were his victim. The State of Connecticut wouldn't send you a letter informing

261

you of his death if he were still around."

"Grandma Naomi was with me when the letter came. I bawled for an hour straight. Everything came roaring back, all the bad memories, the attack, testifying against him in court." I rub my eyes and expel a deep, long breath, then continue. "Those eyes, Ty. The way he would look at me with those ice-cold, blue eyes. They terrified me. I think he would have killed me if he had the chance to get near me, prison be damned. That's how much he loathed me. His life got shredded to bits and all he could do was blame me. Not his own actions."

Ty rubs my shoulders. "I know, Cooper. I remember every excruciating detail, too. It's obvious who the woman in the photo is, although we've never laid eyes on her before."

"Right. His mother. We have to let Lance know about the photo and the backstory. It could help speed things along."

My cell phone vibrates. I grab it from my purse and answer.

"Hello." I draw in a stunned breath as I listen to the caller. Chills spiral down my spine. I want to run, but my body has turned into a petrified block of ice.

"Cooper, what's wrong?" An alarmed Ty, his body tense, looks at me, his eyes bulging with fright.

I say nothing. I manage to nod at my caller, who can't see me, though it seems oxygen is fleeing my brain. I hang up once he's finished speaking.

"Who was that?"

The bedroom seems to be spinning in slow motion. The words leave my lips in slow, painful drips.

"That was Detective Flores."

Panic seeps into his hazel eyes. His body goes rigid, as if preparing for a blow.

"They received a call from the Massachusetts State Police."

"And?" his tone is fraught with dread.

"The state police received a call from a border agent. The U.S.-Canada border near Derby, Vermont."

I place my hand over my mouth as tears form at the corners of my eyes and start to trickle down my cheeks.

"What happened to our boy, Cooper?" he asks, his voice catching.

After several hiccups, I wipe my tears and pull myself together.

"The agent said that around seven thirty this morning, a woman with a little boy about Lucas' age came through his line. The woman said the boy was her nephew and she had a signed letter from the mother granting permission to take him out of the country to attend a wedding."

Ty takes a deep, loud breath. "Go on."

"The agent said all the documentation looked to be in order but then something strange happened. The boy kept making these weird gestures with his hands, a sign of some sort."

I grab Ty's hand, and squeeze, to gather my courage to get the rest of the story out. "The woman told the agent the boy was just goofing off, being silly, that he does stuff like that all the time. He let them go. But he said the boy looked sad and the sign, he couldn't get it out of his head. So, he asked one of his colleagues if they've ever seen that sign before and what it means."

Ty's spine jerks upright. "What did the colleague say?"

"His colleague told him that her niece is deaf. All the close family members had to learn Sign language."

He bites down hard on a clenched fist to suppress a scream.

I force myself to continue. "The gesture the boy made is Sign language for *Help me*."

Ty sniffles, then asks, "Did the agent remember the name of the woman in the car and the little boy? He saw the documents."

"He remembered it clearly. The names on the passports the agent looked at were Brynn Harper and Lucas Jason Rambally."

CHAPTER 58

A FEW HOURS LATER, the Gulfstream G650 takes off from Hanscom Airforce Base in Bedford. Everything is happening fast, and my head hasn't stopped spinning. Christian offered up the Wheeler jet once we looped him in on the recent events. Detectives Flores and Corwin have been in contact with the Service de Police de la Ville de Montréal, and are on their way. We were told in no uncertain terms that this was official police business, and that we couldn't interfere in any way.

Translation: we can't meet with their Canadian counterparts, or be privy to any conversations, or be part of any moves made to find Lucas. But they can't stop us from entering Canada. We intend to be close by when the call comes in that Lucas has been found, safe and sound.

After I hold my baby in my arms, I want to witness Jenna, a.k.a. Brynn Harper, being carted off to jail in handcuffs.

Explosive thoughts race through my mind. Thoughts about what kind of condition we'll find Lucas in, what Brynn has said to him, where she plans to take him, and whether she has revealed her real name, not that it would mean anything to Lucas. Canada may not be her final destination. And that's the scariest thought of all.

I try to empty my head of such distressing deliberations by sizing up my surroundings. The plush, spacious interior designed for both business and pleasure, a stored table that folds out into a conference room table, beige leather chairs that recline almost to the floor, and high-speed internet access.

Zone two, where Ty and I are seated, is what would be considered the living room area, for relaxation. We're seated on a comfortable divan built for three, with a large plasma TV across from us. I don't think we'll be watching any movies or TV shows or doing any relaxing on this trip. The plane is also outfitted with a fully functioning kitchen, espresso machine, dining area, and private bedroom with a shower.

We have one pilot, and one flight attendant—Stephanie, a pretty brunette in her mid-thirties with a dazzlingly white smile and dimples—on board. After we've reached a comfortable cruising altitude, she approaches us and offers coffee and some delicious-looking snacks and pastries. I'm too wound up to eat snacks, and ask for an espresso instead.

After Stephanie busies herself with her tasks, I say to Ty, "I don't know anyone named Brynn Harper, but my mind won't let it go."

"How do you mean?"

"I've heard the name Brynn before, but I can't remember when or where, or why I think I've heard it before."

"The mind is a tricky organ," he says. "You could have heard it in a movie or maybe it's the name of some actress or a character in a book you read. Hearing it now could have triggered that memory."

I ponder his words. I know the name is important. I just don't know why it is. I decided to do a quick internet search and see what comes up.

I tap the search engine icon on my phone and type in

Brynn Harper. The top entry is the social media profile of a product manager for a high-end retailer, then a TV actress and stories and photos of her wedding. I scroll through the entire first page search results and nothing turns up. I sigh.

"No luck?" Ty takes a sip of his coffee then places the mug on the table.

"I'll search the second page, although it's unlikely I'll find anything. We have a couple of hours to kill before this flight lands. I may as well make use of the time."

I click to the second page and scroll through. I find a radio DJ in the UK, a lifestyle blogger, and a plethora of other links to information that has nothing to do with the search term I entered.

"What's the use?" I hold up the phone in a gesture of defeat. "I'll ping Lance. I'm sure he would have much better luck than me."

"I'm sure he will, Cooper. Don't stress out. We need to be cool and calm when we get Lucas."

"I know," I say, leaning into his chest.

I'm about to exit the search when for some inexplicable reason, I decide to look at one more page of results. A link for the University of Michigan Woodford Illustration Award pops up. I tap the link with a trembling index finger.

"I may have found something." I draw the phone to his line of vision so we can view the results together.

WOODFORD ILLUSTRATION AWARD WINNERS ANNOUNCED, the headline screams.

"What does this have to do with Brynn Harper?" Ty rubs the back of his neck as if attempting to drive out some troublesome mass that had formed there.

"Jenna told the kids she was a children's book illustrator. Jenna Payne may not have been an illustrator, but what if Brynn Harper is?"

"So she superimposed pieces of her true identity onto the fake one she was living as our neighbor?"

"Precisely."

"That gets me thinking about something Brynn said while pretending to be Jenna. I think she gave us a clue about her intentions and we missed it."

"What do you mean?"

Stephanie arrives with my espresso, the aroma lingering in the space. I inhale deeply, thank her, and have a sip.

Ty says, "Jenna told us that story about running into her father at the airport on a field trip to Montreal, remember?"

As if it were waiting for this prompt, my brain flashes back to the scene in the kitchen. It was after Lucas was taken and we interrogated Jenna about Katie. I remember it clearly. She had also mentioned that Katie worked for a Canadian family who went back home and that's why she needed a job.

"I can't believe we missed it," I say, shaking my head.

"Missed what?"

"She was dropping clues left and right. We missed them all."

"No way we could have known that, Cooper. Let's read this article and see if it brings anything to light."

The opening paragraph was about the winners being announced, a second paragraph about the prestige of the contest and the history, and then a breakdown of the winners by category. First up, the student category. I click on the link, which takes me to a new page where a large cover illustration appears, obviously for a children's book. Before I can take a moment to absorb the beauty of the cover, my eyes, as if instructed to do so, look downward from the image.

The name of the artist is Brynn Rossdale.

CHAPTER 59

M Y STOMACH GOES cold as if a thousand snowballs were dropped inside me.

"Crap!" Ty yells, drawing Stephanie's attention.

She appeared out of thin air, like a genie. "Is everything okay? Do you need anything?"

"Sorry, I didn't mean to alarm you," he says. "We're good."

Stephanie returns to whatever she was doing. I fix Ty with a firm, somber gaze. "We have our motive. *Revenge.*"

We stay silent for long seconds as the jet powers through the sky. I peer out the window. Fat clouds rush by in the late afternoon sky.

"She blames me for what happened." I continue to focus on the window. "She thinks it's my fault she lost both her brothers. She took Lucas to get back at me, at us. There's no other explanation."

"Maybe," Ty says.

I turn away from the window. "What do you mean?"

"It could be that Canada is where she made her home. It's not unheard of for a person to move to another country and start over after a tragedy. Revenge may have been her motive initially, but knowing what we do now, perhaps it's not that simple. Not that it matters. She needs to pay for what she did"

I shake my head slowly, absorbing his words. "It would explain why she flipped out when I said Lucas' biological father was dead and good riddance. She knew I was talking about her brother." I rub my temples to ward off a monster tension headache. Ty touches my forehead to see if I have a fever.

"Anyway," I continue, "the way she looked at Lucas when she first laid eyes on him, her reaction was genuine. I could see the longing in her eyes, how amazed she was, as if she couldn't believe she was meeting him in the flesh."

"It all fits. Now all we have to do is get Lucas back."

I feel better knowing it was her," Ty says. "She won't harm him."

An awful thought drops into my head like a rock. "Ty, what if Brynn tells Lucas the truth? If she went through all this trouble to grab him, it stands to reason she would explain her motive. What better way to explain away what she did than to tell him she's his aunt?"

Before Ty could formulate a response, my phone rings. It's Lance. I need time to collect my bearings, so I ask Ty to take the call.

"Ty here," he says then pauses. "Lance, hold on a minute." He puts the phone on speaker, and amps up the volume so I can hear. "Go ahead."

"Listen, one of my guys was able to pull up a positive ID on Jenna Payne. You and Abbie were right. Jenna Payne was an alias. Her real name is—"

"Brynn Rossdale Harper," Ty finishes.

"How do you know that?" Lance asks, his tone laced with surprise.

So much has happened in the past few hours that we didn't even have a chance to call Lance and update him.

"State police got a call from Canadian immigration, border patrol."

Ty explains to Lance what occurred over the last few hours.

"That's fantastic news, man. You're getting your boy back. I'll send you an encrypted file with everything we found on Brynn, anyway. The additional information could come in handy. But I may also have a lead on Charlie Payne."

Ty turns to me, wide-eyed. "Go ahead. Cooper is right next to me. You may have to yell a little. We're on a plane."

"You were also right about him. He was using an alias. He could be the one who planned and executed the kidnap for ransom scheme."

"Lance, are you sure?" Ty asks, his tone hopeful.

"Let me look into a few more things to get you as complete a picture as possible. But I'm ninety-five percent sure."

"Can you tell us anything about this guy?"

"Looks like he served time in prison."

CHAPTER 60

I 'M NOT GOING, and you can't make me." Lucas folded his arms, his stare determined.

"Yes, you are going. We talked about this already."

"I don't like you, and I don't like Adrian. You're both mean. And liars. You're mean liars."

At least he stopped calling her Mrs. Payne. She couldn't stand the stupid alias anymore. It had served its purpose, and after that, she had begun to resent it. Now that they were about to take off for Australia, she didn't see the need to stick to it, so she told Lucas to call her Brynn. She would explain things to him later. The whole story and the truth behind who he was to her. She was sure his parents wouldn't have bothered to tell him. The boy deserved to know the truth. Once he was informed, then maybe he would stop hating her. For now, she would tolerate his tantrums and mouthing off.

She and Adrian decided to pack light. Two large suitcases and two pieces of carry-on luggage were all they needed. Brynn and Lucas were in the living room of an apartment in downtown Montreal, thanks to Adrian's friend who was away on business. Adrian was in the shower, and once he was dressed, they'd be good to go. They were taking a nine-thirty p.m. flight out of Montreal-Pierre Elliott Trudeau International Airport to Sydney. They chose Australia because it was far away, and close to Asia. Adrian's firm had a large international practice based in Hong Kong, and the minute an opening became available, they would move.

"You're gonna get in big trouble," Lucas says, sitting on the arm of the sofa. "My mom and dad are coming to get me and you're going to jail."

Brynn's temper flared. "And what do you know about jail?"

"I know people who do bad things go to jail. You did a bad thing. You and Adrian."

She inched closer to him, deciding that reasoning with him might work. She said, "I'll explain everything. There's reason for all of this."

"What reason?" he asked, his gaze dark. "I don't want to go with you and Adrian, but you said I had to. Plus, you lie a lot, so why should I believe you?"

She'd had it. The stress of trying to leave the country without getting caught, all of the plotting and scheming of the past year, Charlie's disappearance, the feeling that nine-thirty was taking too long to show up, all of it was pressing down on her like an overburdened tree branch. She was exhausted, plain and simple, and Lucas was exacerbating the situation with his constant questions and insults. She just couldn't take it anymore. She got right up into his face and looked him square in the eyes.

"Listen, you're coming with us whether you like it or not. You're not going to see your parents for a long while. Get used to it," she seethed. "I'm not here to hurt you, and neither is Adrian. I told you I would explain everything, and I will. But if I hear any more insults coming out of your mouth or you keep giving me a hard time, I swear I will knock you out with the drug in that syringe, and you may never wake up."

His eyes went wide and the tears started snaking down his cheeks. His breathing was hard and rapid. Then his little body started shaking. Loud, gut-wrenching sobs followed as he stared at her through blinding tears, as if he couldn't believe anyone could be that cruel.

She wanted to cry too. She wanted Lucas to like her, yet she just threatened him— a poor defenseless child. What if she wasn't cut out to be the nurturing type? She wanted to console him, but decided it was a bad idea. It was clear Lucas didn't trust her. He would reject any attempt on her part to comfort him.

A fireball of pain and regret sliced through Brynn. Rejected by her father when she was a little girl, when he abandoned the family, and then again as a teenager when he pretended he didn't know her during that airport run-in. Her mother abandoned her by dying. Her brothers were also dead. This little boy was all she had left, and the thought that he would reject her, too, was too much to bear.

But she had come too far to give up now, no matter how emotionally drained she was. She had to see things through to the end. They were going to get on that plane, all three of them, and start a new life on the other side of the world. That's how it was going to be and too bad for Lucas. He would get with the program, eventually. Eight years. That's all she would get, and once Lucas turned eighteen, he could do whatever he wanted.

For now, she was just borrowing him.

CHAPTER 61

M Y PHONE LIGHTS up from its current spot on the bed of a downtown Montreal hotel room. I look at the screen. It's Detective Flores. Yet, instead of snatching the phone to get answers, I'm overcome with paralysis by analysis. Maybe he's calling with terrible news. Brynn managed to make it out of the country with my child, and now we're looking at an international manhunt—well, womanhunt—that could take months or years.

There are over one hundred and fifty-four countries on this planet we call home. Seven continents, five oceans. She could disappear anywhere with Lucas. Or worse, what if he's hurt? What if, like her criminal brother, she has psychopathic tendencies and decided to off Lucas just to get back at me? Is there a psychopath gene that can be inherited? I'm no geneticist, but—

"Cooper, pick up the phone," Ty says impatiently, jolting me out of my morbid thoughts.

I obey and click the speaker button so we can both hear whatever news the detective is about to deliver, together.

"Hello."

"Abbie, it's Gabe Flores. Where are you?"

"At a hotel in downtown Montreal. Why?"

"We got a lead on Lucas' whereabouts."

A primal gasp escapes me. I land on the bed like a large boulder, and hand over the phone to Ty. My hands can't stop shaking. He sits next to me and holds up the phone with steady hands. He's breathing hard.

"Go on, detective. Ty is with me. Where is our son?"

"Cameras captured Brynn Harper inside a convenience store an hour ago. We were able to track her to an apartment building in downtown Montreal."

"Where exactly? Was Lucas with her when she pulled up for gas? Just tell us where she is." My speech is rushed as excitement builds up in my bones. I scuttle to my feet, pulling Ty along with me.

"We have every reason to be optimistic, but we have to do this by the book. You and your husband can't be in the apartment when this goes down, if it's the right apartment."

"We're Lucas' parents and he needs us," I shoot back.

A car door slams in the background, then the detective says, "I understand, Abbie. But we don't know what kind of situation we're dealing with. Not, yet. She could be armed. She could have accomplices. The situation could get dangerous. I need you and Dr. Rambally to stay put until you hear from me or Detective Corwin."

I take in a deep, long breath and expel it in short bursts. "Please, Detective Flores. You don't know the hell we've been living. Lucas is terrified. It's not fair to him to prolong his terror by keeping us away from him any longer than necessary."

A pause. I can practically see his thoughts spinning like a top, trying to come up with a compromise that will work for all parties.

"I'm sorry, Abbie. It has to be this way. Once we have

Lucas, we'll let you know. I promise."

He hangs up. I kick the foot of the bed in frustration, and then yelp in pain from the impact. "He won't give up the location, Ty. Can you believe this nonsense?"

"I know, Cooper. I'm right there with you. I wish there was something we could do in the meantime."

"There is," I say, a smile tugging at the corners of my mouth. I flop down on the bed once more and extend my hand to get the phone from Ty. "Detective Flores wouldn't follow the rules if it were his child missing, and neither should we."

"Meaning?" Ty asks, eyeing me with trepidation.

"I'm calling Lance. See if he can hack into their system or track them or something. I don't know how he works his magic, but we know enough to give him something to go on."

Forty-five minutes later, Lance pings me back. "I had to call in a few favors. I'll spare you the details, but one of the guys on my team got the license plate number of the Chevy Brynn rented, the car she used to cross into Canada. We picked up a GPS signal. I can tell you exactly where the car is."

CHAPTER 62

H URRY UP, ADRIAN. We have to get out of here, now."
Lucas noticed how nervous and upset Brynn was.
She was looking through her bag for something, and kept
muttering to herself. Adrian had brought two suitcases to the
living room and said they would be leaving soon, but that was
a while ago. Maybe that's why Brynn was upset. Lucas thought
the longer it took for them to leave the apartment, the better it
was for him.

All afternoon, he tried to think of a plan to escape, but he
couldn't think of anything. He went to the bathroom earlier
and there was a window, but it was too high up. If he tried
to escape that way, he would fall down and break his neck or
something awful like that. He didn't know the neighbors so he
couldn't ask for help. Adrian and Brynn kept the apartment
door locked, and they were always watching him. Adrian had
even followed him to the bathroom, waiting just outside the
door and talking to Lucas the whole time.

Lucas clutched his teddy bear. He didn't care if it made
him look like a big baby. Mr. Snoopy kept him company and
made him think of home. Sometimes Alexis would invite Mr.
Snoopy to her tea parties. Blake thought Alexis was getting too

old for tea parties, but Lucas didn't mind. He liked seeing his sister smile.

"Adrian!" Brynn yelled, startling Lucas.

When Adrian came into the living room with a backpack and a shoulder bag, he parked on the floor, Lucas knew it was over.

"Checking to make sure we have everything we need and we're not forgetting anything," he said.

"If anything is missing, we will replace it when we get to Australia. Now load up the car. We can't miss our flight."

Lucas focused hard on a colorful mat hanging from the wall, but the tears rolled down his face, anyway. This was it. They would go to the airport, board a plane headed for Australia, and his parents, brother and sister and grandparents wouldn't know where he went.

He hiccupped air, and that got both Adrian and Brynn's attention.

"What's wrong," Adrian asked. "Are you hurt?"

"I want to go home," he said, softly. "I don't want to go to Australia with you. I won't tell on you. I promise. I just want to go home."

More tears flowed down his face, followed by more hiccups, and soon, Lucas couldn't catch his breath.

"Get him some water," Brynn yelled to Adrian. "Hurry."

Adrian took off for the kitchen and Brynn knelt down in front of Lucas, who sat on the sofa.

"Breathe, Lucas. You're going to make yourself sick. Throwing a temper tantrum isn't going to change anything. Just calm down."

He took in several big gulps of air, and soon, he could breathe again. Lucas wished it were Adrian kneeling in front of him instead of Brynn. He would have kicked Adrian hard so he would get mad and it would cause a delay. But his dad had taught him and Blake that it was not okay to hit a lady.

Adrian came back from the kitchen and handed Lucas a glass of water. He was about to take a sip when there was a knock at the door.

Adrian and Brynn froze. Then Adrian made a sign to Brynn. She pulled Lucas off the sofa, spilling some of the water, and told him to be quiet. She dragged him into the kitchen.

"Who is it?" Adrian asked in a deep, loud voice.

"Maintenance. You reported a problem with the smoke detectors last week. Sorry it took so long to come have a look."

The person answered in English. That was strange. Lucas thought they mostly spoke French in Montreal. And then Brynn's eyes went wide and she screamed.

"Adrian, don't open the door!"

But it was too late.

CHAPTER 63

EVERYTHING HAPPENED SO fast that Lucas could barely keep up. A bunch of people came into the apartment. There was a lot of yelling and footsteps and doors being opened and closed. One guy told Adrian he was the police and to put his hands up. A lady said that they had a search warrant for the apartment and they believed a child had been kidnapped and was staying here.

Lucas breathed hard and fast. He squeezed his bear tight. The police were here. Good. Finally, he would go home and he wouldn't have to go to Australia. He tried to wrestle free from Brynn, but she locked his arm in place. It hurt. They were huddled under a square table, with a thick, long tablecloth covering all four sides, so no one could see in or out.

Lucas wanted to scream, but by the time the scream left his throat, Brynn had clamped her hand over his mouth, silencing him.

"Don't say a word and don't move a muscle," she whispered.

The tears gushed from Lucas. Brynn kept her hand clamped over his mouth and his arm hurt where she pinned it down.

"I need to see the warrant," Lucas heard Adrian say. "You obviously have the wrong apartment. This place belongs to my friend Paul, who's away on business in Hong Kong. He doesn't have kids."

A brief pause followed. Then one of the men said, "Search the bedrooms, bathroom and every closet you can find. Look for open windows, fire escapes, and alternate exits."

Then people started whispering in a language Lucas didn't understand. It sounded like French, but he wasn't sure.

He twisted and tried to wiggle free. His hand ached from the pressure Brynn was applying. He couldn't breathe in that tiny space under the table. He was sitting upright, with his head rubbing up against the roof of the table. His neck ached. He couldn't see Brynn. His back was to her. By Lucas' estimation, she was probably curled up into a ball. Otherwise, she wouldn't fit and her legs would stick out from under the table. Then they would be caught.

Maybe that's it, he thought. If he could put up enough of a fight, Brynn would get uncomfortable and the movement would cause one of the police officers to come to the kitchen to see what was going on.

Lucas didn't have to wait long. Footsteps approached the kitchen. They sounded like heavy boots. He strained to pull away from Brynn. She clamped down harder and applied even more pressure to his mouth. The pressure was so intense that Lucas couldn't move his mouth, even one inch to try and bite her so she would release her grip.

The heavy footsteps moved around the kitchen. The refrigerator door was opened and then shut. Cabinets were opened and closed. Then under the sink.

The footsteps drew closer to the table. Closer and closer until Lucas could make out the faint outline of legs, and pants and boots. The person stood there for what seemed like forever. Then he started to move away.

"All clear in here," he said.

Lucas' heart thundered in his chest. He had to try. He had to try and get the attention of the officer. He made a groaning noise. The footsteps stopped. There was a silent pause, then the footsteps started moving again. Lucas tried once more, with as much strength as he could muster which wasn't a lot. He moved his head from side to side, forcing Brynn to release her grip just a tiny bit—but it was enough.

Lucas bit down as hard as he could. She yelped in pain and removed her hand quickly. In a split second, before she could place her other hand over his mouth again, Lucas screamed his lungs out. An army of footsteps and murmurs came barreling into the kitchen. They stopped at the table.

"Who's there?" a voice asked

Lucas sat still. He knew it was only a matter of time before the tablecloth was removed and their hiding place discovered.

He watched as the tablecloth was slowly lifted until it was completely removed.

"Hello, Lucas," a man said.

He peered down at Lucas. He wasn't wearing a police uniform and he had dark hair and dark eyes. He smiled at Lucas. It didn't matter how the man knew his name. Lucas had a feeling this man would take him to his parents.

CHAPTER 64

TY AND I are parked in a rental car, sandwiched between an SUV and a BMW sedan outside a modern apartment complex downtown Montreal. The building sits between Saint-Denis and Saint-Laurent streets—one block south of the famous, bustling Sainte-Catherine Street.

We're prepared to wait as long as it takes to hear from either Flores or Corwin, to see them walk out of the building with Lucas. But the waiting is killing me—death by a thousand cuts. My emotions oscillate between dizzying fear and uncontrollable excitement.

"Waiting sucks," Ty offers, adjusting the side view mirror. "But in this case, it could be a good sign. I bet they're searching the apartment, asking questions, and so on. Any minute now, one of the detectives will call to say they have Lucas."

"I hope you're right. I don't know how much more stress I can take."

"There's one other thing, Cooper. Something we need to be prepared for."

"What are you talking about?"

"They may insist that Lucas be taken to a hospital to be checked out."

"Checked out for what?"

"Injuries or trauma of any kind."

I gape at Ty, floundering for words as I digest this piece of information. "But why would they do that? Do you think Brynn would harm Lucas?"

"Calm down, Cooper. It's protocol from what I understand. In the early years of my residency, we had a missing child case. Luckily the girl was found, but she was brought in to be checked out."

My mind is still grappling with the idea that Lucas could suffer additional trauma when I hear a siren wailing in the distance, behind us.

Ty hears it, too and turns. The sound grows louder, closer. Soon, the flashing lights of an ambulance come into view. The emergency vehicle stops directly across the street from the apartment building.

Panic seizes me. Before I have a chance to verbalize my thoughts, Ty stops me in my tracks.

"Don't assume the worst. This may not have anything to do with Lucas. If it did, the detectives would have called us."

Uniformed EMTs exit the ambulance, two of them carrying a stretcher. A third holds her hand up like a traffic cop, as they cross the street, trying not to get hit by oncoming traffic. They make it safely across the street, enter the building and disappear inside.

My phone rings. I jerk back into my seat, startled. It's Detective Corwin, this time. "It's Corwin," I say to Ty, as if he can't see the screen, sitting in the middle of the console.

"Should I get it?"

My head dips in a quick nod.

"Did you find Lucas. Is he okay?" Ty asks, without preamble, his speech rushed and tense. He holds the phone away from his ear so we can both hear the detective.

Corwin sounds drained when he says, "Meet us at Montreal Children's Hospital. It's part of the McGill University Health Center complex. Lucas—"

Ty didn't wait to hear the rest of the sentence. He hangs up on the detective, puts the car into gear and guns the engine, almost plowing into the car parked in front of us when he floors it without thinking. After performing a three-point turn, he peels out of the parking space.

My shaky hands fumble with the GPS as I attempt to map our route.

CHAPTER 65

W E BARREL INTO the ER of Montreal Children's Hospital, out of breath, our eyes wild, looking for signs of Lucas or Detective Corwin or Flores. We ignore the bustle of the place—doctors and nurses in scrubs passing by, patients in wheelchairs, doctors being paged by the intercom, kids in the waiting area with various injuries and ailments, and even the smell of antiseptic. My eyes are peeled on the nurse behind the glass at reception.

Ty catches his breath first. "My son was admitted here. My wife and I—"

"Abbie, Ty, this way."

We whip our heads around at the same time, and see Detective Flores down the hall, gesturing to us. We rush toward him and practically tackle him to the ground.

"Where's Lucas. Is he okay?" I ask.

"He's fine. He's okay. At least outwardly."

I almost sag against Ty. I cover my mouth with my hands to suppress a sob.

"We want to see him," Ty says. "We're not waiting for him to be examined."

"When we saw the ambulance pull up across the street

287

from the building, we feared the worst," I say. "We thought Jenna hurt Lucas. When Detective Corwin said to meet him here, we almost lost it."

Flores doesn't respond to our comments. Instead, he says, "He's waiting for you in an exam room."

With quick, purposeful strides, we walk down a long hallway, passing hospital personnel, a young teenager being wheeled on a bed, and an orderly using the hand sanitizer dispenser clipped to the wall. The sound of someone coughing up a lung is like wings under my feet. I can't wait to see my boy and get him out of here.

Flores gently knocks on the door of exam room six. I don't wait for a response and push the door open. When I step into the room, the scene before me leaves my heart stuck in my throat. Lucas sits ramrod straight at the edge of the bed with Mr. Snoopy firmly in his grasp, his legs dangling, almost touching the floor.

"Me and Mr. Snoopy have been waiting for you," he says. "Mr. Snoopy was scared you wouldn't come get us in time, but I told him not to worry, you would find us."

In a flash, I'm beside him and pull him into a bear hug, tears of joy flowing down my cheeks. I only slacken my grip when I hear his muffled voice which may be an indication I'm in danger of cutting off his air supply. I ease up, but only a little. I continue to embrace him, gently rocking him. He loved that when he was little. I don't want to let go or think about what he's been through, what he's seen and heard. There will be time for that later. Right now, I just want to hold my little boy, so he feels safe once again.

"Come on, Cooper, I want in, too." Ty's voice spikes up a notch as he stands in front of us.

I reluctantly release Lucas, get to my feet and wipe my tears with the back of my hand. Ty replaces me by scooping him up. Lucas wraps his arms around his father's neck and buries his head in his shoulders. They don't speak either. Words will take too much effort.

I cast a glance around the room for the first time and notice Detective Flores is missing. I could have sworn there was someone sitting in a chair when I came into the room. Maybe a volunteer who sat with Lucas for a while, but I can't be sure. My attention was elsewhere.

Ty sets Lucas down on the bed. We each pull up a chair in front of him.

"Does anything hurt?" Ty asks. "Any cuts or bruises we should know about?"

"No."

"Are you sure?" Ty holds up three fingers and asks, "How many fingers do you see?"

"Three."

"Good." He holds up his index finger and asks Lucas to follow the movement with his eyes.

Lucas does. Then Ty says, "Did the doctor come in to see you yet?"

He shakes his head.

"Okay. I don't want to get in the way. They should be here soon. The staff here just wants to make sure there are no issues. After that, we're going home."

Lucas cracks a smile. I stroke his head. When we get home, we'll take him to see his regular pediatrician, unpack his ordeal and any psychological trauma that may have occurred as a result. For now, we're only interested in restoring order to his world.

A somber expression clouds his face. He asks, "Is Brynn going to die?"

"What?" His father and I ask in unison.

"Brynn. She cut her wrists. She was bleeding a lot."

CHAPTER 66

THE NEWS THAT Brynn Harper tried to take her life in front of my son has me enraged. It was shocking enough to hear Lucas ask if she would die, but when we demanded answers and Detectives Flores and Corwin sat down to tell us the story, we were floored.

Things turned ugly when Brynn grabbed a knife before detectives had a chance to handcuff her, and threatened to slash her wrists. While they were trying to talk her down, she pretended to consider the idea and did it anyway.

Lucas saw all of this.

Unfortunately, Brynn survived and was admitted to the McGill University Health Center in the same complex. Armed officers stand guard outside her hospital room. Flores and Corwin objected vehemently, but I insisted they should take me to see her. I have to face Brynn Rossdale Harper one last time. I promised the detectives that I won't stick a pillow over her face during my visit.

She's asleep, looking fragile and helpless. An IV bag stands off to the side, at the head of the bed. Seeing her like this stirs my compassion. It can't be easy living with a botched suicide attempt, and staring down the barrel of a lengthy prison sentence. Then I remember whom I'm dealing with. A scheming, lying, diabolical sociopath of a woman.

"Wake up, Brynn," I say, shaking her leg. "We have things to discuss."

She groans, then her eyes flutter open. It takes her a moment to focus. "What do you want?" she asks, groggily, the hostility in her tone unmistakable.

"Just some parting words to remember me by." I stand at the foot of the bed.

"I have nothing to say to you," she says, sleepily.

"You're wrong. We have plenty to talk about."

Her skin has taken on a pale, gray pallor, her hair a matted mess.

"So, this was all about revenge? You blame me for what happened to your brothers?"

She matches my cold stare with a defiant one of her own but doesn't answer.

"I asked you a question, Brynn. You terrorized my child, and I want to know why."

She winces, as if offended by my use of the word terrorized. It's the truth, no matter how ugly.

"You have some nerve accusing me of terrorizing Lucas. I would never do that to him. But what you did to my family was unforgiveable. My mother died of a broken heart because of you," she says, jabbing a finger in my direction. "Spencer and Zach are gone because of you."

I take a deep, tight breath. All the anger, and heartache and stress of the past four days swell like a wave gathering momentum before it crashes into the shoreline.

"I won't dignify that ridiculous outburst with a response. Zach was a murdering psychopath. How many lives did he destroy, Brynn? He left me for dead. And almost got away with it. With all of his crimes. Why aren't you blaming him?"

Hot, anguished tears burn at the back of my eyes. Not here, not now, not in front of her. If she wants to be cold, detached, and pretend her criminally insane brother was a saint, I will handle it.

Her eyes shoot daggers at me, the hatred reflected in them so intense, it feels as if they're slicing through me.

I swat away those feelings. I'm not backing down and neither will she.

"It doesn't matter what you say. You took everything from me and went on with your life, didn't you Abbie? You got married, had children. Both your parents are alive, doting grandparents to your kids. You have a large extended family. People who love and care about you. Your career is about to take off too, isn't it?"

I'm not sure what my response is supposed to be, but she looks like she's expecting one. I'll wait her out.

Then she yells, "What did I get, Abbie? Nothing! You're a selfish woman. You have it all. I just wanted to get to know my nephew, the only family I have left, but you couldn't stand the idea of sharing him."

"You snatched my child from his bed in the middle of the night and planned to take him to another continent," I shriek. "He's a little boy. You didn't stop to think how that would impact him, or his family. You wanted revenge. That's all you cared about. Who's the selfish one, Brynn?"

A diabolical smile plays on the corners of her mouth. "You think you've won, don't you? You think you're so smart, that you have it all figured out." She lets out a demented laugh as she adjusts the setting of the bed by hitting a side button. "You don't know anything. In fact, I feel sorry for you. Because once he finds out what happened, he's going to come after you again. And this time, he won't stop until you're finished."

CHAPTER 67

————◦○◦————

"W HAT DO YOU think she meant by *He will come after me again and won't stop until I'm finished?* There was a vindictive air about her when she said it."

"Maybe she's talking about Charlie or whatever his real name is. There could be another phase to their plan, a contingency."

"I don't think so. Brynn and Charlie weren't close. They were two people who, for their own reasons, decided to work together. I still don't understand why. The way I see it, she didn't need Charlie."

Lucas is fast asleep on the divan that pulls out into a sleep bed. Not even the sound of the jet's engines was enough to keep him awake. The cabin is quiet. Ty and I sit across from a slumbering Lucas. Poor kid. He hasn't mentioned what happened except to say that they traveled by car and neither Brynn nor Adrian hurt him.

The minute we were airborne, I sent a group text to family and close friends: *Lucas is on his way home.* Our phones blew up after that. I mostly ignored the messages. Ty answered a few and then we decided it would all have to wait until we get home.

"That's just it, Cooper. Charlie and Brynn were a means to an end for the mastermind behind this whole thing. Brynn

293

confirmed it didn't begin and end with her and Charlie when she told you *he* would come after you once he heard how things went down. Brynn doesn't seem to care where Charlie is."

"Because she had her own plans that didn't involve him."

"Correct."

I begin to twirl Mr. Snoopy, who has been sitting on my lap since Lucas drifted off to sleep. He told me to keep him for Alexis, Mr. Snoopy's new rightful owner. Once Lucas was on his way home, he didn't need the bear to keep him company anymore.

"But it begs the question. Why Charlie?" I say. "Brynn is married. She could have easily used her real husband. We don't know him. So why go through all the trouble of pretending that she and Charlie were a married couple?"

"It may have been easier to use Brynn and Charlie, for whatever reason. Maybe Brynn's husband wasn't available to work that part of the plan, but Charlie was. Everybody had their role to play in this elaborate scheme."

I mull over the explanation. As I do, one of the paw pads on the bear catches my attention. Mr. Snoopy is a dark brown bear with paw pads that are leather, and beige in color. A large one in the center and three smaller ones. The one in the center looks off.

"What's wrong?" Ty asks.

I frown. "The paw at the center. The stitching is weird."

"What do you mean?" He edges closer to get a look.

I trace the radius with my index finger. "There's new stitching layered over the original made by the manufacturer. Look closely. The edges are uneven, not as neat and near invisible as the old one. The thread is a slightly darker color than the beige."

We gape at each other. Ty says, "Someone messed with the bear."

294

I nod slowly. "We need a knife to uncover Mr. Snoopy's secrets."

After Stephanie, our flight attendant, delivers a *pointy knife*, Ty's words, not mine, he makes a neat incision along the perforated edges of the paw and completes a full rotation. He removes the leather patch. At first, we don't see anything but white stuffing.

I reach inside the toy and pull out all the stuffing from the leg, spreading it out over my lap. A small, black, square object, around two by three inches, tumbles out. I hold it up so we can both see clearly.

"A GPS tracker," Ty says.

I nod. "That's how Lance was able to find the location of the car, and by extension, the apartment building. I bet the detectives did the same, searched for a signal from the car once they discovered what Brynn was driving."

"We thought the car had a built-in GPS system and that's how they tracked her. But it was the tracker inside the bear all along."

"That's the most likely scenario. I don't think Brynn was dumb enough to get a car with a built-in tracker, knowing what she was planning."

"So who put the tracker in the bear?" Ty asks, stroking his chin. "We didn't even realize Mr. Snoopy was missing."

"I thought Alexis just got bored with him and placed him in the toy box with the rest of her stuffed animals."

"We can rule out Brynn."

"Her husband?" I speculate. "He had to have been part of the plan. He was in the apartment, getting ready to leave North America with our kid and Brynn. What if he changed his mind but didn't tell Brynn he couldn't go through with it?"

"Sticking the tracker in the bear was his way of helping us

find Lucas without incriminating himself."

"Makes sense," I say. Yet, I'm not ready to concede it was that simple. I pick up the bear again to see if the paw on the second leg has the same odd stitching. It does.

The pilot announces our descent. Lucas stirs briefly but continues his rest. I get to work cutting out the second paw. It doesn't take long to find the piece of paper wedged inside. I hold it up between us so we can read it together.

Abbie,

I'm sorry. I hope you find Lucas before it's too late.

I study the thin strip of paper with the cryptic note typewritten and unsigned, not sure if I should be enraged, thankful or both. It doesn't take a genius to know who sent it. Leaving it unsigned was clever on her part, no culpability if the authorities were to catch up with her.

"She may have saved Lucas," Ty says, his voice soft and soothing. He wraps his arms around me. "I'm not saying she should get away with her part in it, but we still don't have all the pieces of the story yet."

"I know. Like why she was involved in the first place. They had something on her, big enough to ensure her cooperation. She always appeared nervous around me, overly eager to please. I thought it was a personality quirk, but it could have been guilt eating away at her. Placing the tracker in the bear was her way of making up for her duplicity."

"I just have one question left, then."

"What's that?" I ask.

"Where is Katie?"

CHAPTER 68

I T'S AFTER ELEVEN o'clock at night when we pull into the driveway. Ty carries an exhausted Lucas on his shoulders while I fumble for the keys to the front door. As I look up from my task, the door magically opens and various family members spill out. Loud cries of relief, excitement and tears greet us, pervading the tranquil suburban night. The dogs next door bark like mad. Lucas lifts up his head to see what all the commotion is about.

"We better get inside," Ty says. He plants Lucas down. He's wobbly on his feet and lets out a big, wide yawn.

The welcome committee assembles in the foyer: my parents, Ty's parents, Grandma Naomi and my brother Miles. And of course, the twins.

As Ty closes the door behind us, Alexis flings herself into Lucas' arms, almost knocking him down. She hugs him in a vice-like grip, weeping noisily.

"I told you Lucas would come back before school starts next week, didn't I, Blake?" She releases Lucas and turns to Blake, who's desperately struggling to keep his emotions under control.

Blake loses the battle when Lucas pulls him into a giant

hug. "I was afraid I would never see you again, but Alexis kept saying that you would come back," Blake says. "She hit me over the head with her stuffed elephant. She says she didn't like my negativity."

Everyone giggles, including Lucas. When the siblings break apart, my father scoops up Lucas and we all head to the kitchen. It's a tight squeeze, but we couldn't be happier. The twins are already in pajamas. They'll be allowed to stay up a few more minutes. They have the rest of school vacation to look forward to, all three of them.

Both Ty and I are exhausted as well and don't have the energy to do anything else other than plop our butts down on a chair at the kitchen table. The adults have many questions. This is going to be an all-nighter. I'm used to it, though.

My mother says she cooked dinner for everyone and saved us some. While she heats up the food in the microwave, everyone is on eggshells, careful not to ask too many questions too soon. But the kids have other ideas.

"Where were you, Lucas?" Alexis asks. "Did a stranger take you? Was he mean to you?"

Grandma Naomi swoops in. "There will be plenty of time for Lucas to tell you all about his adventure, but for now, let's enjoy some family time and be grateful Lucas is home. Okay, sweetie?" She pats Alexis on the head, so her words don't feel like an admonishment.

Alexis nods, although I can see from her expression she wasn't satisfied with that response.

The adults shuffle around the kitchen, grabbing coffee, water, snacks, and scoping out a comfortable spot from which to catch up on the latest events. The kids will soon be carted off to bed. The truth is, I would rather have all three of them sleep next to us. I can't shake the not-so- veiled threat from

Brynn and the *he* who might try to get me again.

The kids finally fall asleep after Ty and I offer reassurances that Lucas won't disappear again. When we return to the kitchen, the family can't hold back any longer.

"What happened? How did all of this go down, and what's next?" My dad takes charge of the conversation. He stands at the island and chugs down a bottle of water while waiting for an answer.

Ty and I take turns explaining the complicated web of deceit fueled by vengeance that led to Lucas' kidnapping. How Brynn still blames me for her brothers' death, and by extension, her mother's and her plan with her real husband, Adrian Harper, to take Lucas to Australia. How Brynn didn't deny kidnapping Lucas and had no remorse, her defiance and accusation that I was selfish. How she tried to kill herself, and her sinister warning. We also loop them in on the GPS tracker and unsigned note found in Lucas' bear and our suspicions that Katie was responsible.

"There's still a lot we don't know." I take a sip of tea this time, not coffee. "Like the whereabouts of both Charlie and Katie, and who was the true mastermind behind the plot."

Verbal pandemonium breaks out as everyone ventures an opinion and expresses their shock and disbelief all at once. Then the conversation ceases abruptly. Grandma Naomi rocks back and forth in her chair. My brother Miles scowls, and my parents fall silent. Ty's mother Jenny takes a deep, exasperated breath.

"We think Charlie, or whatever his name is, can help answer some of our questions," Ty says. "Brynn wouldn't reveal anything, and I have a feeling the detectives won't have an easy time with her."

Adding to his take on the situation, I say, "We're depending on Lance to find out who Charlie is and where he is. Lance says he has a lead."

The other Dr. Rambally, Ty's dad, Bobby—a small man with a thick head of graying hair, and kind eyes, speaks up for the first time. "The question is whether or not Lucas is now safe. According to Brynn, there might be another attempt."

"Dad, so far we only have Brynn's word to go on, about this so-called mastermind," Ty says. "She could have been bluffing because she was angry and wanted to get Cooper all crazy and paranoid." He turns to me for confirmation. "But Cooper thinks Brynn was serious. That's why we need to find out about Charlie."

"So the kids need protection until this whole thing is solved," my mother says.

"You can't allow anyone who isn't close family in or near the house," Grandma Naomi chimes in. "If Brynn was telling the truth, they could try again, and Lucas may not be the only target this time."

A somber mist blankets the air—a wet, heavy, ugly reminder that our collective nightmare isn't over.

"We'll do whatever it takes to keep our grandchildren safe," Jenny says, with a determined tilt of her braided head. "I don't care if we all have to take shifts guarding their rooms as they sleep at night, and hire security to escort them to school, the park, wherever they go. We can't relax until whoever is behind this is caught and thrown into prison."

When my brother, Miles, pipes up and asks the question we've all been avoiding, the temperature in the room drops several degrees.

"What are we telling Lucas about why he was kidnapped and who Brynn is? We have to be consistent with our story."

My throat clenches with a heaviness resembling grief.

During the date night at my mother's restaurant, Ty and I had decided to tell Lucas the truth. It now seems like an eternity ago when it was only last week. Brynn sabotaged those plans when she took Lucas.

"We had already agreed to tell Lucas," I explain. "Then things got out of hand. We just got him back. Let him enjoy a period of normalcy and readjustment before we lay something this heavy on him. He's just a kid. We don't want to overwhelm him."

"We can all agree on that," Miles says. "But you're dealing with a ticking clock. You don't know if Brynn said anything to him and he might catch you off guard."

I cover my face with my palms to stifle a yawn. There's also the Christian piece of the equation, and his father, Alan Wheeler, Lucas' other biological grandfather. Lucas met Christian and Alan a handful of times. They got along fine. Now we have to tell Lucas that his uncle and grandfather have been under his nose all along, and we kept it from him.

CHAPTER 69

T HE NEXT DAY, Blake and Lucas resume their competitive rivalry in the backyard under the watchful eyes of no less than five family members, including Grandma Naomi, my dad, and Ty's dad. A lively game of soccer is in progress. Blake is determined to beat his brother, who won their last match. As much as I would like to sit back and enjoy the simple pleasure of hearing my children laugh and play again, more serious matters need attending.

Lance Carter had called to say he's on his way. The urgency and seriousness in his tone tells me that I should brace myself.

We meet up in the office Ty and I share on the main floor of the house. Two oak desks, each with a laptop and desk drawers, take up most of the space, in addition to a small bookshelf and two black leather swivel chairs.

A shaft of sunlight slices through the curtains of the fiber-glass windows, brightening the room. We gather at the edge of my desk and lean over Lance's laptop. A mugshot of a young guy with dark hair in a black T-shirt, is displayed on the screen.

"Do you recognize this guy?" Lance asks.

Ty and I peek closer and shake our heads collectively.

"Study the face for a minute," Lance presses. "Imagine if

you changed his hair color to blond, does he look familiar at all?"

"Charlie!" I blurt out.

"You got it," Lance says. "The man you knew as Charlie Payne is actually Brian Rogers, and up until two years ago, he was a guest of the State of Connecticut. He served four years for manslaughter."

My jaw goes slack and then I say, "I need to sit down."

"Me too," Ty says, his tone weary.

We both grab the swivel chairs, and sit side by side while Lance continues to stand. He launches into an incredible story that has us sitting motionless like two bronzed statues.

"Brian Rogers, a.k.a. Charlie Payne, got into a fight during the first semester of his senior year of college. According to court transcripts, he claimed self-defense. Apparently, some guy thought Brian was coming on to his girlfriend and wanted to teach him a lesson. In the process of defending himself, Brian landed a fatal blow."

"What happened next?" I ask, my voice barely making it above a raspy whisper.

"I don't have all the pieces yet, but it could be that while in prison, Brian met this mastermind you're looking for. To know for sure, we need to find him. On that front, my guys and I have made a lot of progress. We've been able to track him through an offshore account on the Caribbean island of Nevis."

"How?" Ty asked.

"It was difficult. The team and I faced layers of asset protection rules and strict financial privacy laws. We had help from an experienced forensic accountant, though. All we needed was the account number the kidnapper provided for the five million dollars they demanded for Lucas' release to give us a start. In the end, we got him."

This is wonderful news, and I should be doing back flips.

We have someone to pursue who can provide answers. Instead, I'm about to crawl out of my skin. Something Lance said is bouncing around my head, looking for a soft place to land, some quiet pearl of wisdom that would convince me I'm being ridiculous. But reassurance is in short supply.

The thought persists: Brian Rogers may have met the real culprit behind Lucas' kidnapping during his prison stint in Connecticut. *He's dead. How many times do you need to hear it, see the proof?*

"Cooper, are you okay?" Ty asks. "You look like you're turning purple."

"Maybe some water would help. I guess I'm dehydrated."

"I'll be right back," Ty says, getting up from his seat. "And I'm going to check you out to make sure you're not coming down with something."

After Ty leaves, a terrible headache takes over. I let out a windy sigh, aching for relief. My brain is determined to drag me back into the past, however. A band of memories assail me in one giant, nausea-inducing montage.

I came for my son, Abbie. He's mine, not Rambally's.

I thought Zach somehow escaped prison and came to steal our baby.

If you shoot at me, I won't hesitate to kill her. If you shoot at my brother, I will also kill her.

Bang, bang, bang.

I come back to the present with a jolt to discover Lance's hand on my shoulder, his face covered in genuine concern.

"Abbie, are you okay? Should I get Ty? You don't look good."

I ignore his concern. "Listen to me, Lance. This is going to sound strange, but I want you to find out if Zachary Rossdale is still alive."

CHAPTER 70

"P LEASE TAKE YOUR time. Tell us what happened," he
said.

Brynn Rossdale Harper sat in an interrogation room at the
Montreal Police Department, two days after she was released
from the hospital. Detectives Flores and Corwin occupied
chairs across from her. There was no table separating them like
you see on TV or the movies. It was quite the intimate scene.

Flores was Hispanic, mid-forties, fit and good-looking
with dark hair and eyes. Corwin was white, younger, with a
buzz cut and average build. Both were unarmed and wore dark
suit jackets and white dress shirts. The room was sparse, dull
and uninteresting with low lighting.

"I don't know why I'm here," she said. "You already know
what happened."

"We don't want to make assumptions, Brynn," Flores said.
"We just want to get to the truth. Truth and facts can be two
different things, as weird as that sounds."

She didn't know exactly what the difference was, but she
had to watch herself, make sure she didn't fall into any traps
they may try to spring on her.

"I was just a lackey, carrying out orders. Someone else was

behind it."

"Go on," Flores encouraged, his hands clasped together.

Brynn expelled a deep breath and began. "He wouldn't give me the details. All I was told was that I needed to agree to pretend to be his wife so we could pose as a suburban couple.

"*He*, who?" Flores asked.

"Charlie Payne."

"Why did he propose this idea?"

"To keep an eye on the Ramballys. They would trust us if we came across as a harmless couple next door. It was easier to befriend them that way."

"And why did he want to do that?"

"Because someone asked him to, but he wouldn't say who the person was. Charlie was supposed to report back. This person was especially interested in Lucas."

"Did he say why?"

"No. He said the less I knew, the better. I just had to do something easy. Get Abbie Rambally to like me, be helpful to her if she needed it. That sort of thing."

"What else?" Corwin cut in.

"That was it until the day I overheard a conversation I wasn't supposed to hear."

"What conversation was this?" Corwin pressed.

"Charlie was on his cell phone in the kitchen. The conversation with the person on the other end of the line was tense, because he was agitated and raised his voice. Charlie told the person no way he would kill Lucas, that he was drawing the line, that he didn't kill kids, no matter how much money was offered."

A dark shadow crossed Flores' face, but he only asked her to continue in an all-too-familiar tone, as if they were two friends catching up over drinks instead of a police interrogation. Brynn observed the body language of the two detectives. It was clear

Flores was the lead in the case.

"The person Charlie was talking to said something, and he agreed to do it. I could tell he didn't want to, but he must have been threatened. The next day, Charlie said he had a business trip to Jersey for a couple of days."

After Flores confirmed the date this conversation allegedly took place, he continued. "Did you tell anybody what you overheard?"

"No."

"Why not?"

"I thought it was up to me to protect Lucas. That's why I had to get him out of the country. I didn't know if Charlie was serious about killing him and I was afraid the person who asked him to do it would keep trying until he succeeded."

Flores cleared his throat. "The Canadian border agent said you told him Lucas Rambally was your nephew. Why did you say that?"

"Because he is. I didn't know that when we first arrived in Lexington. It wasn't until I met Abbie and her family that it dawned on me. She used to date my brother. She got pregnant. I figured Lucas was my nephew. He even looks like my brother."

"Did you ask Abbie who Lucas' father was, if you suspected Ty Rambally wasn't his biological father?"

"Yes. She wouldn't tell me. She would only say that Lucas' biological father was dead, and good riddance." Brynn looked down at her hands like some poor despondent soul. "It hurt to hear her say that. He's gone, and so is my mother. Lucas is the only family I have left."

Flores nodded sympathetically. But Brynn was no fool. They wanted her to take the fall for this. She understood they had a job to do, but so did she: avoiding a long prison sentence.

"How did you meet Charlie Payne?" Corwin asked, rejoining the conversation.

Without missing a beat, Brynn said, "At a party. We struck up a conversation and became friends."

"You didn't think it was strange when he asked you to pose as one half of a married couple?"

"I did, but he offered to pay me a lot of money. Ten times more than what I make in a year as a freelance children's book illustrator. I was almost broke. It seemed like easy money."

"I see," Corwin said, chewing on the base of his pen. He asked, "Do you have any idea where Charlie is now?"

"No. I haven't seen him since he said he was going on a brief business trip."

"Do you have any clue about what the connection is between Charlie and the person who ordered him to kill Lucas Rambally?"

"No, I don't," Brynn said, shaking her head, regretfully.

"Did Charlie ever threaten you?" Flores asked.

"Not directly. But after I found out what he was capable of, I kept my head down, kept my mouth shut, and focused on taking Lucas to safety."

"What do you mean by that?" Corwin prodded.

"I think Charlie killed Olivia Stewart, and her replacement, Katie Nicholson."

CHAPTER 71

T WO NERVE-RACKING HOURS after I asked Lance Carter to confirm whether or not Zachary Rossdale was still alive, a call comes in. I click the answer button, put the phone on speaker, and place it on the desk. Both Ty and I take a seat.

"Go ahead, Lance," I say calmly. "Ty is sitting right next to me in our home office."

"Zachary Rossdale is alive and kicking, still serving back to back life sentences at a state pen in Connecticut. That official letter from the Connecticut Department of Corrections you received, telling you he was dead, was a forgery."

I feel like a nuclear bomb just detonated in my head and the debris is hurtling its way down through my heart and into my gut. The room spins around me. I can't focus that well, but I venture a furtive glance at Ty. The thunderous look stenciled on his face is the exact opposite of what I'm feeling. I'm too shaken to be furious.

"Are you guys still with me?" a sympathetic Lance asks.

"We're still here," I manage to say through my panic and distress. I ask, "Did you find out if Zach and Brian Rogers ever crossed paths?"

"As a matter of fact, they did. Brian Rogers and Zachary Rossdale were in the same cell block."

The pieces of the mystery are beginning to come together with nauseating clarity. The thought that this monster is still breathing air, and still has the power to upend my life, is more than I can handle. It took me at least five years to start feeling normal and safe after the assault. And now, I find out I was lulled into a false sense of security, that this viper was simply waiting for the right time to strike again, ripping open old wounds and inflicting new ones.

"Lance, can we call you back?" Ty says. "Cooper and I need a few minutes."

After Lance hangs up, I sit on Ty's lap and bury my head into his shoulders. My sobs come out in short, angry bursts at first, followed by loud, blubbering, can't-breathe wailing.

Ty wipes my tears while kissing my cheeks. "We'll get him, Cooper. I don't know exactly how yet, but I will make sure Zachary Rossdale never hurts you again."

"WE'RE GIVING YOU one more chance to tell us the truth, the whole truth, this time," Detective Flores said to Brynn.

Gone was the calm, steady detective of a few hours ago. Flores and Corwin had taken turns leaving the room. Now, they were both back, and it did not look good from the black expressions on their faces. Brynn didn't know what they had found out in the interim, but they knew she had lied. Her only chance to save her skin and lower her sentence if she were ever convicted was to cooperate. However, it didn't mean she was going to make it easy for them.

"I told you the truth."

"Just enough to sound credible," Flores said. He shot a

stormy glare in her direction. "There's more to the story than you're saying. You know what happened to Olivia Stewart, don't you?"

Brynn shifted her legs to one side. "I don't know what you're talking about."

"Sure, you do," Corwin quipped. "You led us to believe that Brian Rogers—yes, we know his real name isn't Charlie Payne—was responsible for Ms. Stewart's death."

"I never said that." Defiance radiated off Brynn. "What I said was, I think he had something to do with it."

"We both know that's not true. And when Brian gets extradited back to the States, he'll tell us how it really went down. Better to get your version of the story in before he does. Before he makes a plea deal, and leaves you out in the cold."

The detective's words kicked her hard in the gut, driving out all the breathable air from her body. If they found Brian and were in the process of hauling him back to the U.S., she was all but done. He would provide the cops with every detail of the plan from beginning to end.

Wait a minute. Brian had as much to lose as she did. He didn't hold all the cards, not by a long shot.

Brynn didn't have any proof, but she had a strong feeling that Brian extorted five million dollars from Christian Wheeler when he pretended to have kidnapped Lucas. That alone would ensure he would go to jail for a long time. As for a plea bargain, that was a bunch of hog wash. He was a convicted felon who served hard time. The only thing prosecutors would be giving Brian Rogers was a one-way trip back to prison for much longer than four years.

Detective Flores drew closer to her, his chair making scraping sounds against the concrete floor. "We think this is how it played out. Olivia Stewart either saw or heard something she shouldn't have. I'm thinking she saw something. But you couldn't let her ruin your plans by running to the boy's parents. All your careful planning would have been for nothing. Purchasing a house down the street from the Ramballys, pretending to be Jenna Payne, stalking the family for a year, all of that work you put in would have been for nothing."

Flores adjusted the lapel of his jacket, his gaze sour. "Getting your real husband, Adrian Harper, to do the actual snatching, that was genius, by the way. He's about Ty Rambally's height and build. They're both black. In the dead of night, no one could prove it wasn't Rambally taking his kid out because of some emergency."

Corwin joined in. "See, we don't really believe you were trying to be a martyr by saving Lucas from the grand architect of this scheme. Your plan all along was to kidnap him to make Abbie Rambally suffer. That's right. We know Zachary Rossdale is your brother. And we believe he set this whole thing in motion, with your complete buy-in." Corwin leaned back in his chair, a satisfied smirk on his face.

Brynn didn't flinch. She would neither confirm nor deny anything. "It's a nice story, but you don't have any proof. This is nothing more than a fishing expedition."

Leaning forward, Flores said, "Nice bravado but we're not biting. Abbie confirmed what we just told you. Oh, and by the way, Brynn, we can place you in Framingham in the vicinity of Olivia Stewart's residence the day she was murdered."

CHAPTER 72

"A BBIE RAMBALLY NEVER trusted you from the day she met you, and neither did Olivia Stewart," Flores said. "Abbie observed Olivia acting strangely the night they had dinner at your house, but she never got to ask her about it. Is that where Oliva saw something she wasn't supposed to see? You caught her. Didn't you Brynn? And that's when you hatched a plan to get rid of her."

They're fishing, trying to rattle you, Brynn reminded herself. As long as she didn't say anything, she would be fine. All this is just conjecture to trap her, to get her angry and defensive so she would say something incriminating. Silence would be her best defense.

"Framingham police figured the killer used Ty Rambally as bait by cloning his cell phone number so Olivia would respond when she saw the text message supposedly coming from him. But that was you, wasn't it, Brynn? You pretended to be Ty Rambally to lure Olivia Stewart to her death. We can prove Rambally never sent that text."

Flores took off his jacket, placed it on the back of the chair, and rolled up the sleeves of his dress shirt. He continued, "You told Olivia you would meet her at her apartment. You already knew where she lived a year in advance. You were here doing leg work ahead of time."

Brynn refused to say another word. In fact, this interview was about to be over.

Corwin said, "You got a ticket when you parked on a street near Olivia's apartment. That's how we can place you there. The timing matches the coroner's estimated time-of-death window."

Despair gnawed at Brynn. They were pretty damn close to nailing her. She recalled that day vividly, Olivia's hostility, and how things had quickly reached the point of no return.

When Olivia opened her apartment door, she'd been stunned to see Brynn, posing as Jenna.

"What do you want and how did you know where I live?" Olivia asked.

She had refused to let Jenna in, preferring to stand in the doorway, arms folded.

Jenna didn't answer her question. Instead she said, "Abbie is in trouble. I know how much you care about her. I thought if we could put our heads together, we could help her."

Olivia narrowed her eyes but she was intrigued. "What are you talking about?"

"I think she's headed for a mental breakdown." Jenna let the statement hang in the air for dramatic effect. When Olivia's eyes popped wide and Jenna was certain she had her full attention, she continued, "I hate to even entertain the idea, but Abbie is capable of hurting herself or one of the kids. I saw marks. She tried to cover them up, but I saw."

Olivia went slack jawed and took two steps back.

"Look, I know you don't like me, and I'm sorry I pretended to be Ty, but it's the only way I could think of that you would talk to me," Jenna said, her tone earnest. "I really like Abbie and I'm scared for her and those kids. You adore the children. Ty is always at the hospital. You're the only person I could talk to about this. I don't know Abbie's family at all."

Brynn followed up with fake tears and trembling. Then she said, "I understand if you don't want me in your home. Maybe we can go to the park and just talk. I don't know the area that well, but I hear Cochituate State Park is nice and it's near the water."

"Let me get my purse."

And just like that, Olivia Stewart had followed Brynn out to her car and rode shotgun all the way to Cochituate Park. While walking along a secluded area of the park that Brynn had scoped out in advance, and discussing Abbie's impending doom, Brynn bent down and pulled the gun she had strapped to her boot, and pointed it at Olivia.

"I heard you while you were in the bathroom the night the Ramballys came over for dinner. You were about to rat me out," she said, accusingly. "You saw the car in the driveway. You also saw it that day at the kids' school, when you came up to me. That's how you figured me and Jane Witherby were one and the same. I'm sorry, Olivia, but I can't have you blabbing to Abbie, ruining my plans."

Olivia held up trembling hands. Tears pooled in her eyes. "I won't say anything, if that's what you want. I swear."

"I don't know, Liv. It's too risky." Brynn pretended to give the matter serious consideration.

"I swear. I'll do it for the sake of the kids." Olivia's desperation was thick. "I'll keep my mouth shut and in exchange, you don't hurt the kids, or Abbie, or Ty. I can do that. Abbie confides in me sometimes and I always keep her secrets. I can keep yours, too. Please, I'm begging you. You don't have to do this."

Brynn sighed loudly. "I don't like loose ends, Liv and you're a loose end I can't afford, so we're gonna have to table this conversation. Permanently."

Without another word, she pulled the trigger twice, the silencer muting the popping sound usually made when a handgun was fired. Brynn watched Olivia hit the ground. It was getting dark, just the way she had planned it. She cast a frantic gaze around the area. The idea that she could get caught standing over a dead body suddenly slammed into her. But she saw no one and heard nothing, not even the rustling of tree leaves.

Once she returned home, Brynn placed the gun in a solution made up of nitric acid and water. The chemical composition of the nitric acid reacted to the steel in the gun, dissolving the metal and any identifying serial numbers along with it.

They would never find that gun, Brynn thought. Placing her car near Olivia's apartment wasn't hard evidence. It was circumstantial at best. A good defense lawyer could rip that to shreds. And as the beneficiary of her mother's seven-figure life insurance policy, she could afford the best criminal defense lawyer money could buy. She would get one for Adrian, too.

"We suspect you had something to do with Katie Nicholson's disappearance too," Flores said, hauling Brynn back to her grim reality. "We'll find the evidence, and when we do, you're going down for a double homicide, and kidnapping."

He shook his head as if grappling with some deep, philosophical issue. Then he said, "What is it with you Rossdales and crime? We looked into your brother's record when Abbie confirmed you two were related. "Pretty heinous stuff. I guess it's in the blood."

Brynn had run out of words and the will to keep fighting. The life she had planned for herself was snuffed out, choked by a darkness she couldn't control, the voices that whispered she deserved to be happy and it didn't matter who or what got in her way.

The voices had lied to her. And now they were laughing at her, taunting her, determined to drive her over the dark edge. It was over. And she was only twenty-nine years old.

CHAPTER 73

LIFE HAS SLOWLY returned to normal, although I don't think I will ever feel completely safe as long as Zachary Rossdale breathes air.

Brian Rogers was arrested while dining at Café Henrici, a popular outdoor spot on Niederdorfstrasse in Zurich. He was eager to cooperate with authorities once he discovered he was dead broke, that the five million he extorted from Christian was wiped from his account. He told quite the tale of how he met Zach in prison and that he was the one who hatched the plan and ordered Brian and Brynn to carry it out. He made a deal with prosecutors to testify as to what he knows in exchange for a lighter sentence.

Brynn is being held without bail until trial. We're still reeling from the news that she murdered Liv and Katie to keep them quiet. Liv didn't have the chance to warn us, and Katie did her best to do just that. Because of her, Lucas is with us.

But dissecting all of that information will have to wait.

At the moment, I'm in a room with approximately one hundred people for my dissertation defense. Graduation is in three weeks. I was given an *unusual* and *extenuating circumstances* pass by Boston University, allowing me to move ahead with my oral defense since I missed my original date. Who am I kidding? The notoriety of having my son kidnapped and going on television probably helped my case.

I wasn't sure I could pull this off. I was well on my way to figuring out a plan B for my future, but my kids wouldn't let me give up. Lucas told me he and Blake already had their outfits for my graduation ceremony picked out. They finally relented and allowed Alexis to provide wardrobe advice, advice they actually listened to and acted on. My mother declared I was born to be a warrior and warriors never quit. I had to find the strength to overcome one last time. If not for me, for my children. I couldn't let them see me quit something I had worked so hard for.

Several professors from the Department of Psychological and Brain Sciences along with Ty, my parents, and Ty's parents are in the crowd.

My advisor, Dr. Elroy Ackermann, a twenty-year veteran of the department, and my most ardent cheerleader, comes up to me at the podium. I'm outwardly confident—hair styled in an elegant chignon, decked out in a fitted, sleeveless sapphire blue dress and black, suede, ankle-strap pumps, compliments of uber designer and BFF, Callie Furi.

"You will do great," Ackermann says. "The committee has high expectations from you. You've set the bar high with all the hard work you put in prior to your family ordeal. I have no doubt you will blow us away. I'll be seeing you at graduation, young lady."

"Thank you, professor. I hope you're right."

He takes his seat with the other committee members. My hands are clammy. My family has a front row seat and it looks like the whole department has turned out for this. The defense could last anywhere between one and three hours. If I don't handle the pressure well, they won't sign off. I won't pass. I won't graduate.

I begin to question whether I can do this, pull off a last-minute miracle, and why I let my family talk me into it.

Breathe, Abbie. You got this. Warriors never quit.

I clear my throat and the room quiets down. I squeeze the laser pointer in my right hand for one last extra dose of courage, and position myself for easy access to the laptop. My talk is well structured, and I dive into explaining how my research is relevant to my dissertation, scrolling through vivid PowerPoint slides that back me up. I'm peppered with questions throughout, and I sail through each of them with ease. But there's always that one professor, the skeptic, the doubter, who throws a flaming torch into the mix.

Professor Barlowe. He asks a question that has only a distant connection to the dissertation. The room goes quiet, waiting for my response. Truth is, I don't know the answer. I never explored that line of research.

"I don't know the answer, Professor Barlowe," I say calmly. "I didn't look into that angle because it wasn't relevant."

I move on, but he won't let it go. He interrupts me again, pointing out there is relevance. At this juncture, I'm starting to get irritated, and I hope they can't see it through my fake smile. I'm stuck for a minute or two. I feel my confidence slipping, but I remember my mother's words. *Warriors never quit.*

I shore up whatever courage I have left and decide to turn the tables on Professor Barlowe. In a pleasant tone, I thank him for pointing out the relevance and agree with the connection that he made. We go back and forth for a couple more minutes, and then I continue with my defense.

At the ninety-minute mark, I'm ready to wrap it up. All I can do now is pray and wait.

CHAPTER 74

L ANCE CARTER IS a rock star, and I tell him so as I pour
him a second glass of wine. It's a late afternoon in May,
the sun still shining, casting splashes of warmth and light into
the cool shade of the patio where we're gathered. Christian
sits across from me while Ty and Lance occupy the remaining
chairs. It's just us out here. The kids are inside, baking cookies
with my mom and Grandma Naomi.

"No wine for you," I say to Ty, and remove the bottle from
his reach. "You're going back to the hospital in a few hours."

"Come on, Cooper. Have a heart."

"More for me," Lance says, taking a long gulp.

"Any news on how and why we were sent a letter from the
State of Connecticut stating that Zach was dead?" I ask.

Lance stops in mid-sip and says, "Zach held some serious
leverage over the warden and used it to blackmail him. Got
him to write the letter on official stationary. No one knows
what he has on the warden, yet."

"You never want to meet that monster," I say. "He's as
vicious as a rattlesnake, a bona fide psychopath. Seems like
prison did nothing to diminish his aggression. It may have
even made him worse."

"He planned this for years," Christian says, shaking his head. "Who has that kind of patience? He went in ten years ago and last year, his sister was here in Lexington, spying. It takes incredible tenacity to lie in wait for that long."

"I know," Lance says. "He must loathe you, Abbie. The dude is pretty sick."

That he is. Which makes what I'm about to do that much harder, the conversation with Lucas we've been putting off. What little information we were able to get from Lucas about his ordeal has left us wondering if it was really as straightforward as he says.

He woke up in a car. Adrian was driving and told him a story about some friend they were supposed to visit. He knew that was a lie and asked to be brought home, but Adrian wouldn't let him go. Then Brynn took him to Canada and he begged her to take him home. She just got mad. But she never hurt him and didn't say anything about who she was.

Although Lucas insists he's fine, he's just happy to be home, we worry about his psychological and emotional state. We take him once a week to a child psychologist. He tells her he's tired of talking about it and that he's fine. All he wanted was to be reunited with his family and now that he's home, he's happy again, and we should stop asking him questions because it's annoying.

AFTER LANCE LEAVES, Ty collects Lucas and he joins us on the patio with a giant chocolate chip cookie in hand. He bites into the treat as his father asks him to take a seat next to me.

The three adults ping each other with looks that say this is one of the hardest things we've ever had to do.

"Sweetie, we wanted to talk to you about what happened. Why it happened," I begin.

Lucas takes a bit of his cookie and then says, "Mom, come on. Do we have to?"

"I know you don't want to talk about it, but it's important."

After a loud sigh of annoyance, another bite of his cookie, and a resigned, *Fine,* he says, "Adrian said he and Brynn were taking me to visit someone, but they didn't want to tell you because you and the person didn't get along. But I didn't believe them."

He continues to chew his cookie as if this conversation was the most normal thing in the world.

"I'm glad you didn't believe them because that's not the reason they took you from us."

"Okay. Can you tell me quick, Mom, cause if I don't get back to the kitchen, Alexis and Blake will eat all the cookies and they won't leave me any. Then Great-Grandma Naomi will be upset about it. You know we shouldn't upset her, cause she's really old."

I cover my mouth to stifle a giggle. Ty and Christian look off into space, but I can tell from their expressions that they don't want to burst out laughing in front of Lucas.

I get down on my knees so I can meet Lucas at eye level. "I know how much you love those cookies, but what we have to say is much more important. Maybe if you ask Christian nicely, he can be your lookout. Make sure a few are stashed away for you. Would that work?"

With youthful enthusiasm, he looks at Christian and says, "Please. Can you go to the kitchen and save me some? I'll split it with you."

Christian, with a twinkle in his eyes and a smile on his lips, leaves his chair and says, "Sure thing, Lucas. I won't let you miss out. Even if I have to wrestle Blake for the remaining cookies."

I get off my knees after Christian leaves. "Sit here, baby,"

I say, patting the chair next to me. Ty sits on the other side so Lucas is sandwiched in between us.

Lucas looks at me and asks, "Is this about what you told Mrs. Payne? I mean Brynn, but back then we thought she was Mrs. Payne?"

"What do you mean?"

He looks down and kicks a leg against the table. Then he looks up again, his face mirroring guilt. "I know I'm not supposed to eavesdrop, but it was an accident, Mom. I came down to get a drink, but then I heard you talking. I didn't want to get in trouble so I didn't say anything. Sorry."

Ty and I exchange puzzled glances. Then Ty says, "It's okay, Lucas. Just tell us in your own words what you overheard. You won't get in trouble. We promise."

"Mom told Brynn that my father was dead and she was glad about it."

I wince. Ty tilts his head as if contemplating how to proceed. Then he reaches for Lucas and plants him across his knees.

"I *am* your dad, Lucas. And I always will be. You remember all those pictures of Mom in the family album, when she was pregnant with you, and I had my ears resting against her tummy?"

Lucas nods.

"I was trying to hear you in there. I would talk to you, so you would know my voice, know that I was your father."

Lucas looks confused, and I can't blame the poor kid. I know what's coming next and brace myself.

"Then what did Mom mean when she said my father was dead?"

I take in a deep, painful breath and plunge in. "A long time ago, Lucas, when I was in college, before you were born, I met a man. At first, he seemed nice and we started dating. Well, it turns out he was only pretending to be nice. Like Brynn was pretending to be Mrs. Payne and pretending to be my friend. This man was very mean. Anyway, we got into a huge fight and I got hurt."

He starts to hiccup and rub his nose, the way he does when he gets emotional and wants to burst into tears, but doesn't want to come across as a baby. I have to get this out before I break wide open in front of my little boy. He must never know the true horror of his conception and the burden and pain I carried for years. Pain that has recently resurfaced, peeling the scab off a wound that was all but healed.

I look up to see Christian rooted to the spot. His face sags with emotion. Ty looks like he's about to fall apart. He pinches the bridge of his nose repeatedly to ward off a breakdown. Christian quietly retakes his seat. I place one arm around Lucas and palm his face with the other, dropping a long, wet kiss on his cheek.

I continue the story for Lucas' benefit. "This man I'm telling you about, well, he died before I found out I was expecting you. It's never a good thing to be glad someone is dead, but I was upset when I said that to Brynn."

"Is that why I look different from Blake and Alexis? Because the mean man was my original father and then you got me a nicer daddy?"

"That's right, baby. I got you the best daddy in the whole world." I can barely control the emotions circling, tugging at me, forcing me to unravel. I won't yield. Not right now.

I search my son's face for signs of hurt, anger, confusion. What I find instead is a quiet understanding and acceptance that his origins don't matter. What does is the here and now. That he's part of a loving family with siblings and grandparents and uncles and cousins. Parents who adore him.

"You don't ever have to worry about the mean man. Your daddy is right here," I say, gesturing to Ty. Alexis and Blake are your brother and sister. You know, they're twins so they kind of have to look alike."

I wink at him. He smiles and then says, "I'm glad you got me a new dad. And I promise I won't get mad at the man who was mean to you."

"Thank you, sweetheart. But you know what else?" I ask, pulling myself together.

"What?"

I look at Christian before I answer. "We didn't know it at the time, but the mean man had the same dad as Christian, but a different mom. Remember Mr. Wheeler?"

"Yes. Grandpa Jason says he's a son of a —"

"Shhh," I interrupt. "We don't repeat bad words, remember? Even if it was Grandpa Jason who said it."

"It was funny."

"I'm going to have a word with your grandfather about his use of language around you and your siblings." I ruffle his hair to shore up the courage to tell him the truth about who Christian is. "Sweetie, because the mean man and Christian have the same dad, that makes Christian your uncle, and Mr. Wheeler your grandpa, too."

His eyes pop wide. "No way." He looks at Christian as if needing confirmation.

Christian gives him a nod and a smile.

Lucas offers a small wave as if to say, 'nice to meet you, uncle.'

Then he starts counting on his fingers. "So I have three grandfathers? That's way cool. More birthday and Christmas presents. I can't wait to tell Blake and Alexis. Blake is going to be mad that I beat him. I have three grandpas but he only has two."

Lucas then takes off like a rocket before anyone could stop him, leaving us to pick up our collective jaws off the ground.

"Um, what happened to the emotionally traumatized child

I was promised?" I croak. "Do you think he's in denial and this will cause deep-seated psychological problems later on? I need to prepare. I need to know what I'm up against."

Ty leans all the way back in his chair with his hands threaded behind his head.

Christian wipes the melted chocolate from handling cookies with one of the napkins on the table.

"He's a kid who grew up with love and security all his life," Christian says. "He's back where he belongs after his ordeal. All is right in his world again. The mean man is dead and you got him a new daddy, the only daddy he's ever known. That's how he sees it through his child's eyes."

Christian swats a bug attempting to crawl up his arm. Then he continues, "As for the future, who can tell? But I think my nephew is going to be fine. He has an army of people pulling for him, and don't underestimate his resilience."

I shake my head, impressed by Christian's wisdom. "I guess you're right. I'll take it and try not to worry so much."

Ty's beeper goes off. He sits up straight in his chair and retrieves the pager from his pants pocket. "I'll be back. I have to call the hospital."

After Ty leaves, I ask Christian, "When did you get to be so smart about kids?"

He gives me a wry smile. "Picked up a few tips here and there. But Abbie, we need to discuss something serious."

I frown. "I don't know if I can take any more for today. I'm kind of fresh out of stamina to deal with serious issues."

"What are we going to do about Zachary Rossdale?"

I give noncommittal shrug. "I don't know, Christian. But I'll tell you something. The next time I get news that he's dead, I want to see the body for myself."

EPILOGUE

---◆---

THREE WEEKS LATER

T Y WHISTLER RAMBALLY leaned against the giant oak in the backyard, one hand in his pants pocket and the other holding a bottle of beer. He was a lucky man, he mused as he took a swig. He couldn't take his eyes off the woman in the fitted, strapless floral dress and three-inch stilettos. Legs for days, toned and slender. There was a tropical flower tucked neatly behind one ear. Her straightened black hair cascaded past her shoulders and down her back. Her round, sable brown eyes had that playful, mischievous sparkle he often feared was gone for good.

Yes, *his* Cooper was back, and he wanted to keep it that way.

She laughed at something a neighbor said and then shook her head. The house and backyard were overflowing with the murmurs and laughter of family, friends and neighbors who came to celebrate with them. The barbecue grill crackled as the aroma of grilled meats and smoke floated in the air.

The long, painful journey was over. Cooper nailed her dissertation defense and earned her Ph.D. The kids couldn't have been prouder and neither could he when she walked across that stage to receive her diploma only hours ago. Come September, she would begin a postdoctoral fellowship in Clinical Neuropsychology at Mass General Hospital, with academic appointments as a Clinical Fellow at both Mass General and Harvard Medical School.

Christian caught his eye and raised a bottle to him.

Ty reciprocated. He was no fool and knew he would owe Christian Wheeler for the rest of his life. He was okay with the debt, though. Christian helped him take care of a plague on humanity named Zachary Rossdale. Not surprisingly, Christian was more than eager to offer his assistance.

That was the best graduation present he could have given his wife: peace of mind. No longer would she have to worry about Zach reaching from behind prison bars to traumatize her again, to steal her peace and security. Ty couldn't allow that to happen. Not ever again.

Cooper had been through enough, and it was her time to shine and fulfill her true potential, free from the shackles of her past. He couldn't wait to watch her soar. Later in the week, he would deliver a second graduation present: a surprise visit to a tattoo parlor. She had expressed an interest in getting one for her thirtieth birthday earlier in the year, but it never happened. He had the image already picked out—a Phoenix rising with the sun as a backdrop.

Christian approached and then stood next to him.

"You have news?" Ty asked.

Christian wore a pair of designer sunglasses, so Ty couldn't read his expression. "Sure do."

"Tell me."

"Apparently, Zachary Rossdale made a lot of enemies in prison. He got confrontational with another inmate and a violent scuffle ensued. Unfortunately, during the fight, the inmate grabbed a baton off an unsuspecting guard. Alas, Zach was beaten to death, his skull crushed."

"How tragic," Ty said, his tone laced with feigned sympathy. "You know, it doesn't surprise me. Some would say karma paid him a visit."

"Exactly how I feel," Christian concurred.

"I hope you insisted on an autopsy."

"Of course."

"When can I see the coroner's report?"

"Soon."

"And the death certificate?"

"You'll get a copy." Christian removed his sunglasses and glanced at Ty. "Are you okay with how this went down?"

"Why do you ask?"

"You're one of the good guys."

"Maybe I've turned a bend in the road."

Christian nodded. "We're all capable of taking that same bend, given the right circumstances."

Ty said, "I just couldn't watch her suffer anymore."

"He wouldn't have stopped."

"Exactly. And she never finds out. Ever."

Christian looked Ty square in the eyes, and clasped his hand in a powerful grip of solidarity. "You didn't even have to ask. That's a given."

"Thank you."

Christian saluted him and went off to go mingle.

"What were you two talking about?" Her voice startled him as she came up behind him.

He turned as she came to stand in front of him. "Nothing. Christian and I were just talking about how amazing you are. You did it, Cooper."

"I did, didn't I?" she said, cocking her head to one side.

"I'm going to get you a plaque for your desk at Mass General that says Dr. Abigail Cooper Rambally, The Most Fearless Woman in the World."

"Too long. I think Badass will do quite nicely."

They both laughed and she took the beer bottle from him and emptied it in one, long chug.

"Speaking of Mass General, tell the nurses in your department that they better watch it. I'll be keeping an eye on them."

"Come on, Cooper. No one pays me any mind."

"You say that with a straight face? The term 'smoking hot, young doctor' was invented because of you."

"Wait, you think I'm hot?" he asks, his tone incredulous. "You've never said that before."

She treated him to a gaze of disbelief, as if he should know this already and she couldn't believe he was clueless. "Okay, if you want to play dumb."

When she started to walk away, he caught her arm and pulled her closer to him, snaking his arm around her waist.

He leaned in and whispered in her ear, "Are you going to show me how hot I am later, or was that just talk?"

"It depends."

"On what?"

"Whether you can handle the heat," she purred suggestively. Her eyes danced with sensual mischief.

She returned to the guests, leaving him with a big, stupid grin on his face, and a pleasant hum warming his blood.

Nothing and no one would ever come between them. Not even Christian Wheeler, the man to whom he owed a monumental debt—a man who was still in love with his wife, after all these years.

NEXT IN THE FEARLESS SERIES

After a series of tragedies and setbacks, Abbie Cooper Rambally has finally achieved it all—she's a respected neuro-psychologist, devoted wife to a world-renowned surgeon, and mother to three wonderful children. But she's about to feel the earth-shattering repercussions of a promise made long ago.

When Abbie runs into Kristina Haywood in the lobby of a London hotel, a brief exchange between long-forgotten acquaintances sparks a dangerous obsession—a ferocious game that will destroy one woman, and forever alter the life of the other. Because thirteen years ago, Abbie took something from Kristina, and she will stop at nothing to get it back.

In the gripping and emotionally charged conclusion to the Fearless Series, power, jealousy, love, and betrayal—all come to a dramatic head in a raging battle where the ultimate prize is having it all.

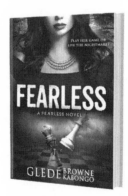

"No one writes a thriller like Gledé Browne Kabongo."
—LaDonna's Book Nook

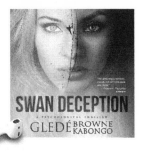

ACKNOWLEDGEMENTS

Thank you to Detective Arthur Brewster of the Boston Police Department for your advice, guidance and expertise on the law enforcement elements of the book. It's always a pleasure speaking with you.

Thank you to my editors, the fabulous Natasha, Jessica and Esther.

Thank you to my readers, especially those of you who take the time to write to me, leave a review or strike up a conversation at a face-to-face event. I'm grateful for your support.

To family and friends who are always cheering and encouraging me, I owe you a debt of gratitude.

Finally, thank you to my favorite boys—my sons Amini and Maximillian, and my husband Donat who's always my first reader, sounding board, and biggest fan. Here's to the next 25 years.

ABOUT THE AUTHOR

Gledé Browne Kabongo is an award-wining author of gripping psychological thrillers—unflinching tales of deception, secrecy, danger and family. She is the Amazon Bestselling Author of The *Fearless* Series, *Swan Deception, Conspiracy of Silence,* and *Mark of Deceit.* Her love affair with books began as a young girl growing up in the Caribbean, where her town library over-looked the Atlantic Ocean.

Gledé holds a Master's degree in Communications, and has been a featured speaker at the Boston Book Festival, *Author Hour,* Epilogues Podcast, and various industry panels. She's also an instructor with the New Hampshire Writers Project. Gledé lives outside Boston with her husband and two sons.

CONNECT ONLINE

⊕ www.gledekabongo.com
✉ glede@gledekabongo.com
f gledekabongoauthor
⊙ @authorgledekabongo

Made in the
USA
Columbia, SC